The
CUPID
CHRONICLES

DENNIS COPELAN

APRICOT
SPRINGS
PUBLISHING

Apricot Springs Publishing
Orange County 🍎 California

Publisher's Note: This is a work of fiction. Names, characters, places and incidents are a product of the author's imagination. Locales and public names are sometimes used for atmospheric purposes. Any resemblances to actual people, living or dead, or to businesses, companies, events, institutions, or locales is completely coincidental.

The following story originally appeared in The Forsaken: Stories of Abandoned Places: "The Theater" Copyright 2017 by Cemetery Dance Publications.

Cover Art and Book Design by Veronica Van Gogh Design
www.vvgdesign.com

Back Cover Art by Roger Dolin, roger@artofrogerdolin.com

ISBN: 978-1-7377122-0-6

To my mother and sister

Praise for THE CUPID CHRONICLES

"Dennis Copelan is one of those writers who is not only imaginative, but versatile. His writing can move from grim, noirish Los Angeles to a jolly theme park that is a wicked parody of a popular California institution. From competing stands selling orange juice in the rural San Fernando Valley to a far-flung future where even dating is regulated by the government. From a silent movie theater with a strange and wonderful secret to Heaven itself. Ordinary joes, cops, ghosts, magic potions, angels, and gods, all of them populating the worlds he has created. And all written with a marvelous eye for character and detail—by turns magical, hilarious, horrifying and sublime. Many's the time Dennis has told me an idea for a new story, and I'd say, "Damn! I wish I had thought of that!" Had he been born some two decades earlier, I know he would have been writing Twilight Zone episodes for Rod Serling—his stories have the same balance of poignancy, eeriness and terror, and ordinary people encountering the supernatural, running headlong into the fantastic. If this is your first time reading the short stories of Dennis Copelan, you've picked an excellent collection, and you're in for one hell of a ride!"

— Mark Onspaugh, Author of
THE FACELESS ONE and DEADLIGHT JACK

Praise for THE CUPID CHRONICLES

"Dennis Copelan's superbly-written stories are full of laugh-out-loud humor, heartwarming vulnerability, and ultimately, redeeming relationships. His talent for sympathetic characters with wide-ranging emotional roller-coaster experiences and unique settings, draws the reader with page-turning enthusiasm."

— Michele Khoury, Author of
BUSTED

"I'm a big fan of Dennis Copelan. His remarkable imagination produces quirky characters in delightfully sinister situations. Original and entertaining!"

— Judith Whitmore, Author of
COME FLY WITH ME

"Dennis Copelan is one of those writers that can make you laugh and then shock you. Surprise and twists will pull you through the smart and witty, The Cupid Chronicles. You'll love the story."

— Wally Runnels, Author of
TWISTED LOVE and IN-KO-PAH SPIRIT

CONTENTS

THE CUPID'S OATH

I swear by Venus, by Eros, by Mars, and by all the gods and goddesses, making them my witness, that I will carry out, according to my ability and judgment, as Cupid or as a fully deputized Cupid's assistant, this covenant.

I promise to do my best by the gods and the people I am helping in order to bring love, desire and happiness to everyone.

I promise to be honest and fair, helpful, considerate and caring, and to use any provided resources wisely to their greatest ability and judgment, and to not cause any emotional distress.

I promise to be loyal, friendly, kind, obedient, cheerful, and clean. In order to make the world a better place and help people at all times, I will also respect myself and authority.

Furthermore, into whosoever's life I enter, I promise to abstain from all intentional or negligent wrongdoing and harm, abusing the bodies of man or woman in providing any service, and causing any injustice to them.

If I keep this covenant, may I forever gain a commendable reputation among the Gods. But if I break it this Oath may the opposite befall me and be subject to banishment or sent to the lower regions thus forswearing heaven for all time.

CHAPTER ONE

CUPID-1637, PART ONE

JUNE 2063
PARADISE CITY, HEAVEN

After a restless weekend, bleary-eyed Pixel Millet, wearing a black suit, white shirt, and tie, staggered his plumpish two-hundred-pound frame into a small cluttered one-man office. Stacks of work files towered on the metal office furniture that filled the room. There was barely enough space for his undeveloped wings, sprouting from the back of his suit, to flutter before he sat down.

As a social worker in the Paradise City Department of Discipline, Mythological Gods Division, Pixel knew Monday was their busiest day, so he wanted to start work early.

Settling into his desk, he looked at the framed photo of his former dog, Gibson, and smiled. He'd loved the little pooch and missed him. The miniature terrier and beagle mix was now running around the real field of dreams up here with the other dog packs. Maybe, if he had time, he'd search out Gibson later in the week so they could see each other again and play fetch.

The office phone rang, and he picked it up. "Pixel. What is it, Peg?"

"Morning, Mr. Millet," said Peg, his nasally voiced assistant. "How was your weekend?"

"It was okay. Thanks. Just a little worried about some work, that's all."

"Oh, Mr. Millet, you always feel this way on Monday. You're too hard on yourself."

"You're right, Peg. I know I do a good job. I just wish the people in charge would notice sometimes."

"Now, you listen to me," she admonished. "You're the best angel-in-training up here. You do a great job, unlike my last boss on Earth."

"Dr. Goodman?"

"Yes. The man was a therapist and should have been locked up and committed. He was nuttier than a fruitcake. You know what else is nutty?"

"What?"

"The rules up here. I saw Marilyn Monroe last week and she looked younger and prettier than when she died. Why can't we look like that?"

Pixel let her talk. He'd heard it a million times, but it was their Monday morning ritual. Pixel knew Peg was right about one thing—the afterlife.

Life in heaven wasn't much different than Earth, except that you were dead, and there were some pretty weird rules, like the one she'd just mentioned. In the hereafter, only celebrities were allowed to revert to their youthful and healthy selves. Otherwise, everyone else looked just the same as when they died. And to make matters worse, you also retained some vestiges of your past maladies like headaches and allergies and bad habits like smoking. Pixel didn't understand it. And, like a lot of things up here, it made absolutely no sense. You just had to accept it. Didn't you?

"Well, thanks for the pep talk, Peg. Anything else I should know?"

"Oh, I forgot to tell you. Judson's bringing you more files."

"Great. Talk to you later."

Peg hung up and he stared at his office.

That was another thing about heaven. On arrival, everyone received a job, and they expected you to work and work hard before earning your full wings. Then, after you got those, you were either promoted into management or granted permanent vacation.

Pixel had been assigned to his current job for twenty-five years and still hadn't grown full wings or been promoted.

He tried not to be disappointed about it but wondered why it was taking so long. He only wanted to make a difference up here and felt he could *if* they ever elevated him into management.

But then he thought about heaven and sighed a heavy sigh.

The place was busy and bureaucratic for a reason. The Big Guy hadn't been seen for thousands of years, flitting around the universe creating other heavenly communities. That left the people in charge, both former mortals and all-knowing deities, to organize a rapidly growing population on their own. And left to their own devices, they proceeded to copy all the Earthly institutions and infrastructures they could remember. To Pixel, it seemed all too familiar and frustrating. The red tape inherent in the system probably contributed to him not getting his full wings.

The door banged open, rattling the glass windows in the office. Pixel's wings fluttered.

Into the room wandered eighteen-year-old office assistant and angel-in-training Judson Femur. The cherubic-faced teenager wore a white shirt, tie, and chinos and held an armful of folders. He dumped them on Millet's desk.

"Here you go, Mr. Millet," said Judson joyfully.

Pixel groaned.

"Mr. Biggle, the division head, said you should read the red folder on top first."

Pixel scrunched his face: a red folder. He knew what that meant. Some Roman god in one of the high-profile departments had a problem employee and needed the underling culled from the herd today—permanently.

"I think he's sitting in the waiting room now," added Judson. His tone was upbeat as it always was, no matter the direness of the situation.

"Who?"

"The guy from the red folder," Judson said, smiling.

Pixel ran a hand through his thinning hair. "Fine. Peg will announce him in due time."

"Okey-dokey, Mr. Millet."

Judson turned, exited the office, and gently closed the door.

Reaching over, Pixel pulled the urgent red folder from the top of the pile. His eyes widened. It was three times the width of any regular file. Whoever "the guy from the red folder" was must be a bad apple.

A bad apple, he thought, smirking. Ha! That was a good one. Feeling immediately guilty, he looked at the ceiling and hoped the Big Guy didn't hear him. Bad apples were still a touchy subject around here.

The office phone rang for the second time and Pixel answered it.

"Your eight o'clock client is here," said Peg.

"Is it—" Pixel squinted at the red folder tab "—Cupid-1637?"

"I'm not really good with names."

"I'll just assume it is."

"Good. And can you hurry up? He's cleaning his nails with the tip of an arrow."

"Okay. Just put the Cupid's assistant in the conference room. I'll be right there."

"Thank heaven. I mean, thank God. Oh, the hell with it," she said. "Why does the Big Guy have to be such a narcissist?" Peg hung up.

Flipping open the fat file, Pixel browsed through the pages. In all his time in the afterlife he'd never seen so many cases of alleged intentional and negligent violations of the Cupid's Oath by a fully deputized agent of love.

Pixel shook his head. The role of Cupid, the Roman god of love and desire, and his deputized assistants, should have been easy. They'd shoot their arrows at people on Earth to make them fall madly and deeply in love—until someone decided to codify it. Now, the job was filled with all kinds of nebulous and poorly written rules—implying an expansion of duties, including the planning and facilitation of romances—many of which Cupid-1637 was claimed to have breached.

He slammed the folder shut. What did they want him to do? Flush the guy?

Pixel stared at the file, his face somber. He'd only represented one other client who'd gotten flushed to the lower regions, and it wasn't pretty. But you never know, he thought, feeling hopeful, maybe he could make a difference for this guy. Help save him. After all, wasn't that what his job was all about?

When he got out of his squeaky chair, Pixel grabbed the heavy file, left his office, and closed the pebble-windowed office door behind him.

He walked, head down, through the air-conditioned office that pumped in fresh-baked cookie smells, past ringing phones, and clacking computer keyboards. No one watched him.

Pixel knew what his co-workers thought, that he always appeared quiet and hard-working. When he had arrived in heaven, he tried to become more gregarious and outgoing. But he is what he was, and it was difficult to change. He wasn't the life of the party, or someone who called attention to himself. He was just a nice, low-key guy that some considered an old softy. And, after all these years, he liked who he was and had finally come to accept himself. He just wished he'd get a little recognition now and then. Isn't that what everybody wants?

Turning left, Pixel made his way to the conference room and entered. The fluorescent-lit office had an oblong, cherry-colored table which was surrounded by six black executive chairs. A whiteboard was attached to a beige wall.

Cupid-1637 slumped in a chair at one end of the table. He failed to acknowledge Pixel and continued picking his nails with a heart-shaped arrow tip.

Pixel gazed at him and grimaced. The romance agent was inappropriately dressed for the job he'd been assigned. He wore a white T-shirt, black Levi's, biker boots, and a pompadour haircut that looked like it came out of an Elvis Presley movie. His angel-in-training wings were barely sprouting, as if they'd been stunted, and a red archery quiver containing his bow and arrows hung over an empty chair.

Pixel sat down in an adjacent seat and placed the thick red file on the table. The faint, musty odor of his client's clothes wafted toward him. "You Cupid-1637?" he asked.

"Could be," replied the curt Cupid assistant.

"I'm Pixel Millet, your social worker. You have a hearing today at four. Do you know why you're here?"

"Yeah," he said, looking at Pixel. "They wanna flush me. What's it to you, Pops?"

"I'm here to help."

Cupid-1637 laughed. "Help me? What're you? Another do-gooder?" He leaned back in his chair. "Well, lay it on me, fat man."

The insult annoyed Pixel, and he tried to let it go. He was in no mood to take any crap from a guy like this. But to help him, he had to keep his cool, so he forced himself to curb his anger.

"Listen, you're up to your neck in this thing," Pixel said. "Without me, you don't have a chance. And that's the truth. I'm not just some guy going through the motions or putting in his time so he can grow a full set of wings and get promoted. I work hard and care about my clients. And I do a good job, too. You might not get that from someone else." He paused. "If you don't want my help, fine. I'll understand. But you're making a mistake if you think you can defend this case on your own. I don't think you want to get flushed, do you? Is that what you want?"

"No," the Cupid's assistant said, staring down at his hands.

"Then you'll listen to me?"

"Alright, alright. Don't get your shorts in a knot. What do you wanna know?"

Pixel let out a breath, opened the file. A conversation like this with a new client was not enjoyable. But if he was going into a hearing to defend their conduct, they had to be on the same page.

Cupid-1637 leaned in and nodded to the folder. "What's that?"

"Your infractions." Pixel pulled out a loose two-page letter from the folder and eyed it. "Here are a few of the things they claim you've breached under the terms of the Cupid's Oath. The failure to bring happiness; the failure to be honest and fair; the failure to use all provided resources wisely; and failure to be clean."

"What's clean mean?"

"Your clothes smell musty. And you're out of uniform."

"Hey, man. I ain't wearing no diaper."

"I wouldn't either if it were me," said Pixel imagining himself in a Cupid's outfit. It made him cringe. The image wasn't pretty.

"What else?" said the Cupid's assistant, frowning.

"The failure to help people at all times." Pixel turned to the letter's second page. "And the big one: alleged intentional and negligent wrong-doing and harm. There are others," he said, returning the document to the file.

The Cupid's assistant whistled. "That's a big list, Pops. There was only one violation the last time."

Pixel narrowed his eyes, concerned. "You mean you've been through a hearing before?" he asked.

"Yeah, about fifty years ago."

"What did you do?"

"Well, there was this actor, see. Some guy named Dirk Krieger." The Cupid smiled as if he was proud. "I arranged for a newspaper to think he'd died in a jaywalking accident. Then, when he spent all day trying to convince people he wasn't dead, I had him meet the woman he was supposed to marry, who was working as a bartender."

"And what happened?"

"He got flattened by a six-thousand-pound wheel-lift tow truck after leaving the restaurant."

10

Pixel gaped. "Good Lord!" He slapped a hand over his mouth and looked upward. "Sorry."

"Hey, it's not my fault that truck lost control. It was an accident, man. I felt terrible about it. Okay?"

Pixel rubbed the back of his neck. Cupid-1637 was a disaster. "Why are you still here?"

"Oh, they put me on probation or something."

"I meant before. How'd you get into heaven?

"I don't know. I musta done something right. Maybe 'cuz I saved that kid's life hoppin' the rails back in '38." He shifted in his seat. "We were both running from the bulls, see, to catch the freight train. The kid tried to jump into an open boxcar, missed, and was dragged with it. I raced by his side and pushed him up onto the boxcar floor until I slipped and fell under the wheels. Next thing you know, I'm up here. I tried to tell the old guy at the gate it was probably a mistake after the life I'd lived." He nodded to the quiver. "And then they gave me that friggin' bow and arrow and told me to report to Cupid. Ain't that a bite? I asked 'em if they had a body shop to work in or any day jobs for mechanics, but they ignored me."

"I see." Pixel put his hand on the folder. "You've got a pretty thick file here."

"Hey, man, what do I know about romance? If there's no carburetor or crankshaft to fix or cash register to boost, it's above my paygrade. I did the best I could."

"Apparently," said Pixel, unimpressed. He flipped open a report. "How about this. We'll go through each violation, discuss what happened, and see if we can mount some defenses."

Cupid-1637 crossed his arms. "Whatever."

Reading the file, Pixel scanned an infraction. He turned toward

11

his client. "A business burned down?"

His client shrugged. "It was nighttime. The flames were crackling. I thought it looked kind of romantic."

Pixel moaned. Defending Cupid-1637 was going to be tough.

"Hey, c'mon, man. The couple got together, right?"

Once again, Pixel questioned why it was so difficult for him to get his full wings. Didn't he deserve them by now?

Pixel stopped himself before his thought process went any further. He didn't want to feel negative about heaven. There was a good reason for the way things happened up here. And perhaps someday, with a little more wisdom and experience, he'd figure it out. He just had to trust the process.

Cupid-1637 smirked. "You look like you were praying I wasn't your client."

"I wasn't thinking that."

"It wouldn't matter anyway," responded Cupid-1637. "From what I can tell, they don't listen to anybody up here."

Time was ticking. Pixel wasn't going to let his client's attitude bother him. "Are you ready?" he asked.

The agent of love moved closer to Pixel.

Feeling pressure to get through all the material before the late afternoon hearing, Pixel cleared his throat and began to read the cases out loud.

CHAPTER TWO

CASE NUMBER ONE: PENNY AND THE MAGIC LAMP

ALLEGED VIOLATION: Causing emotional distress
ALLEGED VIOLATION: Exceeding authority
ALLEGED VIOLATION: Not using resources wisely

MAY 2018
LOS ANGELES, CALIFORNIA

Penny Palmer, with her bobbed hair and sepia-framed glasses, entered the musty-smelling Hollywood antique store that was cluttered with old curiosities and curios. She immediately eyed the strange-looking brass lamp sitting on top of the bargain bin. Feeling lonely that day, and with nothing better to do, she picked up the lamp and examined its odd shape.

The battered and tarnished item felt light in her hands. She adjusted her glasses for a better look and squinted. All she saw in the dull-colored surface was a 32-year-old, slightly pudgy and depressed unemployed actress with a ski slope nose—things that could probably be fixed by having better looks, a ton of money, or a new boyfriend. Good luck with that.

As she rotated the metal object, Penny gazed at the thing from different angles. It reminded her of Aladdin's magic lamp with its curved handle at the lamp's tail, its long spout for pouring, the geometric patterns and jewels on top, and the brass horn-shaped base. She'd hoped for something more practical like a teapot, gravy boat or even an incense holder for whenever she smoked her "medical" marijuana. She didn't need another piece of junk cluttering up her apartment, especially a cast-off lighting fixture that probably used oil instead of a 60-watt bulb.

Turning over the lamp, she noticed a blackened and faded engraving that read:

WHOSOEVER OWNS THIS LAMP AND RUBS IT TWO TIMES SHALL POSSESS THE POWER OF A GENIE FOR NO MORE THAN THREE WISHES.

Penny grimaced. Was this for real? Who ever heard of a magic lamp in real life? The whole idea was absurd.

But then she paused. What if it were true?

She mulled that thought over for a moment, then eyed the lamp with more focus. Imagine what a person could do with three wishes.

Her pulse quickened. If she wanted, she could become an incredibly famous movie star, idolized and desired by everyone; or maybe even a wealthy international sex symbol.

Or both.

Unable to contain her excitement, Penny pivoted toward the middle-aged woman at the cash register. "Excuse me," she said. "How much is this lamp?"

The long-faced cashier wore too much pancake makeup on her face and purple streaks highlighted her gray hair. The woman stared at Penny through tortoise shell glasses. "Was it in the bargain bin?"

"Yes."

"Three bucks."

"You're kidding," said Penny, unable to believe her good luck.

"I'd sell it to you cheaper, but you know, rent."

Penny approached the ancient cash register and rifled through her purse, pulling out three dollars. She handed them to the woman, who rang up the sale.

The machine dinged and a compartmentalized drawer opened.

The saleswoman hesitated before putting the cash into a money tray. "Now, you're sure you want to buy this?"

"Why wouldn't I? It's a bargain."

"Okay then," said the old woman, seeming as if she knew better. "A deal's a deal!" She dropped the money into the register, sighed, and slammed the drawer shut.

Wide-eyed, Penny admired the lamp in her hand.

"Well, it's your problem now," said the saleswoman.

"Wait a minute," said Penny, narrowing her eyes. "What do you mean?"

"You'll find out."

"Did I just get ripped off?" she asked, pursing her lips. Penny folded her arms across her chest. "I don't think I want this lamp anymore."

"No refunds." She glowered at Penny, pointing to a sign on

the back of the register. "A deal's a deal. All sales are final."

When Penny returned to her untidy one-bedroom apartment, decorated with her ex-roommate's second-hand furniture, she was still steamed at the salesclerk. It wasn't the money involved, but the principle. And to imply something wrong existed with the lamp and then not refund the sale. Well, it was a pretty lousy way of doing business just to con her out of three lousy bucks.

She looked at the lantern. Shook her head. All this aggravation over a crappy brass lamp. How could she let her imagination get out of control? The thing probably wasn't even magic.

Tossing it onto her cloth couch, Penny opened a drawer in her TV bench and pulled out her stash of marijuana. She needed to calm herself with a toke.

After six puffs of sweet, pine-scented Laughing Grass, a tumbler of Two-Buck Chuck from Trader Joe's, and three old episodes of *Sex and the City* on Blu-ray, Penny had regressed from despondency to full-blown depression.

Here she was, an aging ingenue, lonely and unmarried, with no relationship in sight, not pretty enough for lead roles, and in perpetual debt from student loans and acting classes. The express lane to nowhere loomed ahead.

Penny took another sip of red wine, spied the magic lamp on the couch, and placed it on the coffee table in front of her. The brass felt cold.

"Worthless piece of junk," she said in her relaxed, medicated state. "I bet you don't even work." She stared at the dull object. "You want me to rub you and prove it?" she said sarcastically, spilling some wine on the carpet. "Maybe. I. Will."

Penny picked up the lamp and rubbed it hard, three times with her free hand. "Oh, great genie of the lamp," she said. "Cometh out and grant me some life-changing shit. Whatever."

The lamp vibrated, a small tremor in her hands. Blue smoke steamed from the spout, billowing upward. When the casing became blistering hot, she screamed in pain and dropped it on the coffee table.

A figure appeared, outlined in smoke-filled haze.

Staring slack-jawed, Penny fell onto the carpet.

When the smoke dissipated, a middle-aged, balding man was sitting at a wooden desk in the middle of her beige living room.

"Wh-what the—"

In front of him sat a silver laptop, and a whirring desk fan. He wore a rumpled black suit, white shirt and maroon tie. The man looked around her less-than-impressive apartment.

Penny climbed to her feet, her heart racing. "Who are you?"

"Sid Wiffle. Senior Accountant and Regional Cost Control Manager." He looked at a Post-it Note. "Is this 2231 Curson Street, Apartment 16C?"

"What happened to the genie? Wasn't I supposed to get a genie?"

"Oh, we laid them off after the buyout. Too expensive, you know. Gotta get these costs under control." Wiffle shook his head and resumed working on the laptop.

"What do you mean buyout?"

He stopped working and gazed at her. "Oh, it's really quite technical," said Wiffle. "All business theories, pie charts and line graphs, if you know what I mean. You'd be bored."

"Really?" Penny said, worried she would get cheated out of her three wishes. "Try me."

"Ever heard of the Magic in a Lamp Company?"

17

"No."

Wiffle cleared his throat, then drank water from a plastic bottle. "Magic in a Lamp formed during the Bronze Age and hired genies as their main source of labor. The work was hard and oppressive—too many hours stuffed in tight spaces and not enough pay—until the disgruntled *djinns* organized and formed the IBGOSC."

"The what?" she asked.

"Union. International Brotherhood of Genies and Other Supernatural Creatures. A royal pain in the ass."

"Oh."

"Anyway," he said, taking another sip of water, "sometime during the Islamic Golden Age, the unlimited cost of granting expensive wishes and the pressure of an organized trade union became a financial burden for Magic in a Lamp. They limped along for a few hundred years, but poor management, corruption and bad labor contracts finally did them in." Wiffle smiled. "That's where I come in."

"Where?" said Penny, not understanding his involvement.

"I work at a secret hedge fund. Organized for the sole purpose of transacting the largest corporate buyout in the history of the world, which we completed last year. We moved the company out of the Middle East, relocated to a warehouse in Topeka, Kansas, and filed incorporation papers in Delaware—for favorable corporate tax laws, of course."

"Of course," said Penny, attempting to focus through what she thought were the hazy effects of smoking Laughing Grass. "Am I going to get my three wishes?"

Wiffle appeared surprised by the question, but addressed her concerns.

"Oh, most certainly, Ms. Palmer. Customers are the lifeblood of our company. But there are some limitations."

"Are you serious?" She raised an eyebrow. "Like what?"

"Well, you heard about the genies," said Wiffle. "But, on the other hand, we successfully cut employee benefits by sixty-three-point eight percent, making us a leaner and more efficient company." And almost as an afterthought. "And we've had to cut down on the COW."

"I don't understand."

"The cost of wishes."

"That doesn't seem fair," Penny protested, frowning.

"Now, I see you're upset," Wiffle said, feigning compassion. "After all, I would be too. It's no fun to be on a budget. But the company wants to make things right."

"Give me a break."

He typed on his laptop. A pie chart appeared on his computer screen, which he showed to Penny.

"We've looked at the figures, crunched a few numbers, and rebalanced some particularly bad long-term losses and investments. And I can safely say," he said, "the company can offer you a complimentary fourth wish, free of charge, no strings attached." He smiled. "Now, how does that sound?"

"Wait a minute," she said, tilting her head, skeptical of the offer. "If you're losing money and slashing budgets, how can you afford to give me an extra wish?"

"Good question, Ms. Palmer, but it's like this. We've determined a fourth wish wouldn't add any additional costs if averaged over a three-year period against other similar customers." Wiffle shrugged. "And besides, most people run out of expensive desires after the third wish anyway."

"So, I can ask for anything?"

"Anything," he said.

Penny's mind swirled with the possibilities. She could get all the beauty, wealth, and popularity she wanted, and still have an extra wish left over. Maybe even help mankind. Maybe not. "It's a deal," she said, shaking Wiffle's hand.

"Excellent," Wiffle said, nodding. He reached down and opened a desk drawer, pulling out a heavy, one-foot-thick contract, and dropped it with a thud onto his desk. "I just need you to sign the WPA."

Her eyes widened. "The what?"

"Wish Protection Agreement."

"Is that a contract?" she asked.

"It's mostly boiler plate. You know these lawyers. Nothing to worry about."

Penny hovered over the document and flipped through it.

"Exclusions?"

"The contract doesn't cover any request for extra wishes, intentional or fraudulent acts, or if the customer is already a genie." He gazed dubiously at Penny. "You're not a genie, are you, Ms. Palmer?"

"Of course not."

"Then nothing to worry about."

She studied the agreement further and grew perplexed.

"Indemnification?"

"Certainly, even you can understand that the company has a legal right to seek full or partial reimbursement against you for any harm or loss caused to a third-party *if* sued over any wish you've requested."

"I don't like this."

"It's no different than buying an insurance policy or a car," said Wiffle. "There are always restrictions." He held out a black pen for her to take. "You want your four wishes, don't you?"

Penny snatched the ballpoint and signed the contract.

Wiffle surveyed her signature. "Great. We're all set." He rubbed his hands. "Ready for your first wish?"

"I guess," she said, still irritated over all the red tape.

"Once you try the first wish, you'll feel better. Most people start with something simple."

"You mean like money?"

"Oh, you'd be surprised," said Wiffle, appearing concerned. "Money is more difficult to conjure than you think. If you don't use the right language or exchange rate, I could fill your coffers with Pesos. And you know how cheap those are."

She pinched her lips together. "You're making this difficult."

The senior accountant stroked his chin. "Why don't you ask for one of your deepest, darkest desires. Something you've always wanted but knew was impossible to obtain. Surely, there must be something."

Penny pondered his suggestion. She had to admit—she'd always wanted to be beautiful. Someone tall and willowy with a great figure, natural beauty, and alluring to men. A sex symbol. There was nothing wrong with being born moderately attractive, but good-looking people always had the world and opportunities open up to them.

"Have you decided yet?" asked Wiffle.

"I want to be pretty," Penny said, her pulse quickening.

"Drop-dead gorgeous, if you want to know the truth. Is that too difficult?"

"It's as simple as snapping my fingers."

She closed her eyes, clasping her hands to her chest. "Then that's what I wish," she said. "To look like—"

"I know, somebody who is a goddess," said Wiffle, clearly bored. "A vision. A bombshell. A stunner. A beauty queen. Arm candy. A looker. A hottie. A woman who is a cross between Marilyn Monroe and Kate Upton. Margot Robbie. I've heard them all before."

"Yes," she said, practically trembling. "And can you give me Jennifer Anniston's hair? I love her hair."

Wiffle shrugged. "Okay," he said, then snapped his fingers. He took a sip from his water bottle and eyed Penny. "Well, it's done."

Penny dashed over to the bathroom before he finished, almost knocking off the wall the watercolor print hanging in the hallway.

Slamming open the door, grinning, anxious to see the radiant vision she had become, Penny stared at her reflection in the mirror above the sink. Looking back was the same moderately attractive, slightly overweight, puffy-eyed, flat-haired woman she'd always been. The smile on her face flatlined.

Nothing had changed.

Heat rushed through her body. Her face turned beet red. Wiffle had lied to her.

Turning, she stormed out of the bathroom toward him. The senior accountant still sat at his desk in the now crowded living room, working on his computer. "What're you trying to pull?" she barked.

Wiffle raised his head, appearing surprised. "I don't quite know what you're talking about, Ms. Palmer."

Standing by the desk, Penny glared at him. "What happened to my wish?" she snapped.

"We granted you your wish."

"No, you didn't," she shrieked. "Just look at me. I'm the same."

"Really, Ms. Palmer. You must control your obvious anger issues."

The sudden spike in her blood pressure made her lightheaded. She cupped her forehead.

Wiffle motioned her over to his computer. "I want you to see something."

Penny peered at the PC.

Typing furiously, Wiffle clicked on the return key and an Instagram account popped up on his HP screen. Hundreds of photos appeared on the monitor that had a slender, seductive, voluptuous, wavy-haired blonde cavorting, posing, eating, modeling, laughing, smiling, mugging at the beach, a pool, a State Fair, fashion shows, Paris, Rome, Tahiti, cathedrals, a castle, in bed, dressed in bikinis, revealing sundresses, clingy blouses, low-cut Ts, short-shorts, tight jeans, sexy and lacy lingerie, and stiletto heels.

Wide-eyed, Penny gaped at the photos. "Who is that?"

"Why that's you, Ms. Palmer. One of the most beautiful women in the world. You have over eighty-five million Instagram followers."

"But that looks nothing like me. I've never been to those places or had those pictures taken," she protested.

"I know," said Wiffle, smiling. "Isn't that the magic of Photoshop? We were able to cut and paste the attributes we liked from other women's photos, meld them with your picture, and liquify and sculpt your body to make it more attractive. Then we digitized the main image and inserted it into various props and locations. And the best part—we were able to save close to one-hundred-twelve percent in fees and costs from previous beauty wishes. Usually, the price for body manipulation and plastic surgery is prohibitively expensive."

Her sweeping arm gesture almost hit Wiffle. "This isn't what I asked for. I could have used Instagram and Photoshop myself instead of wasting it on a wish."

"You know, we just discussed this Wish Fulfillment phenomenon with Antoon Krishna at the Grant-A-Wish Conference in Reno last year. He said, 'When you make a wish, it seems impossible. When you get a wish, it seems inevitable.'" He looked at Penny and dabbed his misty eyes. "Isn't that beautiful?"

"I want a new wish," she demanded.

"Now, now—"

"I want it!"

Wiffle's face seemed to balloon with apparent anger. He pulled out the heavy WPA contract and slammed it on the desk. This time the thud resonated louder. "Let's look at the contract, shall we?" He rifled through the pages until he stopped. "Page 857, Conditions, Section 3, subsection (b), and I quote: 'The wish grantee'—that's you—'shall not request of the wish grantor'— that's Magic in a Lamp Corporation—'duplicate wishes. Failure to abide by the terms and conditions of this agreement will result in an immediate breach and termination of said contract, subject to binding arbitration in the jurisdiction of wish grantor's choice.'" He stared at Penny, adjusting his glasses. "I can do nothing on this point."

Penny sighed.

His face relaxed. "Perhaps you should think about your second wish, Ms. Palmer."

"What if it turns out like the last one?"

Wiffle gave her an understanding nod and spoke with a soothing tone. "You're being too hard on yourself. Making a wish isn't that difficult. It's like riding a bike. Fall off and you get back on. You just have to be careful about your choice of words, that's all."

Her indignation dissipated. He sounded sincere. Could she trust him? "So, you think the next one will be better?"

"You seem like a bright person," he said, giving her an encouraging smile. "I'm sure you can figure it out. Now, what's your wish?"

Penny pondered his question. She had to admit—she'd always wanted to be a wealthy and world-famous actress. Admired for her talent and well known enough to get the parts; you know, the good ones—maybe even Academy Award® winning roles—without struggling to get noticed. And why shouldn't she wish for that? She had the aptitude, but was a Hollywood nobody. Imagine being recognized for her talent and taking acting risks without worrying about paying her bills or putting food on the table.

"Did you decide?" asked Wiffle.

"Yes, I did," she said with renewed zest. "I wish to be a rich and famous movie actress."

A sour expression appeared on Wiffle's face. "I see," he said.

"What's wrong?" she asked.

"That seems to be two wishes. Rich and famous."

"No, that's only one wish."

"How do you figure?" he asked, clearly eyeing her with suspicion.

"Well," Penny explained, "I asked to be rich and famous. Not rich, comma, and famous. The latter is two wishes. Since I asked for the former, it's only one wish because I requested to be a rich and famous person, which are connected. Therefore, it's one wish."

The senior accountant folded his arms. "And you expect me to believe that?"

"Yes," she said adamantly. "You told me to be careful with my words. I can't ask to be just a famous actress. If I did, you could make me a poor one. And I'm already poor. Why would I want that? I think it's inferred that if you ask to be famous, you're wealthy."

"I think you're missing the point."

Penny raised her voice. "Listen, you told me wishing for money was difficult because I had to be specific. Well, now I'm being more precise. I want to be a rich and famous actress. And I want my wealth to be in U.S. dollars."

"This is most distressing," commented Wiffle, typing on his computer.

"What're you doing?" Penny asked, concerned.

"Letting corporate legal know that they need to amend future contracts to add a CWC."

"What's a CWC?"

"Compound Wish Clause. Any other questions?"

Penny swallowed hard. "So, I'm not getting my wish?"

"Oh, no, no," said Whiffle, preoccupied. "You're getting your wish. We just need to close this contractual loophole so future customers can't take advantage."

Wiffle's comment touched a nerve. "Now, wait a minute," she protested. "I didn't steal a wish from the company. I'm a principled person, you know."

"If you say so," said Wiffle, shrugging. "Ready for your wish?"

She glared at her wish giver. Oh, she'd make a wish all right. Make this cheap company pay, big time. "Yeah, I'm ready for my wish."

"To make you a rich and a famous actress, right?"

"Yes. Make me a famous actress and one of the richest women in the world. U.S. dollars, and I don't mean Confederate or greenbacks, online, bitcoin or other cryptocurrencies, either."

Wiffle looked bored stiff. "As you wish." He snapped his fingers.

In a nanosecond, Penny stood in the middle of an exquisitely decorated living room that smelled of sweet coconut, citrusy scented orchids, and fresh jasmine. She wore a lacy embroidered long gown that covered a skin-tight black miniskirt and a top with a plunging neckline, and strappy gold Jimmy Choo stiletto sandals.

Gazing around the posh room, she spied a diamond-studded, glossy black rhinoceros' leather sofa framed with Zimbabwe pure pink ivory wood. A coffee table with a patchwork of mixed metals and an emerald slate top. A solid gold fireplace with a marble mantle that displayed her three Academy Awards®, six Emmy Awards, two Tony Awards, and a Nobel Peace Prize. And a shiny floor, made of expensive Brazilian walnut, that stretched into other rooms. On the walls hung original Picasso, Hockney, and Lichtenstein artwork.

Trembling, she glanced out a wall-sized window at the far end of the living room. It overlooked ocean waves slow-rolling against a white sandy beach rimmed in tropical flowers and palm trees swaying lazily in a light breeze. An infinity pool jutted from the house. The sun sparkled off its languid water.

Penny hugged herself and burst out laughing, jumping up-and-down and squealing like a little girl.

Wiffle strolled into the room, eating a turkey sandwich. He asked, "Does this satisfy your wish?"

She stood misty-eyed, a wide grin on her face. "Yes. Oh, yes. Thank you, Mr. Wiffle. Thank you."

"Good," he said, taking a bite from his sandwich. "If you're happy, don't forget to fill out the five-minute marketing survey after all the wishes have been completed. The company would appreciate it."

"Of course, of course."

At that moment, Penny had never been so happy in her life, until her cell phone vibrated and rang with a distinctive *Gone with the Wind* theme.

❦

"Where's the phone?" she said, hastily touching her body and glancing around. "I don't have a purse."

Wiffle reached into his pocket and pulled out her iPhone. "You left it in the apartment."

She snatched the device out of his hand and stared at the screen, which indicated Tully, Peterson & Marley were calling.

"Who are they?" said Penny, confused.

"Your financial managers," said Wiffle.

She lifted the phone to her cheek. "Hello."

"Ms. Palmer," said a scared, young male voice. Mayhem erupted in the background. People yelled and screamed over each other. "You don't know me." His voice trembled.

"Gotta talk fast. You're our largest account. Money stolen. Turn on TV. FBI at the door."

Her chest tightened. "What? What're you saying?"

Over the phone, she heard a muffled bullhorn and then a door crash open. "FBI. Drop what you're holding."

The iPhone screen went blank.

Panicked, she jammed her hands into her armpits. "Oh, my god! Oh, my god! Where's the TV?"

Wiffle, chewing, pointed to a hallway. "Around the corner."

Penny bolted toward the foyer, almost falling off her Jimmy Choo heels. She stopped, ripped the strappy shoes off her feet and swore before running into another room.

She skidded to a halt in a large home theater filled with six white leather reclining movie seats, a fully stocked bar with three bar stools, and a ninety-six-inch TV screen on the wall. Dim ambient lighting illuminated the entertainment center in a dull seashell hue.

Searching from seat-to-seat, Penny looked for a remote control.

When Wiffle wandered into the room, she barked, "Where's the clicker? The whatchama-call-it."

"You mean the remote?"

"Yes!" she shouted frantically.

"It doesn't have a remote. Just tell the room what you want and it'll show up on the screen."

"Turn on the news," she shouted.

The large TV screen lit up and exploded with color. Standing in front of a high-rise in Beverly Hills, surrounded by police cars and FBI vehicles, was a middle-aged female reporter with brunette hair, overinflated lip fillers, and hard-angled eyebrows.

She talked into a handheld microphone. "In a Ponzi scheme reminiscent of the Bernie Madoff scandal, the securities investment concern of Tully, Peterson and Marley has defrauded thousands of investors, including their biggest client, world famous actress Penny Palmer, out of tens of billions of dollars, leaving her completely broke," she said with a noticeable vocal fry at the end of her sentence.

Penny stared at the TV. She cupped her hand over her mouth.

"It's been an especially trying day for movie actress and entertainment icon Penny Palmer—," said the female reporter, "—after news broke in the *New York Times* this morning that she had suppressed a secret, early career as a fetish, lesbian porno star named, Penelo-Pee Palm-Her. Upon hearing the news, CBS cancelled her hit, the number one rated sitcom, *The Girl Next Door*."

"What?" screamed Penny.

Wiffle finished the last bite. "Looks like you hired the wrong people to handle your money and career. That's the problem," he said, licking his fingers. "You can't trust anybody these days."

Penny pointed at Wiffle. "You did this to me," she accused.

"I did nothing of the sort. You made a wish, and I granted it. The management of that wish was your fault."

"But I'm not a lesbian or a porno star," she protested. "I don't even get undressed or have sex with the lights on when I have intimate relations with a guy," she ranted. "And about the wish. I never even got a chance to spend my money. And you tanked my acting career before it even got started."

"Under the terms of the agreement, all complaints must be formally lodged with—"

"Screw the contract," she interrupted. "You've acted in bad faith."

Wiffle's mouth fell open. "I beg your pardon. That is a very serious allegation."

Her cell phone whizzed by Wiffle's face, almost clobbering him, and shattered against the bleached wood-paneled wall. "What'd you do that for?" he said.

"I want my wish back," she shrieked.

"We complied with your wish. And we saved eighty-seven percent in the usual costs by renting the house for one day instead of purchasing, and—"

Penny angrily pulled out a bottle of Chateau Lafite Rothschild from the bar and brandished it. She slowly walked toward Wiffle.

He took a step backwards. "I was right. You do have a temper."

"Are you going to give back my wish?"

"Now, let's not be hasty. Do something you might regret," he said coolly. "You know I can't do that."

She came face-to-face with him, flourishing her weapon. "Why not?"

"Because under the terms of the agreement, by hitting me you'd breach the contract and forfeit your remaining wishes. And, besides, you'd be financially responsible for the physical injuries you caused and would have to reimburse Magic in the Lamp under the liquidated damage clause."

The last statement confused Penny. "What are you talking about?"

"Oh, it's quite simple," said Wiffle. "If you breach the contract you have to pay the company full market value of the fees and costs we expended in your two prior wishes, not to exceed fifteen million dollars."

As if she'd been thrown into a cold storage unit, a chill ran down her body. "Wha—what?" she stuttered.

"I suppose that would be kind of harsh since the news indicated you were broke."

Panting in consternation, Penny turned toward one of the movie seats. "I need to sit down."

Plopping onto the soft creamy marshmallow leather seat, Penny hyperventilated, shoulders heaving as she drew short harsh breaths. She dropped the wine bottle on the floor and it rolled to a stop.

Wiffle walked over to Penny and patted her on the shoulder. "Breathe," he said. "Breathe. That's it."

"What am I gonna do?" she said, holding back tears.

"Oh, come on. It's not as bad as all that. You haven't even breached the contract yet."

She wiped her eyes. "I don't have any money, my TV show was cancelled, and I'm a national disgrace." She wailed, "And I don't even have a good porno name."

He pulled a beige handkerchief out of his coat pocket and handed it to Penny. She grabbed it and dabbed her eyes.

Wiffle bent down, peered at her. "Look, I'm not a bad guy," he said, "but the rules are the rules. How about this?" Taking a cell phone out of his pants pocket, he tapped the display.

A digital version of the contract appeared on the screen.

"What if I return you to the way things were before the first wish, and we agree to arbitrate over whether you're entitled to a replacement. That's the best I can do."

Penny sniffled. "But it'll cost me my third wish if you return me back to my old life."

"Not according to the contract. On page 752, under Arbitration, Section 2, subsection (d), it indicates that the grantee will not surrender any unused wishes if they agree to arbitrate over the fairness or good faith execution of the used wish in question."

"Did you just make that up?" she asked.

She studied his face, but it remained impassive. She didn't know if he did or didn't.

"Are you agreeable?" he asked.

When Penny nodded, Wiffle raised his arm, snapped his fingers, and the room blurred into darkness.

Four walls came into focus and her dreary apartment promptly reappeared, just the way she'd left it. The magic lamp lay on the floor, the living room still had the lingering stink of Laughing Grass, the kitchen sink overflowed with dirty dishes, and Wiffle was back at his desk working on his laptop.

All her tension immediately dissipated. She flopped onto the lumpy couch, sinking into the saggy cushions, and exhaled a sigh of relief. Penny was grateful to be back.

Wiffle faced his laptop. "Have you decided on your third wish?"

His question took her by surprise. She hadn't even thought about it.

"I don't know," she confessed.

"Don't know what to wish for?" said Wiffle. "It's a classic case of WCC."

"What's that?" she said sarcastically. "Wish confusion conundrum?"

"Right you are," he said, appearing surprised. "I see you've been reading Edgar Stavinsky's groundbreaking paper on the subject."

"Who?" she said, running her hands through her hair.

Wiffle swiveled in his chair and eyed her. "Perhaps, you should consider asking for something that isn't so materialistic. Now, what's your wish?"

Penny pondered his question. She had to admit—maybe Wiffle was right. She'd made two wishes—beauty and wealth—and look what happened. She needed to look inside herself and figure out what would make her happy.

Wiffle stared at his watch. "Having a problem?" he said.

Annoyed, she glared at him. "Do you mind? This is a very important decision. I'm not going to rush it."

She thought about a wish. Her biggest fear had always been loneliness, the most insidious emotion in the world. She didn't want to grow old and be alone. She wanted a man she could share her life with, feel safe with, and be her protector. Someone who could share a deep, emotional, resonant love, and who would accept her for who she was. And it wouldn't hurt if he had long flowing hair and good looks either, she thought.

She bit her lip. But could she trust him to give her what she wanted? He'd misrepresented the other two wishes. What would keep him from doing it again?

Wiffle tilted his head back, gazing upward.

Penny sighed. What choice did she have? He was the only middle-management Senior Accountant and Cost Control

Regional Manager who granted wishes that she knew. She'd just have to be more precise on how she worded her next command.

"I know my third wish now," she said.

"Go on," said Wiffle, folding his arms.

"I want a lifelong relationship, with mutual love and respect—"

"I see," he said, looking bored as usual. "Someone who is invested in you emotionally and is attentive, assertive, and vulnerable, but stable. Someone who will treat you as an equal. A good personality. Did I miss anything?"

"Yes. He has to be a male, good-looking and have long golden hair. He has to be straight, no substance abuse, and not older than me. No seniors, understand? And lastly, no shenanigans. I'm looking for lifetime companionship."

"I can do that," said Wiffle.

"And if money's involved, no skimping."

Wiffle sighed. "You ready?"

Penny clasped her hands together. "I want to meet my prince."

Wiffle walked up to her. "Okay," he said then snapped his fingers.

There were three knocks on the front door.

She looked at Wiffle, who nodded.

Making a mad dash to the door, Penny could feel her heart race. What would she say? She didn't want to be tongue-tied when the man of her dreams appeared.

Penny reached for the knob and stopped. Taking a deep breath, she tilted her head back, fluffed up her flat hair, then opened the door.

A dog barked, meek and high-pitched like a puppy.

Looking down, Penny spied a golden retriever pup with floppy ears and soft, furry flaxen hair. The puppy sat peacefully in a wicker basket, a red bow tied around its neck, staring up at her with wide, soulful eyes. His tail wagged rapidly against the woven willow twigs.

A note on the basket proclaimed: Hi! My name is PRINCE, your new dog.

Penny angrily jerked toward Wiffle. "What the fuck?"

"You said you wanted a lengthy relationship with mutual love and respect, someone with long golden hair, and a lifetime companion."

"But he's a dog!" she screamed.

"Yes, but he's the *best* dog."

Penny paced. "What're you trying to do? I said a guy."

"No, you said a male. Prince is a male."

"But money was supposed to be no object. I can't afford to feed a dog. I can barely even afford to feed myself."

A frown crossed Wiffle's face. "Do you know how much breeders cost?" he said sharply. "Frankly, I'm a bit surprised at your thankless attitude."

She pointed her finger at him. "Out!" she shouted. "I want you outta here, and don't ever come back."

"Is that your fourth wish?"

"Yes!" she hollered.

Wiffle smiled. "Funny, that's what everybody asks for when they get to their fourth wish." He looked proud. "No costs expended."

"Go!"

"Okay." He raised his hand.

"And don't forget to take the—"

She never finished. Wiffle had already snapped his fingers and disappeared, leaving only the dog.

Stepping out of the basket, the puppy trotted to her, sat on his hind legs and whimpered.

"I'm not a dog person," she said to Prince.

The puppy gently pawed her leg with his oversized, furry forepaw.

Penny bent down and stared into the pup's sad eyes. The dog nuzzled close, wagged his tail and licked her hand.

Her heart melted. She picked him up, feeling the warmth of its cuddly body and soft puppy fur that smelled of vanilla, hay, and sweet fresh cream.

When Penny kissed Prince on the head, she knew love had come.

While walking Prince six months later, Penny strolled by Hollywood Blue Ribbon Antiques. When she looked at a bin outside the front entrance, she spied the magic lamp with a price tag attached to the handle that said FREE in bold black letters.

Her skin tingled. She didn't want to be anywhere near that thing.

She turned, pulled her puppy's leash, and said, "C'mon, Prince, let's go."

"Is that you, Penny?" said a familiar voice from within the lamp.

Penny stopped. Her heart raced. Was that Wiffle?

"I know that's you," said the voice.

"Wiffle?" Penny asked.

"You do recognize me," he said, his speech muffled. "You know we still have some unfinished business together."

"No, we don't," she objected. "I wished you away."

"Put the lamp on the ground so I can talk to you better."

"That doesn't make any sense."

"It does if you want another wish."

"How do you figure?" she asked. "I used my four wishes." Penny cocked her head, curious. "I'm entitled to another wish?"

"Yes, just put me on the ground."

Slowly approaching the bin, she reached for the lamp. A pit formed in her stomach. What if it was another trick? She no longer trusted Wiffle.

"You think it's a trick, right?" said the lamp.

"Yes," said Penny.

Prince wandered to her side and sat down. His worried eyes looked up at her.

"I know we've had some rough times, but just put me on the sidewalk so I can explain about the contract."

Against her better judgment, Penny grabbed the lamp. The metal still felt cool in her hands.

Bending down, she placed the lamp on the sidewalk. Prince leaned forward and sniffed the dull and muted yellow object.

"Now," said the Wiffle voice. "Let me explain."

She crossed her arms. "Why am I entitled to another wish?"

"Remember when you contested the second wish?"

"Yes."

"I submitted it to the home office, and, well—" Wiffle's voice paused "—they took it to legal, who agreed with you. They said my actions were in bad faith and, technically, you're entitled to a new wish. Not to mention that human resources placed me on an action plan after that incident, with a six-month probationary period. It's ageism, I tell you." His voice expressed anger. "I'm the only one in the office who's over fifty and then they try to push you out, see. Hire young, new MBAs or millennials who don't know squat about what we do and get paid more than I make, and—"

She interrupted. "So, I'm entitled to a new wish?"

"Oh, yes," said Wiffle's voice, regaining composure. "Just rub the lamp and I'll come out and have you sign an amended contract.

Penny pondered his question. She had to admit—maybe having another wish wouldn't be so bad. The first two wishes didn't turn out, but look how lucky she'd gotten with the third wish. She absolutely loved her dog. He was the best thing that had ever happened to her.

She sat on her haunches, ready to reach out, rub the lamp, but deep-seated suspicions seeped in.

Why did she need another wish? She was enjoying her life right now. Maybe she wasn't the richest or most beautiful woman in the world. But did it really matter? She'd learned that having those things doesn't necessarily make you happy.

"Well, what are you waiting for?" barked Wiffle's voice.

"I'm thinking," she said.

"It's not that difficult. Do we have a deal?"

She asked Prince, "What do you think?"

Sniffing the lamp, Prince sidled up to it, raised his hind leg and urinated.

Wiffle's voice gagged.

Penny looked at Prince with wonder. He really *was* her protector, wasn't he? "Sorry, Mr. Wiffle," she said, suppressing a laugh. "No deal."

"But, your wish—"

Smiling, Penny tugged on the leash and led Prince away from the store. She didn't need a wish. It had already come true.

CHAPTER THREE

CASE NUMBER TWO: MOONLIGHT SERENADE

ALLEGED VIOLATION: Failing to use wise judgment
ALLEGED VIOLATION: Causing emotional distress

JUNE 1945
NORTHRIDGE, CALIFORNIA

Betty McCallum jolted upright in the middle of the night, gasping and laboring to breathe. Once again, her dead husband Mickey had appeared in her dreams.

Blood had oozed from the bullet holes in his combat helmet, covering his left eye and cheek. His bloodstained Marine uniform hung in tatters from where his right chest and shoulder used to be, the images still vivid.

She'd recoiled when he reached out with his left arm, straining to touch her. But when she stared back at the man she'd once loved, her heart ached and longing filled her.

"I'll be back, babe," he'd said, grinning.

She remembered feeling a nudge inside at his charm; it had always affected her. She'd covered her face to hide the tears.

Mickey took a step backward, fading into darkness. "Just like I promised," he'd said. "I'll be back."

ॐ

Thinking of Mickey, Betty trembled on her lower bunk bed. A thickness formed in her throat, signaling more sorrow. If only she could talk with her sister Evie now. They'd been so close once but hadn't spoken in almost two years. All because she eloped.

In the distance, Glenn Miller's "Moonlight Serenade" wafted through the window, distracting her. The music's slow, melodic tempo sounded like it was coming from a distant radio. She wiped her damp eyes and wondered who in the world would play music so loud while people were trying to sleep.

Viv roused in the upper bunk. "You okay, hun?"

"I don't know," she said, her voice cracking.

Wearing pink curler pins and a cotton nightgown, Viv jumped down hitting the floor with a thud that rattled two nearby wooden lockers in the cramped, undecorated room.

Viv gazed at Betty with evident concern.

She was the closest friend Betty had made since volunteering for The Women's Land Army of the U.S. Crop Corps during harvest season. It was a far cry from the counter job she'd left behind at the Wilshire May Company after Mickey died at the Battle of Peleliu eight months ago.

"More dreams about Mickey?" Viv asked.

"Yes," she said, rubbing the back of her neck. "I wish they'd stop. And I wish they'd turn off that music."

"What music?

"You know, 'Moonlight Serenade,' coming from outside."

Viv appeared puzzled.

"You don't hear it?" Betty cocked her head, but the song had disappeared. The room was silent now. Had she imagined it? Her stomach tightened. "It's stopped," she said, lowering her chin, breaking eye contact.

Viv plopped on her bed. "Maybe you should see Dr. Perry in Reseda. The girls say he'll make house calls to the farm." Viv's face lit up. "They also say he's kind of dreamy looking."

"I'll be okay," said Betty, wondering if she would be.

"Are you sure?"

"No," she admitted. "Mickey said he'd come back."

"You've gotta get over this, hun," Viv said. She clasped Betty's hand. "I know it's hard, but he's *never* coming back."

Betty scrunched her eyebrows. "Then why are the dreams so real?"

After taking a sedative, Betty awoke at 5:30 a.m. to the clanging sound of an alarm clock and the sweet smell of lemon blossoms drifting in from the citrus fields. A sliver of moonlight, shining through the window, crested on a corner of her bed.

Noisy women in the hallway jabbered excitedly outside her room as they hurried toward the communal washroom.

"C'mon, sleepyhead," said Viv, towering above her, holding a towel. "We're due in the fields soon."

Betty, still groggy, dragged herself out of bed and into the bathroom, where she joined six other women preparing for the day.

Four hand-washing basins lined one pale green wall. A long silver mirror showed Betty squeezed between two girls, her eyes dulled and puffy. The pain of Mickey's death after all these months had made her fine, fresh-faced looks appear weary. Craning in front of the reflecting surface, she washed her face, brushed her teeth and combed her thick shoulder-length brunette hair.

Back in her bedroom, she pulled out denim overalls and a light blue sport shirt from the wooden locker where she kept her clothes and Mickey's old, beat-up trumpet case and trumpet.

She gazed at the case. Betty knew she needed to move on and start life fresh but wasn't ready to give up "Old Blew" just yet. The instrument had meant so much to Mickey. It was one of the last things he'd left behind that bound her to him.

After putting on her "Farmerette" outfit, Betty headed to the door. When she touched the doorknob something cool brushed her back. She tensed, fearing someone else was in the room. The smell of Mickey's mentholated Aqua Velva aftershave lotion wafted into her face.

Is Mickey here?

Her heart racing, she jerked around. The room appeared empty.

Sheer curtains covering an open window swayed lazily in the morning breeze.

She leaned against the door to calm herself, jamming her hands into her armpits. Her dreams, she feared, were affecting her, making her imagine things. She stared at the trumpet case.

"C'mon, Betty," hollered Viv from downstairs. "Breakfast is getting cold."

"I'll be right there," she yelled back.

Taking a deep breath, Betty straightened her uniform, then rushed downstairs as if nothing were wrong.

In the dining area, a group of fifteen Farmerettes ate breakfast at three long picnic tables in the middle of the plain room. A framed needlepoint sampler that read HOME SWEET HOME hung on a nearby wall. Underneath the wording someone had sewn a small embroidered farmhouse, surrounded by a fancy decorative border. Betty liked the cross-stitched picture. The piece caught her attention whenever she entered the room.

Viv waived to her from the table, saving her a place.

Betty approached a cast iron cooking pot on the food counter and ladled a bowl of lumpy oatmeal. She took a spoonful and grimaced.

"I told you so," said Viv, referring to Betty's late arrival.

Moving to the crowded table, Betty sat down.

Mabel, a chatty, frizzy-haired redhead, spoke up first. "Didja hear the news last night?" she said, excitedly. "The military thinks they found Glenn Miller's plane in the English Channel." Her lips formed a pout. "Hard to believe he's been gone since December."

"Glenn Miller?" asked Betty, perplexed by the coincidence with the tune she'd heard earlier.

"Yeah," said Mabel. "It was on the radio."

Betty addressed everyone at the table. "Did any of you hear his music in the middle of the night last night?"

Viv rolled her eyes.

"I was sleeping," said one girl.

"Me too," said another.

"Didn't *anybody* hear Glenn Miller?"

"Oh, Betty," giggled Mabel. "Everybody knows old man Filbert sometimes cranks up his radio at night. Doesn't he, Viv?"

"That's right," said Viv. She patted Betty on the arm. "It was probably Mr. Filbert, hun." Viv turned to the group and explained. "She had a dream about Mickey again."

The women nodded in evident understanding.

"You poor dear," said Cora Baker, squinting through her coke-bottle glasses.

"Wait a minute," said Susie Farren, a petite blond, taking a semester break from her classes at USC. "Who thinks they found the plane?"

"The Army Air Force," answered Mabel.

"Why would they do that?" asked Susie. "It's a waste of our military money. He was just a musician who died in the war. And when you're dead, you're dead. You can't do anything about that."

Betty dropped her spoon. It clinked on the bowl. The color drained from her face.

Tension silenced the table.

"What'd you say that for, Susie, yuh little dip," growled Viv. "You know Betty's husband was a trumpet player."

"It's okay, really," said Betty, trying to defuse the situation. "She didn't mean anything by it."

"Did, too," said Viv, glaring at Susie. "The little dip."

"We still have a war going on against the Japanese, you know." said Susie.

An iron triangle clanged.

Mr. Filbert, a middle-aged farmer as sour as the lemons he grew, lumbered into the room. "Okay, girls, time to go," he said, clapping his calloused hands. "Let's move it. Pick up some grub from Mrs. Filbert outside the building, grab your buckets, and get to work."

Moods somber, the women filed out of the shabby two-story dormitory into the morning darkness on their way to the lemon orchard, one-quarter mile away.

As they trudged down the road together, their feet crunching on gravel, a rooster crowed in the distance, welcoming the slow rising sun.

Betty, leading the pack, hoped work would help her forget about Mickey and her dreams. But she still wondered where the music and the scent of Aqua Velva had come from.

After reaching the lemon groves, the women fanned out. Each Farmerette was given a ladder to lug around and set up. Betty picked up hers and dragged it to a tree.

Placing the legs on stable ground, she climbed three steps, reached up, and twisted a fully yellow lemon from a branch, releasing sharp, fresh oils. She dropped the fruit into the bucket.

It was tiring, mindless work. But as the sun beat down, her daydreams returned. They were always about Mickey.

They'd met two years ago on a warm summer night in June 1943. An evening so hot she'd worn a light blue skirt and short-sleeved blouse in an effort to feel cooler.

Activity hummed around her. She stood across the street from The Hollywood Canteen on Cahuenga Boulevard, waiting for her favorite movie star, Van Johnson, to enter.

While she lingered, people paraded up and down the crowded sidewalk, past open bars and other bustling businesses, to catch a glimpse of the arriving celebrities. Cars inched forward in slow-moving traffic; some rowdy fans darted into the street, causing traffic to halt and horns to blare.

When she looked around to see better, someone nudged her. A man six feet tall, with black hair, a wide smile, and wearing a drab light-brown Marine uniform and matching garrison cap, sidled up to her. He held a beat-up trumpet case that was clutched to his chest like a sleeping baby.

She'd given him a polite smile and resumed observing.

"See any stars yet?" he asked.

"Not yet," she responded, noticing his soulful brown eyes. When their gazes met, she was taken aback. Her pulse raced. She was not one to believe in love at first sight, but there was something different about him. Maybe it was the way he looked in his uniform, or how the corner of his mouth curved up when he smiled.

"I'm Mickey," he said with a big grin. "Mickey Baker. Have you been standing here long?"

Her knees weakened. "Betty McCallum," she said, smiling shyly. "I'm waiting to see some stars. Silly, I know. Imagine a grown woman standing in the heat waiting to see some movie stars enter a building." Tilting her head, Betty looked up at him. "Don't you think?"

"They don't go in through the front door, you know."

Her eyebrows raised. "They don't?"

"You wanna see some stars?"

"What're you gonna do?" she asked flirtatiously. "Tell me to look up at the sky and then sneak a kiss?"

Mickey blushed. "No, no. Nothing like that," he protested. "We'll go inside. Just follow me."

He held out his hand and took a step toward the curb.

Betty hesitated. "I can't go into that club. I'm not in the military."

"Old Blew and I will get you in," he said patting the trumpet case. "Trust me."

She eyed his good-natured face. Without even thinking, she took his hand. "I can't believe I'm doing this."

Jumping off the curb, they'd dashed into the gasoline-choked air and plodding traffic, laughing while they zigzagged between vehicles. Cars slammed on their brakes and horns honked.

☙

Outside the famous club, lighting illuminated the large rope-lettering sign that read HOLLYWOOD CANTEEN FOR SERVICE MEN. Six red-painted stars had been affixed above the nondescript doorway.

Two long lines of military personnel, leading to the canopied entrance, crowded the sidewalk in front of the seven-foot-high wooden fences that partially hid the famed club.

"Let's go around the back," said Mickey, pulling Betty past the soldiers.

Her black wedge shoes clomped on the sidewalk, and she struggled to keep from falling.

Some of the service men whistled and howled.

"Nice gams, baby," crowed a leering sailor.

Turning a corner, Mickey tugged Betty to the rear of the building where a few people talked and smoked between the volunteer help entrance and the stage door.

"Has Jimmy Dorsey gone on yet?" Mickey asked a hefty-looking actor smoking a cigar. Betty recognized him as actor Jack Carson from *The Strawberry Blonde*.

"Not yet, pal." When they moved past him, Carson yelled, "Hey, where'd you get the doll?"

"Mickey," Betty said, excited, "That was—"

She never finished. They reached the rear stage door entrance, where a hard-nosed guard stood holding a clipboard. Nearby, wearing a busboy smock, Gary Cooper leaned against a white wood-paneled wall, staring past them, smoking a mentholated Kool cigarette. He gave them a two-finger salute.

"You volunteering this evening?" the guard asked Mickey.

"Well," said Mickey hemming and hawing. "I wanted to sit in with the Jimmy Dorsey Band tonight."

The guard gave him the once-over and rolled his eyes.

"Yeah, and I'm Clark Gable."

"But I'm a trumpet player."

"Beat it, kid. Professionals only. Stand outside with the other Marines."

"Maybe we should go, Mickey," said Betty.

Inside the club, a silhouetted figure wandered in the backstage area.

Mickey craned to see him better. "Jimmy," he yelled out, waving.

The figure stopped, looked over, and hollered, "Mickey."

The guard gave Jimmy Dorsey an incredulous stare. "You know this guy, Mr. Dorsey?"

"Yeah," said the voice. "Mickey Baker, second trumpet in Glenn Miller's band." Jimmy Dorsey appeared in the doorway now. He wore a white shirt with a cream-colored tuxedo jacket and a black bow tie. "Sure, I know him."

Betty gaped.

"Listen, Jimmy," said Mickey. "I'm on leave 'till I go back to Camp Pendleton on Tuesday. Can I sit in for a few songs?"

"We're on in ten minutes. Bring your axe and find a seat on the stand. We'll fit you in."

"Thanks, Jimmy."

Dorsey waved. "See you on stage—Corporal."

Mickey smiled at Betty. "C'mon, let's go."

She'd followed Mickey into the musty-smelling backstage area behind a large hanging backdrop.

Members of the Jimmy Dorsey band, wearing black suits and matching bow ties, were lined up, ready to enter the main stage. Mickey joined them.

She'd peered out from behind the curtain into the busy nightclub. Wagon wheel light fixtures with glowing antique lanterns illuminated the western-themed nightclub; cartoon murals were painted on the walls; and service men jammed the dance floor.

Betty Grable, Hedy Lamarr and Rita Hayworth wandered through the lively crowd, serving sandwiches and cake to hungry soldiers. And on stage, comedian Bob Hope stood at an open mike and regaled the audience with his jokes. The audience howled.

Jimmy Dorsey marched his band onto the stage to thunderous whistles and applause.

"...and now," said Hope, leering out at the audience for a laugh. "No, it's *not* Virginia Mayo, you happy howling hounds—how about a big welcome for Mr. Jimmy Dorsey, right here."

Dorsey raised his hands and kick-started his sixteen musicians into a rousing, fast-paced rendition of "King Porter Stomp."

The crowd exploded. Service men jitterbugged with Lana Turner and Joan Crawford. Unattached soldiers clapped along to the beat, while Jimmy Dorsey's melodic, trilling clarinet solo soared over the sound of the hard-driving ensemble.

Betty swayed to the rhythm, keeping an eye on Mickey, who seemed to be enjoying himself. But it wasn't until the band played a slower number called "Tangerine" that she realized how much she liked him.

Before the songs' bridge, Jimmy Dorsey called out to the crowd, "Ladies and gentlemen, we have a very special guest tonight. Sitting in on trumpet—a regular in the Glenn Miller Band and now the Marines—Corporal Mickey Baker."

The soldiers cheered.

Standing, Mickey glanced at her peering through the curtains, put the horn to his lips, and played a trumpet solo in the middle of the tune. The moment she'd heard his soft, dulcet serenade, her heart fluttered and cheeks heated. At that moment, Betty knew she was falling hopelessly in love.

After the show, they'd left the Canteen, borrowed a friend's Pontiac, and driven down to Will Rodgers State Beach, where they walked hand-in-hand on the sand.

Lights glittered in the Palisades hillside homes. Faint carousel music floated in from the Santa Monica pier. In the distance, a boat with a clattery diesel engine and weak spotlight slowly cruised the coastline.

Mickey spread out a wool military blanket, and they lay down, staring up at the Milky Way. Yellowish moonlight lit their faces, while waves crashed and lapped nearby.

"So, you want six kids?" she'd asked, smiling.

"Yeah, I think so. A whole brass section."

She giggled. "And who do you think is going to help you with this little project?"

"Well, I—" He blushed. Mickey glanced down and then snorted out a tiny laugh.

"Cat got your tongue?"

He looked back at her smiling face.

"Geez, Betty, I didn't mean you. I mean...oh, I don't know what I mean. You know I like you a lot, and—"

She leaned over and *shushed* him, placing her finger on his lips. "Don't say anything. It's more romantic that way."

Their eyes met and they both grinned.

Mickey leaned on his elbow. "How many kids do *you* want, Betty?"

"I figure my husband will be the first. After that, who knows?"

He laughed. "You're funny. You know that?"

"My sister Evie thinks so." She caressed his arm. "Can I ask you something? Why do you carry that trumpet around like it's your baby?"

"Old Blew? Why, we've been together forever. I guess cause one day it just talked to me."

She raised her eyebrows. "What do you mean?"

"Well, when I was eleven, and we lived in Trenton, Ohio, I followed my brother, Randy, into Griffin's Music Store on Grand Avenue. It was a musty old place with sheet music and band instruments hanging on the walls.

"Anyway, while I was looking around, Mr. Griffin cranks up this Victrola and plays this crackly old 78 record by Bix Biederbecke called "Riverboat Shuffle." He shook his head. "Man, that record changed my life."

Mickey's face brightened as he described the visit.

"It's a real fast-tempo song, see, but all I heard was Biederbecke on the cornet, playing that tune as easy and pure as he could. Each note was big and round, exploring melodies and harmonies I'd never heard before."

He looked at Betty. His voice took on a wistful tone. "It's almost like he'd wanted me to reach out and touch those notes, but you couldn't because they were too perfect. Always out of reach.

"When the record ended, I asked Mr. Griffin who it was, and he said, 'That was the greatest cornet player who ever lived: Bix Biederbecke.'

"And then I saw some instruments in a glass display case and wished I could play just like Bix."

He looked solemn. "There was Old Blew, stuck in the corner, its shine faded and scratched. Old Blew stared at me and I heard a voice in my head say, 'We can play like that. We can do it together,' and I believed him." He nodded to the trumpet case. "I bought Old Blew by working at that store for a year after school; lessons, too. And we've been chasing those perfect notes ever since."

"Play me a song," she'd said, nudging his shoulder with hers.

"You mean out here?"

Betty nodded yes. Mickey clicked open his trumpet case, pulled out Old Blew, and played.

Tears glistened in her eyes.

He stopped.

Impulsively, she leaned over and pecked Mickey on the cheek.

There rose a flush of red in his cheeks and neck. "What was that for?" he asked.

"Just because."

She drew him in with her eyes. Mickey set aside his trumpet.

When their lips touched, he slowly, softly kissed her until she quivered. His body pressed against hers.

She threaded her fingers through his hair, tugging him closer, smelling his Aqua Velva, enjoying everything about him. She kissed his lips, his chin, his nose, his cheeks. Her heart pounded faster and faster. She never wanted to let go or stop.

"Let's get married," Mickey panted.

"But we barely know each other," she said.

"What does that have to do with anything?"

There was no music in the air. No little voice in her head. Just Mickey and her, and she trusted him. Had confidence in him. He was her perfect note.

"All right," she said, placing her arms around his neck. "Shut up, and get the license."

They kissed again, melting into each other, lulled by the sound of breaking surf.

Within twenty-four hours they were married at the courthouse in downtown Los Angeles and had boarded a train to San Diego, joining a cluster of soldiers on deployment. When they arrived at the Santa Fe Depot, they stepped outside the Spanish-style building and wandered up Broadway, looking for the U.S. Grant Hotel. She held his hand, beaming with happiness, proud to be his wife.

While they walked, the sidewalks bustled with activity. People shopped, sailors strolled, and noisy buses drove by.

At Horton Plaza, a small park at the corner of 4th Avenue and Broadway, Mickey spotted the eleven-story hotel across the street.

After checking into the luxuriously decorated establishment, they withdrew to their room and didn't leave until Mickey was due at Camp Pendleton on Tuesday morning.

On the train ride back to Oceanside, they sat in silence, holding hands and giving each other loving looks to remind themselves nothing was wrong.

But Betty was terrified.

She wondered what would happen if Mickey was hurt. Or worse, killed in action. If he died, she wouldn't be able to bear it.

At 10:27 a.m. the *San Diegan* slowed to a stop at the small, red-shingled, Oceanside depot near Camp Pendleton.

Standing up, she followed Mickey and a group of Marines toward the vestibule door.

On the threshold plate at the top of the passenger car steps Mickey embraced her. She hugged back, holding him tight, not wanting him to leave.

"I've gotta go, babe," he said. He brushed a strand of brunette hair away from her forehead and she started to cry. He raised her chin. "Don't cry, Betty."

"I can't help it," she said, her voice breaking.

"I'll be back. Trust me."

She leaned in and clutched him again, feeling his wide, comforting shoulders around her. "Please don't go."

"Listen. Uncle Sam owns this body until I can come back home, but my heart belongs to you." He caressed her cheek. "You gonna be all right?"

She nodded.

"Okay. I'll write you every day."

Blowing her a kiss, he bounded down the steps.

The whistle blew and the passenger car jolted.

He stood in the dirt field near the tracks. As the train pulled away, Mickey waved. "Take care of Old Blew for me while I'm gone," he called out. "And don't forget, I'll be back." He pretended to dance with her. "We'll make a night of it. I promise. I'll be back." He smiled his big stupid grin.

Her tears flowed freely. "I love you," she shouted.

That was the last time she ever saw Mickey alive.

Betty stepped down from the citrus ladder and wiped her brow. Thinking about Mickey had only enlarged the hollowness in her heart. She yearned for him even more.

As she dragged the ladder to another tree, the midday sun sizzled on her arms. Sweat trickled down her cheeks and back.

After setting up, Betty climbed three steps to pick more fruit. The leaves rustled around her, while a cold gust of wind swept through, catching her by surprise. The moisture on her back cooled instantly. In the distance, the faint sound of Glenn Miller's "American Patrol" grew louder as it floated through the grove.

Her pulse raced. She glanced around, looking for the source of the notes. Then she looked at the other Farmerettes. Had they felt the cold air or heard Glenn Miller, too? To her dismay, everyone was working hard, oblivious to what she was experiencing.

She touched her forehead with her hand. *No, no, no. This can't be happening.* Was she crazy?

Feeling light-headed, Betty fanned herself before losing balance; she tumbled down the ladder, landing on her feet. Her head throbbed and she labored to breathe. She wanted to run off and lie in some grassy field until her faculties calmed.

But that wasn't going to be possible, for standing in the distance amongst the unpicked lemon trees was a lone familiar figure.

Betty strained to see. A man stepped out from the shadows, wearing a light-brown military uniform and holding a shiny metal object.

She brightened. "Mickey?"

The figure stood at attention.

"Is that you, Mickey?"

The soldier lifted his arm. The shiny metal object glinted in the sunlight.

Was he holding Old Blew?

Dropping her basket of lemons, Betty took a slow step forward, then another, and another, until she launched into a full-bore sprint, charging over the gravelly and uneven dirt. Tears rolled down her cheeks.

"Is that you, darling?" she cried out. Her heart pounded. She wanted to kiss him, squeeze him, and hold him tight. Maybe the death certificate had been wrong. "Mickey," she screamed.

But as she approached, the figure faded away, the last vestiges of his shadow disappearing into the light.

Winded, Betty lurched forward and dropped to her knees, skinning her shins on the coarse dry dirt. "Mickey," she wailed. "Come back, please."

When the rest of the Farmerettes caught up to her, she was sobbing uncontrollably.

That afternoon, the lowered window shades darkened her dormitory room. Betty lay in bed, weak and frightened.

Mr. Filbert leaned against a wall. Standing next to her bed stood a man with a concerned look on his face, a stranger who'd introduced himself as Dr Perry. He wore black-framed glasses.

"So, what's wrong with her, doc?" asked Mr. Filbert, crossing his arms.

"I'm not sure," said Dr. Perry. He took off his eyewear and looked at Mr. Filbert. "It could be heat stroke, but she doesn't have a high temperature. As a matter of fact, it's normal." He put his specs back on. "I talked with some of the girls, and they say she didn't have heat cramps or nausea before this happened."

"What could it be?"

"Possibly dehydration. It's been warm lately."

Mr. Filbert frowned. "I gotta tell you, doc, she's been nothin' but trouble from the day she got here." He pinched his lips together. "These girls, some of 'em got boyfriends and husbands in the war, and they don't complain about nothin'." His eyes turned hard. "The missus and me, we lost a son in Italy and I kept mum. But Betty's been moonin' about this Mickey fella every day for months. Been upsettin' the other girls, and I can't have it."

Betty winced. What if Mr. Filbert kicked her out of the farm? Where would she go? An institution?

She moaned.

"Maybe she just needs a day or two of rest," said Dr. Perry. "Let's try that."

"Whatever you say," said Mr. Filbert. "But I'm tellin' yuh, I'd boot her out in a second if I didn't need the help."

Tears welled up in Betty's eyes. She began to lose focus. *Mickey...*

Dr. Perry answered in a sharp tone. "She's the one who needs the help."

"You're not much of a business man, are yuh, doc?"

Mr. Filbert stormed off.

Dr. Perry sat on the edge of her bed.

"So, how are you feeling?"

"Worried," she said, her voice trailing off. "Mickey..."

"Did you hear what I told Mr. Filbert about heat stroke?"

Stroke? Had she had a stroke? Was that the cause of her dreams? Betty shook her head.

"We're gonna keep you out of the sun for a few days, and make sure you drink plenty of fluids."

"Okay," she muttered. "Boss... doesn't like me."

"Don't worry yourself about that. He's just a farmer concerned about his harvest."

Dr. Perry bent forward, and she smelled something familiar: a peppermint and vanilla odor.

Aqua Velva.

Betty bolted upright; her eyes wide open. "Mickey." she cried out. "His shaving lotion."

The doctor placed his hand on her shoulder. "Betty, listen to me."

"Saw him," she rambled on, unable to stop the images. "In the field. He's here." Her gaze darted about. Just one more glimpse of her love. "Mickey, are you here, darling?" She raised her voice. "Mickey?"

Dr. Perry grabbed her hands.

She felt jerked into the present.

Doc was gazing hard at her. "It's not Mickey you're smelling," he said. "It's me."

"No," she protested, struggling to break free.

"It's *my* aftershave. Whatever you saw this morning wasn't real."

Betty looked into his stern eyes and lost energy. She fell limp on the bed, all visions vanished.

"We're going to give you a sedative now. Let you sleep. We'll see how you're doing later today."

"Don't want any," she murmured. She didn't need drugs; she needed her husband.

Dr. Perry mixed Veronal powder in a cool glass of water. After she drank the tasteless drug, Betty stared at the top bunk box spring above her, yawned, and drifted off.

She awoke hours later, feeling refreshed: no anxiety, no dreams, and no Mickey.

Summer light streamed through the window. She looked around the warm room. Everything seemed the same; she breathed in the fresh scented air.

Viv stood by her dresser, sifting through clothes. "Welcome back, hun. Have a nice nap?"

Betty stretched. "Yes. What time is it?"

Viv turned and faced her. "Five o'clock. Dinnertime."

"I'm not hungry."

Crossing the room, Viv sat down on Betty's bed. "You had us worried. Even that little dip, Susie."

Betty lowered her chin. "I'm sorry, I didn't mean—"

"It's okay." Viv touched her hand. "Why don't you come down and join us. You don't have to eat or nothin'." She smiled. "Just come down and prove my roommate doesn't belong in the looney-bin."

Betty smacked Viv with her pillow and chuckled. It was the first laugh she could remember having in a long time.

"That's the spirit," said Viv, rooting her on. "You're gonna be all right."

While Viv finished dressing, Betty slid out of bed and slipped on a white cotton robe over her nightgown. She tightened the belt around her waist and ambled over to Viv, waiting at the door.

"Need any help?" her friend asked.

"I'm okay."

Viv grabbed her elbow anyway and guided her downstairs, their feet clomping on the wooden steps.

Betty marveled at how calm she felt, as if she'd turned a corner. Maybe Dr. Perry had been right: Mickey was only a hallucination, brought on by dehydration. If that were true, she wasn't going crazy at all.

At the bottom stair, she glanced into the dining room. All the other Farmerettes sat at the picnic tables, eating dinner.

"Look what the cat dragged in," announced Viv, grinning.

The girls broke into cheerful applause.

"Thanks, everybody," Betty said, blushing. She turned away to hide her embarrassment.

Looking at the wall, she spied the framed needlepoint sampler. It appeared different. The cross-stitched picture no longer said HOME SWEET HOME, but had Mickey's face embroidered on it, instead with a new message that spelled I'M BACK.

She dashed to the wall and stared at the sampler close up. A frisson of excitement crossbred with fear ripped down her spine. "Mickey," she cried out. "Mickey."

The girls bolted from their seats. Chairs screeched on the floor.

Viv raced to her. "What are you talking about?" she asked.

The Farmerettes surrounded them.

"He's here," Betty said in an emotion-choked voice. "The sampler says he's here."

Viv's eyebrows drew together. "It says Home Sweet Home like always."

The girls agreed.

"You're wrong," Betty said. She gazed at the dining room door. Mickey, standing casually in his khaki Marine uniform, leaned against the jamb, a big toothy grin on his face, his wounds still evident. "He's over there," she squealed.

"There's nothing there but that stupid door," said Viv.

"You're lying to me," Betty yelled. She pointed. "Can't you see him?"

The rest of the Farmerettes stared at her as if she were crazy.

Trembling, Betty jerked her head to Mickey before darting toward him.

"Grab her," hollered one of the girls.

From behind, Viv reached around and applied pressure to Betty's chest to keep her from moving forward.

"Help me, Mickey. Help!" Betty screamed. She thrashed about with manic energy. Her face reddened. "Let go of me."

The girls surrounded Betty and guided her to a chair. She struggled and flailed against them, but there were to many.

"Somebody call Dr. Perry," yelled Viv.

When the doctor arrived, Betty was already upstairs resting. Viv sat shotgun by the bed, protecting her from anyone who entered the room.

In the hallway, Dr. Perry and Mr. Filbert argued loud enough to be heard.

"I want her out tonight," said Mr. Filbert. "She's nuttier than a fruitcake."

Betty closed her eyes, a nauseous feeling roiled inside her.

"You can't do that," said Dr. Perry. "She needs to stay in a safe environment until her sister picks her up tomorrow."

"Sister? Whatdayuh mean, sister?"

"Your wife gave me a referral number and I called her. She's driving down from Fresno with her husband in the morning."

"What'd you do that for?"

Betty cringed. She didn't want to live with her sister. They hadn't spoken since Evie called her reckless and stopped talking to her after she'd married Mickey. Now, what would Evie think if she needed psychiatric help?

"Don't you know anything about these girls?" said Dr. Perry, raising his voice.

"What do I care? They're nothin' but lemon pickers to me. And not even good ones at that."

"Fine," said Dr. Perry harshly.

Dr. Perry pointed his finger at the farmer. "I'm her doctor and I'm ordering you. For health reasons, she can't be moved until her family arrives. Are we clear?"

"I liked it better before Doc Matheson moved away. He knew what was what."

"I'll let Betty know."

"Yeah, yeah," said Mr. Filbert, stomping down the stairs. "Can't wait until we beat those damn Japs and get this war over with so's I can get some *real* men around here."

Viv shook her head. "Stupid hillbilly," she muttered.

Betty, on the verge of tears, sniffled, and worried about whether she was just sick or becoming unhinged.

That evening, Dr. Perry medicated her with more Veronal.

At 3:15 a.m., the melodic rhythm of Glenn Miller's "Moonlight Serenade" seeped through the window, waking her. She squeezed her eyes tight to will away the song, but it wouldn't disappear. It continued to play.

Frightened, she reeled out of bed and glanced at Viv who slept peacefully in the upper bunk, oblivious to the music.

Betty stifled a whimper by slipping a hand over her own mouth. Was she going nuts?

Beads of sweat dampened her lip. She had to leave, but to go where? One thing was for sure, she wasn't going to move in with her sister, or be admitted to some crazy looney bin.

Being careful not to make any noise, she put on some black wedges and changed into a day dress hanging in her wooden locker. Grabbing Old Blew in one hand and her purse in the other, Betty slowly tiptoed to the door and put down the trumpet case on the floor. When she turned the knob, the door creaked open.

She froze.

Viv rustled in her bunk but resumed snoring.

Exhaling, Betty gingerly picked up Old Blew again, sandwiched herself through the opening, and rushed downstairs and out the building.

Once outside, she heard nothing except crickets singing in the nearby bushes. The Glenn Miller music had completely disappeared. It hadn't been real.

A light flicked on in one of the dorm rooms upstairs.

Worried she'd be caught, Betty headed toward the lemon groves and the paved roadway adjacent to the farm. A full moon peeked through the dark clouds, dimly lighting a pathway for her to see.

As she lugged Old Blew, sweat trickled down her back. With each step, the case handles made her hands ache more and more until they finally cramped, and she dropped the luggage on the ground. Betty wiped her forehead and sat on the trumpet case, clenching and unclenching her fingers.

Gravel crunched in the lemon grove.

On edge, Betty jerked. Then she saw something move and jumped up.

As Mickey stepped out from behind a tree, wearing his Marine uniform, the handsome, six-foot, black-haired soldier beamed. His war wounds had disappeared. "Betty," he called out.

She recoiled, prepared to run.

He abruptly materialized before her, stopping her from fleeing. "I told you I'd come back."

She shut her eyes and shook her head. "No, no, no, you're not real," she said before breaking down in tears. "You're dead. They told me so."

"True," said Mickey, agreeing. "But I just *had* to see you. I don't have much time."

Betty opened her watery eyes and looked at the dead soldier. "What-what do you mean? Mickey's gone."

"C'mon, you know it's me. I wouldn't lie to you."

She stared at him. He was whole and complete. Just like the day she'd said goodbye to him in Oceanside.

"Go on, touch me. I won't bite."

Betty hesitated. Reached out. She cupped Mickey's ice-cold cheek with her hand. His low temperature made her body shiver and she took a step back.

Mickey's smile faded. "What's wrong, baby?"

"This isn't you. In my dreams, your face, your arm—" She dropped her gaze.

"In heaven, we're all perfect, especially entertainers." He leaned in and lifted her chin with one icy finger. "Isn't that the way it's supposed to be?" He grinned, a twinkle in his eyes. "I'm still the same goofy, trumpet-playing, fun-loving guy. Just a little dead, that's all."

His humor made her laugh, and she melted into his freezing body. She draped her arms around his neck. "Oh, Mickey, I missed you so much."

He kissed her fervently, holding her tight.

While they embraced, an intense, blazing light shot out from the sky and illuminated the ground near the lemon trees. The sound of Glenn Miller's "A String of Pearls" drifted through the grove.

Betty, blinded by the brightness, shielded her eyes.

"They're here," said Mickey.

"Who's here?"

He grabbed her hand. "We don't have much time."

Tugging her, Mickey approached the light.

When they reached the edge, Betty paused. Her heart raced. "I can't."

"What's wrong?"

She stared at the unearthly brilliance. Her shoulders tightened. Images of heaven, or what she remembered of it from catechism, flashed through her mind. "I don't—," she said. "I don't want to die."

"Die?" He broke into a hearty laugh. "You're not going to die. What makes you think that?"

"You said there's not much time."

"You're being silly. Trust me."

She looked at Mickey and knew he was right. Just like the evening when she'd blindly taken his hand and crossed the street to get into the Hollywood Canteen. She'd trusted him then and trusted him now. "All right," she said, giving him a reassuring smile.

He eased her forward, and they stepped into the circular beam of light together.

They were not alone.

In the middle of the grove, white lattice surrounded a large Victorian gazebo. On top, a domed roof crowned the structure, which was supported by eight symmetrical pillared columns adorned with twinkling lights. Wooden stairs led up to the pavilion bandstand where a group of twenty-two musicians fiddled with their instruments, belching out notes and riding the scales on melodic roller coasters.

Betty, fascinated, struggled to see. "Who's that?" she asked, pointing to a stern-faced bandleader with horn-rimmed glasses.

Mickey whispered, "That's Glenn Miller."

Her eyes widened. "You mean *the* Glenn Miller?" She stared in wonderment.

Mickey pointed to a few other musicians. "And over there on trumpet from the Duke Ellington Band is Bubber Miley. Next to him, the baby-faced guy with the slicked back hair is Bix Beiderbecke, cornet. On his right, Chick Webb, King of the Savoy ballroom, sittin' in on drums."

Webb raised his drum stick to acknowledge them.

"Fats Waller—the harmful little armful—on the piano."

Waller smiled and twinkled some keys.

"And in the back," continued Mickey. "Bunny Berigan, second trumpet, Charlie Christian, guitar, and—"

Betty asked, "Are they all—"

"Dead?" Mickey interrupted. "Yeah, just like me. Some of the best jazz musicians who ever existed, black or white, now playing in harmony without prejudice.

Rubbing the back of his head, Glenn Miller stomped out of the bandstand and yelled, "You ready? We're due back soon."

"In a minute," Mickey hollered.

"Musicians," muttered Glenn Miller, shaking his head. He looked at his wristwatch, then stormed back into the gazebo.

"Hey, man, let's get this gig rolling," called out Bubber Miley.

Glenn Miller raised his hands in front of the band.

"What's going on?" asked Betty.

Before Mickey could answer, the sound of a clarinet and saxophone playing the melody flowed from the bandstand. Glenn Miller's slow, romantic "Moonlight Serenade" had never sounded better.

"Look, Mickey," said Betty, pointing.

Bright light surrounding the lemon grove lessened to a semidarkness, allowing thousands of stars to flicker overhead. It was the most romantic setting ever. She squeezed Mickey's arm in joy.

"Remember how I said we'd dance when I came back?" he asked. Betty nodded.

"This is it."

Her eyes welled. "You're a fool."

"I know," he said, sighing. "But a happy one."

When he pulled her close their eyes met. There was nothing left to say. She leaned against him, and they swayed in place to the slow, tender song as if they were the only two people in the world.

Betty closed her eyes to remember everything she could about her husband. The way he looked—his dark hair, strong chin, powerful arms. And the scent of Aqua Velva, so familiar. The moments they'd shared together. This dance. She didn't want to forget anything.

When the song ended, they continued to hold each other, dancing to their own music.

Glenn Miller rushed off the gazebo and strode toward them with a fixed stare.

"Pack up, Baker," said Miller, pointing to his watch. "It's time to go."

"Already?" said Mickey.

Betty looked at the bandstand. The musicians were putting away their instruments.

The famed bandleader frowned. "I told you this gig would take too long. We're behind schedule."

Mickey turned to Betty and gazed into her eyes. "I've gotta go, babe."

"What do you mean?" she said. "You just got here."

He gestured toward Glenn Miller. "Major's orders."

The thought of Mickey leaving scared her. She didn't want to lose him again. In a desperate attempt, she grabbed onto him. "Don't leave me, Mickey, please."

Glenn Miller rolled his eyes. "C'mon, Baker."

"In a minute, Glenn. Okay?"

Miller appeared to seethe.

Mickey firmly placed his hands on her shoulders. The firmness of his touch relaxed her.

"It's time for me to move on, Betty. My stay here is over."

"But I don't want you to go," she said, weeping. "I can't live without you."

"Listen to me. Can you do that?"

She nodded.

"It's time for you to move on, too," he said. "Experience life, find new relationships. You need to make up with your sister. It's the right thing to do." He cocked his head. "C'mon, Betty, you'll meet another guy."

"But I don't want to find anybody else." She closed her eyes. "I'm afraid I'll forget you."

Mickey reached out and placed his palm on her heart. "I'm not going anywhere. You can't forget me. I'll always be right here, with you."

She seized his hand and set it to her lips.

"Our time is up. The rains are coming," said Glenn Miller.

Mickey took a step back. The light surrounding the lemon grove began to fade.

A large opaque bubble cocooned over the famous bandleader first and then the musicians. Betty noticed one enfolding Mickey.

"I love you," she yelled, crying.

"Take care of Old Blew for me, babe. I love—"

His voice disappeared in a crack of thunder. Betty followed the floating cocoons as they ascended into the sky and disappeared. As she stared into the heavens, a droplet of water hit her cheek.

A bolt of lightning lit up the darkness. Thunder rolled across the valley.

After soft drizzle fell first, it intensified into a torrent.

Betty stood in the cloudburst, savoring the cool liquid soaking her body.

The breeze on her face soothed her.

The pain in her heart eased.

Was Mickey real, or just a dream?

She looked upward and smiled, something she thought she'd forgotten how to do.

The questions didn't matter anymore. She and Mickey had expressed their love and had their last dance. The memory of him would live in her heart forever.

"Goodbye, Mickey, my love. You're right. It's time to move on." She blew him a kiss and closed her eyes. "I love you, darling, always."

Picking up her belongings, she walked back to the gravelly path that led to Mr. Filbert's farm. Evie would be there in the morning, and she'd ask her sister if she could stay while she got settled again.

Thanks to Mickey, she had a life to resume—and a relationship to repair. Now she could live in peace.

CHAPTER FOUR

CUPID-1637, PART TWO

JUNE 2063
PARADISE CITY, HEAVEN

Pixel stopped reading, put a smile on his face to stay positive, and turned toward his client. He knew the violations in both cases would be hard to defend.

In the first case, Cupid-1637 had hired a third-party vendor, Magic in a Lamp Company, to spend thousands of dollars on wishes outside his given authority. Then, after he granted the love wish, Penny Palmer ended up with a dog as a companion instead of a human.

In the second case, his client had terrorized Betty McCallum by bringing back her maimed husband Mickey, dead of horrific war wounds, which caused her severe emotional distress. Then, to make the violation worse, he disrupted at least fifteen departments by rounding up all those dead musicians to perform with Glenn Miller, and yet, the lovers still decided to move on and part ways forever.

The two cases raised a critical question. Why was Cupid-1637 so actively involved in the planning and facilitation of both romances? Because the Cupid's Oath ambiguously claimed that, "…I will carry out, according to my ability and judgment, as a Cupid or as a fully deputized Cupid's assistant, this covenant" and "Furthermore, into whosoever's life I shall enter, I promise to abstain from (a) all intentional or negligent wrong-doing and harm, (b) abusing the bodies of man or woman in providing any service, and (c) causing any injustice to them."

Both pledges, taken together, imply Cupid or a Cupid's assistant can expand their authority beyond using just a bow and arrow because "carry out, according to my ability and judgment" and "into whosoever life I shall enter" leaves the Oath up to interpretation by the assistant. Usually, most Cupid's assistants continue to limit their actions to the old tried and true method of using a bow and arrow, but some improvise.

Cupid-1637 certainly improvised.

If he had to take a guess, Pixel assumed that the panel would most likely claim his client had used poor judgment and decision-making ability by resurrecting a love affair between a human and a ghost. He suspected that type of substitution was not what the gods and goddesses had intended when they authorized Cupid or any of his fully deputized assistants to implement the Cupid's Oath. The same with matching a human with a dog.

Cupid-1637 leaned back in his chair, hands clasped behind his head. "So, what do you think, Pops?"

Pixel was careful to answer. Unlike Earth, a social worker in heaven had to be an advocate, a therapist, and a lawyer, all in one. He didn't necessarily like the attorney part, but he had no choice. Most of the lawyers hadn't made it up to heaven, and there was a shortage in the system.

He cleared his throat. "It's not good. Maybe, before we talk about the cases, we should discuss your life on Earth. Something we can use to explain—"

"Oh, man," moaned his client. "You guys are all the same."

"What do you mean?"

"All this psychological mumbo-jumbo. How do I know you're even qualified to help?"

Not qualified? Pixel stared at his impertinent client and pursed his lips. "I happen to have a master's degree in social work from the University of Southern California."

"You mean you were also a social worker before you died?"

"Yes."

Cupid-1637 burst out laughing. "Oh, man. Have they got you pegged!" He slapped the table. "You're just another one of those shufflers; somebody who'll do anything the bosses want just to please them. Bet you're underappreciated up here, too, just like on Earth."

"You don't know anything about me."

"It's written all over your face, man."

His comment pushed a button. People had been judging him like this his whole life. On Earth, in heaven, even at his own funeral. He was either too heavy or not good-looking enough. His ex-wife treated him like trash. He should have had a better job. Made more money.

Pixel stood and shoved the chair hard into the table.

His actions startled Cupid-1637, who immediately lost the grin on his face.

Grabbing the file, Pixel barreled toward the door.

"Hey, man, where are you going?"

"I think you should request another social worker. I'm not sure we can work together."

His face ashen, the client bolted from his seat. "Hey, c'mon," he pleaded. "I was just bustin' your balls. That's all. I didn't mean it."

"I'll help you find somebody else. Although, it might be too late."

As Pixel reached for the door handle, Cupid-1637 grabbed his arm. There was desperation in the Cupid assistant's voice when he said, "Don't—"

Pixel stopped and stared at his client, who wore a pained expression.

"You can't leave," said the romance agent softly. He lowered his gaze. "They're going to flush me." The hold on Pixel's arm loosened. "I'll answer whatever you want."

There were things Pixel had wanted to say but didn't. To his detriment, a familiar feeling reappeared, and the "old softy" hiding inside him made an encore appearance. In his heart of hearts, he knew he had to put aside his anger to help this lost being.

It was the story of his life. He'd always helped people. Maybe that's why his supervisor, Mr. Biggle, had assigned him this case because he knew Cupid-1637 was a problematic client and needed additional support.

Still, it seemed odd that he'd received the assignment because his co-worker and angel-in-training, Scot Adams, usually handled the larger and more complex cases like this one.

He wondered why Biggle had done it.

"So, will you help me?" asked Cupid-1637.

"Okay," Pixel said to Dean, "Let's try it again."

The two went back to the table and seated themselves.

Pixel reopened the file and studied a page. "It says here you were born in Gary, Indiana."

His client squirmed in his chair. "Yeah, I was born Dean Aloysius Webster on April 23, 1913."

"Can I call you Dean?"

"Yeah, whatever, man."

"Okay, Dean. It says here your parents were Joseph Webster—"

"You mean, Big Joe," said Dean, snorting a laugh.

Pixel drew his eyebrows together. "Good father?"

Dean's expression tightened. "He was a real sonuvabitch! And a rummy too. After hurting his leg during the 1919 steel strike, he left me to go boozing. Ain't that a bite? I had to kipe our meals just to survive."

"What about your mother, Dorothy?"

"She died during the 1918 Spanish Flu epidemic."

"What was she like?"

"Let me tell you something, Mr. Millet—"

"Pixel."

Dean pointed his finger. "Let me tell you something. The only good in me came from my mother, see. Too bad I only got five years' worth. She was a saint."

"Do you think the upbringing by your parents had any impact on your performance as a Cupid's assistant?"

"I don't know, man," said Dean, shrugging. "What does my file say?"

"It only contains your infractions and has minimal background information. So, I need to ask you these questions to figure out what your problem is."

"Well, it seems pretty obvious. I'm a troublemaker."

"I doubt it. It's usually something deeper."

There were two knocks on the conference room door, interrupting the meeting. Pixel and Dean jerked toward the sound.

The door swung open, and an attractive woman in her early forties stood in the entrance. She had light ash-brown shoulder-length hair and wore a conservative black pencil skirt with a matching blazer and high-heeled shoes. A white open-collared blouse showed beneath her coat. She held two red files.

Aside from noticing that she was beautiful, Pixel saw two small wings sprouting from the back of her clothes. A newbie. His heart skipped a beat. He then looked down, afraid he was staring.

"Is this conference room C?" she asked, smiling.

"It's conference room B," said Pixel, trying to avoid eye contact. "C is on the other side of the office, past the working bullpen."

"Thanks. My name's Carrie Lansdale. I just got transferred in from the Department of Discipline, Pre-Columbian American Division. Guess there aren't many cases involving the Aztec gods anymore."

"I don't mean to be rude," said Pixel, masking his attraction with a brusque tone, "But we're working on a difficult case right now, and we've got a lot to finish before our hearing this afternoon—"

"Hey, let her talk," interrupted Dean.

Pixel grimaced.

Carrie raised the palms of her hands. "I understand perfectly," she said apologetically. "I've got a case, too. And now I should find my client." She grabbed the handle on the door, then tilted her head and smiled again. "It was nice to meet you. Maybe we'll run into each other at the hearings."

As she closed the door, Dean shouted out, "His name is Pixel. He's my social worker. That's Pixel."

Pixel frowned. "What'd you do that for?"

A smug grin appeared on Dean's face. "I think she kind of likes you, Pops."

"I don't think so."

Dean chuckled mildly. "Boy, are you ever clueless."

"What do you know about it?"

"I'm a Cupid's assistant, remember? I know these things."

"According to your file, you're not very good at your job." Pixel gazed down, looked at the open folder. "Hey, I didn't mean that. I'm sorry."

"Listen, Pops, I may not be the best Cupid up here, but I've seen enough chicks in my life to know when they're interested." Cupid-1637 smiled, and said earnestly, "Anyway, I saw how you looked at her."

Pixel raised his head, staring directly at Dean. "Are you through yet?"

"Yeah," said Dean, leaning back in his chair. "For now."

Pixel ignored him and silently read the file. "Says here you left home at seventeen and traveled around the Midwest and Texas, working odd jobs."

"It was the Depression, man."

"And then you died at twenty-five." He exhaled. "There's not much to use here. What about the two cases? Why the woman and the ghost?"

"I was new on the job, see. I wanted that Betty McCallum dame to have the kind of goodbye I couldn't give to my girlfriend."

Pixel raised his eyebrows. "Girlfriend?"

"Yeah, I had one before I croaked. Her name was Sue Woods."

"And you loved her?"

Dean's eyes revealed his sadness. "Course I did. She was the sweetest thing this side of Fort Worth," he said wistfully. "The gods were looking out for me on the day I met her."

Nodding his head, Pixel felt relieved. He gave Dean a knowing look. "Good. Maybe we can mitigate some of the liability and the panel's concerns by claiming you were working with a broken heart. What about the other case?"

"You mean the one with the magic lamp?"

"Yes. Penny Palmer."

Dean appeared pensive and shrugged. "The reason she got a dog instead of a man was that—" he paused. "—she seemed kind of nice, and I didn't want her to end up with a guy like me."

His answer surprised Pixel, who sat there speechless. He rubbed his face. "A guy not like you? You just told me you loved your girlfriend."

Dean leaned forward. "You know why I was running for that train?"

"The one that killed you?"

"Right, the one that killed me. I was trying to run away."

"From what?"

"I'd just gotten Sue Woods pregnant."

Pixel felt his throat tighten. He exhaled. *Great*, he thought, *that probably weakens the defense in both cases.*

He looked at his watch: 10:00 a.m. Two hours had gone by fast, and he needed to finish reviewing everything before the 4:00 p.m. hearing. It was a big file.

"Let's go through the next set of violations," Pixel said. "Maybe there's something there."

"I don't think it gets much better."

So, once again, Pixel began reading the file out loud. But something was bothering him.

He'd had enough work experience to know that his client, in all likelihood, had other reasons for the way he'd acted on these cases. He wasn't even sure Dean himself knew why.

Pixel hoped that *he* could figure it out before they met with the panel.

CHAPTER FIVE

CASE NUMBER THREE: LOVE POTION NUMBER NEIN

ALLEGED VIOLATION: Intentional or negligent wrongdoing
ALLEGED VIOLATION: Failure to use wise judgment
ALLEGED VIOLATION: Abusing the bodies of man or woman

APRIL 2013
CULVER CITY, CALIFORNIA

Kirby Briggs, naturally thin and young-looking for his twenty-seven years, carried a small bowl of Fancy Feast for the feral cat lurking near his apartment door.

He bent down and set the ceramic dish on the walkway by a red-flowering begonia. "Here, Graycie," he called out.

The frightened feline stayed hidden beneath a concrete stairwell, staring at him.

"You can eat it later," he said, knowing his furry friend would wait until he left.

Kirby smiled and brushed his hand through his wavy brown hair. He wasn't a cat fanatic or anything but figured everybody deserved a little love.

Worried about the time, he looked at his watch and grimaced. He didn't want to be late for work today as a part-time clown at the Gower-Atascadero Farmers Market in Hollywood. The market owners frowned upon employees who weren't punctual, so he had to leave now.

A noise distracted him.

His new neighbor, Maxine Liu, rushed across the courtyard, her high heels click-clacking on the concrete.

Kirby's pulse raced. Maxine was beautiful. She had a tall, slender frame and wore a black pencil skirt with a white blouse that caressed her olive-skinned body in just the right places.

Appearing preoccupied, she disappeared down the stairs to the underground garage, probably on her way to work.

He sighed. He'd been a goner from the moment she'd first moved into the apartment building. She appeared self-confident and smart, and, according to his other neighbors, she was a financial adviser and friendly with everyone.

But what really attracted him to her was the way she smiled and how it brought a radiance to her face. And for a part-time clown who noticed those things, her cheerful demeanor came across like an irresistible ray of sunshine. Now, how could he not want to be with somebody like that? It was love at first sight.

Then reality set in, and he shook his head. Who was he trying to kid? He was just a silly party clown, not the kind of guy Maxine would date. She didn't even know he existed. If he wanted to go out with her, he'd need a miracle.

While working at the Farmers Market, Kirby wandered through the crowd, wearing red floppy shoes, striped baggy pants with suspenders, rainbow hair, and holding a bouquet of balloons. As he strolled past the tables piled with row-on-rows of grapefruits, oranges, avocados, cucumbers, tomatoes, root vegetables, and bunches of cilantro and onions, the people gave more attention to the food than him.

He thought it seemed stupid to hire a clown to entertain when all the customers wanted was to buy their food and leave. Besides, he'd never even seen a clown perform at a Farmer's Market before. What did he even "perform"? Wasn't he just added color or a curiosity for the kids?

Kirby ambled past a kettle corn booth and thought about Maxine, which he seemed to be doing quite a lot lately. What would she think if she saw him working here? Had he made the right career choice, acting? Wouldn't office work, even filing and running errands for a corporate hack, seem more admirable? He could work his way up. His gut grabbed at the thought of giving up his dream.

He tried to ignore his inner thoughts and clear his mind. He had a job to do. But when a woman with a blue canvas stroller rolled up, he sprang into a funny dance, made a goofy face, and handed her child a big shiny balloon.

After the kid burst into tears, Kirby figured it was time for a break.

He wandered into No Man's Land, located in a far corner near the trash bins where Julie Moreau hawked her Scandinavian Beet Sauce; Vic Trumbo, the blind violinist, played his fiddle; and SanDee Beaches sold her autographed photos. People rarely visited this area.

Kirby, deep in thought, sat on a wooden bench next to SanDee's table. Maybe he did need a new career. He'd been a psychology major at UCLA before getting the acting bug in his senior year, just around the same time his girlfriend Paige had broken up with him. She'd called him a Peter Pan. Hell, even Dr. Langford, his faculty advisor, was so upset about his defection to the arts that he'd practically promised him a spot in the Clinical Psychology Graduate Program if only he would take the GREs.

And what about his parents? He shook his head. They'd yelled at him for three months, calling him irresponsible and immature, which was the main reason he'd moved out of their house—to prove them wrong. One thing he knew he wasn't was irresponsible and immature.

But should he go back to school? Now, that was a good question. He wished the answer were easy because, face it, being an entertainer wasn't all that rewarding.

Movement caught his eye, and he looked left.

SanDee adjusted the FORMER TV STAR OF "FRIENDS" sign mounted on her card table. "Kirby," she called out in her raspy voice.

"Oh, hey."

"C'mere," she gestured.

A heavyset blonde in her late forties, SanDee wore a too-tight black leather miniskirt and black leggings. Hoop earrings swung from her ear lobes.

Kirby trudged to her table and gazed down at the glossy photos for sale. One of them, scattered amid bottles of scented oils and a "Magic Make-up" cosmetic line, was a picture of the *Friends* cast sitting around a table at Central Perk, the fictional coffee shop in the show.

"Where are you in the shot?" he asked, puzzled.

She pointed her finger to a woman drinking coffee at a table in the background. "I'm an extra."

"I never saw you in the show."

"I was the star," snapped SanDee, clearly annoyed. "I just had a bad agent, okay? Do you think it's easy drinking coffee all day on the set? Jennifer Aniston couldn't do it. Matthew Perry couldn't do it. Courtney Cox couldn't do it." She pointed to herself. "I could do it," she said, anger rising. "I could drink the coffee, but they conspired to keep me from getting a credit. Assholes," she shrieked. "Assholes!"

He raised his palms. "Yeah, right," Kirby said, taking a step back, not wanting to get involved.

"So, why are you here, moping around?"

"I'm not moping," he said defensively, wishing he were back in the fruits and vegetables side of the market.

"What's the matter? Girl problems?"

"No."

"Course it is," she said. "It's always girl problems." She looked at him with knowing eyes. "Lonely?"

His skin tingled. "How did you know?"

"I'm a psychic and a Wiccan."

"You mean like witchcraft?" he said, realizing SanDee might be certifiable.

"I make an honest living, honey."

He jerked his thumb at the market. "I've really gotta get back to work, SanDee." Kirby forced a smile. "The bosses don't like me taking breaks."

She held out a business card. "I can make you a love potion if you want. Doesn't cost much. That's because it's a high-volume item."

Kirby shook his head. "I don't think so. I believe in love the old-fashioned way."

SanDee rolled her eyes. "Puh-lease, take the card. Think about it. The old-fashioned way takes too long."

Reluctantly, Kirby took the card.

"Listen, hun," she said, smiling. "If you want to do business, there's a sale on this week. Three spells for the price of two. I take Mastercard."

Once again, wandering the market searching for kids to entertain, he'd reconsidered SanDee's offer. But why complicate his love life by involving a phony witch? Still, he kept her business card in his pocket just in case.

That afternoon, Kirby returned home, opened the mail—another GRE application sent by his parents—and checked the web to see if there were any acting auditions. He gave up after learning a local production of *Hamlet* required him to speak fluent Mandarin.

When it neared four o'clock, he changed into his slip-resistant shoes, black pants, white shirt, and skinny tie for the job that really paid his bills—he was a food server over at Cinder's Deep-Water Grill in Culver City.

Cinder's, a new wave restaurant near Sony Studios, attracted the thriving millennial crowd. The eatery, a steak and seafood house, dimly lit with pendant lights and picture-sized lighting fixtures attached to the brick walls, had a warm and cozy ambiance that reminded him of his Uncle Ted's Shadyside Inn chophouse in Pittsburgh. Kirby liked working at Cinder's. The tips were good, his co-workers were nice, and he could walk there from his apartment.

As usual, his shift started slow, but by 7:30, the place was rocking. Kirby was primarily responsible for taking orders, delivering food, and providing good customer service. Since he could do all three, and because the owner knew his Uncle Ted, he'd gotten the job. It certainly wasn't because he had an undergraduate degree in psychology.

Inside the kitchen, he heard clanging pots and pans, garlic and butter crackling, and cooks shouting "Yes, Chef" and "No, Chef" from their assigned stations. The mellow scent of brandy-flavored Steak Diane wafted around him.

Kirby handed an order to the expeditor, the liaison between the cooks and the waiters.

Pablo Muvelli, another pony-tailed, out-of-work actor employed as a waiter, approached him. He pulled out a Pall Mall and shoved it between his lips. "Hey, Kirby, bro, do me a favor. Cover my tables for me while I grab a smoke." Backing up toward the door, he flicked his brushed chrome lighter and lit the cigarette, taking a puff. "There's a new party of two on eighteen."

"Sure," said Kirby, his smile slipping. He couldn't refuse without seeming like a jerk.

Muvelli coughed and hacked. "Thanks, bro. I owe you one."

Bursting through the kitchen door, Kirby entered the crowded dining room and made a beeline for table eighteen near the illuminated brick wall.

He would be as professional a waiter as could possibly be. "Yes, sir" and "No, ma'am," and "Might I recommend the Chilean

Sea bass tonight?" His smile widened the closer he got to the table until he realized Maxine Liu sat there.

Could anything be worse? He didn't want Maxine to see him working as a lowly waiter. It was just as bad as being a clown. First impressions were so important.

He slowed, hoping it was someone else. But there she was, sitting in the black leather booth, looking at her cell phone. She wore yet another white blouse and a perfectly tailored navy pantsuit. And when she moved, her raven hair glistened in the light of the wall sconces.

He gathered confidence and arrived at the table. "Hello," he said to Maxine, who appeared to be reading her email. "My name is Kirby. I'm your waiter tonight."

Maxine glanced up and smiled. "Hi, Kirby," she said, showing no sign of recognition.

He stepped backward, feeling awkward. "I'll return in a few minutes with your menu."

She eyed him with evident curiosity. "Don't I know you? You look familiar."

Kirby paused before answering. He had to tell her the truth. "We live at the same apartment complex," he said. "I see you every morning."

She thought a moment. "Are you the guy who feeds the cat every day?"

He nodded. "That's me."

"What's your last name, Kirby, the-guy-who-feeds-the-cats?"

"Briggs. Kirby Briggs."

"Maxine Liu." She held out her hand.

He shook it. Her soft, reassuring touch warmed him, and he relaxed.

"Have you worked here long?" she inquired.

"About a year. Only in the evenings."

She seemed intrigued and leaned forward. "Why? What do you do during the day?"

"I clown around," he said, covering his reluctance with irony.

"You mean you goof off?"

"No. I mean, I'm a clown. Like for parties."

"Now, that's interesting," she said. "For a minute, I thought you were going to tell me you were an unemployed actor."

"I'm that, too," he admitted. Did she think he was a loser?

"You're a funny dude, Kirby Briggs, the-guy-who-feeds-the-cats." Maxine laughed.

Kirby chuckled, too. His heart filled with joy. He was actually talking with Maxine Liu. What if she liked him? Maybe he could get her phone number.

"Move over," barked a tall, handsome man who wore a designer golf shirt of baby blue and knife-edged tan slacks that bespoke money.

She slid to the right. The man sat beside her.

"Hey, babe," Maxine said, pecking him on the cheek.

The elation Kirby felt seeped out like a fast-deflating balloon, but he kept a professional demeanor.

"Kirby, this is my date, Brad. He's a film sales executive at Red K Media."

He eyed Brad, who looked like George Clooney's better-looking younger brother. "Nice to meet you."

"Kirby lives in my building," Maxine explained.

"Yeah, great," Brad said with unmistakable disinterest.

"What do you recommend tonight, Kirby?" asked Maxine.

"Just get what we always get," snapped Brad.

"The Chilean Sea bass with lemon sauce," he said, ignoring Brad completely, and slipping into the role of the professional waiter.

"That sounds good," said Maxine.

"I hate fish," Brad barked. "Bring me a Jack and Coke. And two menus."

"Yes, sir," Kirby responded.

Disappointed, he turned and walked toward the hostess. Whatever moment he'd had with Maxine, that small spark of affinity was over.

☙

That night, Kirby couldn't sleep. He tossed and turned, thinking about Maxine. How could she be with such a jerk? And what did Brad have that he didn't, other than money, a successful career, and movie star looks?

Rubbing his neck, he decided to get out of bed and drown out his sorrow with sweets. Of course, emotional eating wasn't the answer, but at that moment, it seemed like the right solution.

Kirby trudged down the hallway to the living room. There wasn't much in the way of furniture except for the gray couch and coffee table he'd bought at Ikea.

His only piece of artwork, a framed poster of Claude Monet's *Water Lilies*, hung on a wall over the sofa. He'd bought it because he loved the colors and its depiction of light. Someday, he hoped to see the original at the Musee-D'Orsay in Paris. Then, maybe, if he were lucky enough, he'd visit the museum with someone like Maxine.

After he turned left into the kitchen, he pulled a pint of Baskin Robbins Rocky Road from the freezer, grabbed the box of Twinkies sitting on the countertop, and sat at the kitchen table. He pried open the cardboard lid of the chocolate ice cream and scooped out a bite. The creamy goodness made him murmur,

"*Mmmm.*" His troubles were easing when he spotted the Potions by SanDee business card. It seemed to stare back, mocking and challenging him.

He picked it up and gazed at the phone number.

Should he call her? The woman was a nut case. Magic spells and incantations only existed in old movies and Harry Potter books. Her "love potion" couldn't possibly work.

Could it?

Kirby sighed. He did like Maxine; he liked her a lot. So, what harm could it do to use a silly spell? He'd be no worse off, right?

He envisioned Maxine wearing a floral print flared sundress; her long-lashed eyes closed, her lips pouted, leaning in to kiss—

This is pathetic, he thought, shaking his head. He crumpled up the card. Magic was fake, and no amount of fantasizing could make him change his mind.

But Maxine's image lingered. He imagined her soft, moist lips pressed against his.

"Oh, crap!" he said, picking up the crinkled card. He punched in SanDee's number on his iPhone.

Her phone rang, and she answered.

"Hello, SanDee," he said. "It's Kirby. I'm calling about the love potion."

He arrived at SanDee's tree-lined street in West Hollywood and parked in front of her apartment building. As an educated person who should have known better, he hated himself for having given in to his desperation by resorting to the love potion.

Getting out of his car, he tramped up the weathered concrete steps. When he reached the locked glass door, he looked at the multi-unit mailboxes embedded in a stucco wall to his right and pressed the button that had SanDee's name printed underneath.

The metal box buzzed.

"Helwo," slurred an inebriated voice.

"Hello, SanDee? It's Kirby."

"I doh know any Furby," said SanDee, clearly irritated. "Whadayuh want?"

"I'm here about the love potion. I called about an hour ago."

"Kirby. Is that you, Kirby?"

"It's me."

"Kirby, why didn't you say so? Some guy named Furby said he was you."

The glass door buzzed and clicked open.

He knew it was a bad idea, especially with SanDee sounding so drunk, but he went in anyway because love makes you do stupid things. At least that's how he rationalized it to himself.

Once inside the courtyard, Kirby walked past an empty, water-stained koi pond. Shattered mosaic tile fragments littered the ground as if smashed by a sledgehammer. Kirby had no desire to find out what'd happened and hurried to SanDee's apartment, hidden behind a slatted staircase.

He knocked on her faded door three times. "Hello, SanDee," he called out.

Nothing.

"SanDee?" He debated whether to leave.

"Hold on. Hold on." A bloodshot eye peered out from the peephole. "Kirby, what're you doing here?"

"I called. Remember?"

"Right, right," SanDee mumbled.

The door opened, and the unmistakable smell of incense flowed out. SanDee greeted him wearing a rumpled black Adidas sweatsuit and holding a half-empty jar of Julie Moreau's Scandinavian Beet Sauce. Grabbing the sleeve of his hoodie, she dragged him inside and shut the door. Then, after the fact, she said, "Kirby, come on in here and have a drink!"

"No thanks," he said, shaking his head.

"Oh c'mon, don't be a poop. It's just some Scandinavian beet sauce—with a little vodka added in," she cackled. "*Shhh*—don't tell anybody."

Her boozy, beet-infused breath reached him, and he recoiled. "You alright?"

"Maybe I should go," Kirby said. "I'm—I'm not feeling very well."

"Nonsense. I promised you a potion—just as soon as I finish this brew." She chugged from the jar.

Kirby eyed her apartment. It overflowed with Wiccan home décor: dangling pentagrams near the kitchen entrance and a colorful, embroidered tapestry hanging on a wall, featuring an impassive-faced sun surrounded by half-moons, planets, and stars. There were vases of flowers and mismatched candles, some burning brightly, on cabinets and tables. In a corner stood a shrine to Elizabeth Montgomery from *Bewitched*, encircled by burning pillar candles, a *Bewitched* metal lunch box, and a *TV Guide* cover. Next to the shrine, he noticed a framed photo of Sonny Bono on a nearby table, with Cher crossed out of the picture. Kirby wondered what that was all about.

"This way," garbled SanDee as she brushed by him.

He reluctantly followed her to the kitchen. A weird smell wafted from the doorway.

Once inside, Kirby noticed she hadn't decorated the room like the rest of her apartment. Other than a sign near the stove that said KITCHEN WITCH—STIRRING UP A LITTLE MAGIC, there was nothing Wiccan about it. Just an old Kenmore refrigerator, a bunch of tired-looking cabinets, and a shelf with cookbooks that included a dog-eared copy of *Witchcraft for Dummies* next to *Joy of Cooking*.

"So, you want a dove potion?" asked SanDee.

"Love potion," corrected Kirby.

SanDee plunked her juice jar on the counter. "Great! I'm not so good with birds." Pulling open a drawer, she lifted an old leather-bound book that had a pentagram on the cover and small shiny rubies at each point.

A chill ran down his spine.

She opened the musty-smelling tome and turned the fragile pages. "Can't find no dove potions."

"Love potion, love potion."

"Luff potion, right."

She took a swig from the beet juice, made a face, and set down the jug while leafing through the pages. "Ah hah!" she chuckled, pointing to the book. "C'mere, Furby."

He apprehensively moved toward her.

SanDee squinted to read. "Go to that top cabinet and get me some dried Jasmine flowers, withered Rose petals, and vanilla extract."

"In your cupboard?"

"No. My cauldron!" she said, shaking her head and scrunching her eyes. "Course my cupboard."

Kirby swung open the cabinet door. There were all types of colored jars and corked glass containers intermixed with cooking condiments. He pushed aside the Morton salt and spied the dried jasmine flowers in a yellow-tinted apothecary jar. He also found the vanilla extract and dried rose petals.

After gathering the items, he plopped them on the kitchen table. "Now what?" he asked.

"Get me an'napple, a strawberry, a lemon, and a chocolate pudding."

"Pudding in the potion?" said Kirby.

"No, I'm hungry," grated SanDee.

He opened the refrigerator and collected everything, including the pudding, which he thought ludicrous given her drunken state.

When he turned toward SanDee, she teetered near the sink, filling up a silver saucepan.

"Get yourself over here," she said. She made a twisting motion with her outstretched arm. "I can't seem to turn on the stoveff."

Kirby dumped the food on the tile counter and stepped to the range next to her. "Here," he said, turning on a top burner.

SanDee wavered toward the ingredients. "Who brought out the pudding?" she snarled. "There's no potion in the pudding."

"You said you were hungry."

She gave a little shrug. Then, peeling back the paper lid, she lifted the cup to her lips and took a slurp. Pudding dripped from her chin. Tears stood in her eyes, and he didn't have a clue why.

His heart sank. This was a total disaster. "I'm gonna go, SanDee. Seriously, this is a bad idea."

"No, no, no," she said, waving her arms. She jostled the saucepan. Water spilled from the lip. "We're almost done." Tears streaked down her cheeks. "I promised you a luff potion, and I'm gonna make it," she sobbed.

"Please, SanDee, don't cry."

She paid no attention, already hovering over the stove, cooking.

"I need cinna-mum."

"Cinnamon?" asked Kirby.

"And amber oil."

"Where are they?"

"I don't know," she snapped. "Do I have to do everything around here?"

He searched the kitchen, hunting through the cluttered cabinets without success. Finally, when he wandered into the living room, he spied a Mason jar full of cinnamon sticks and some amber Oil near the Sonny and Cher photo.

Kirby grabbed the items and rushed into the kitchen.

He found SanDee slicing fruit with a dull-edged knife. More like squishing it.

"Less start," she slurred.

Turning toward the saucepan, SanDee pinched something over the boiling water that caused it to bubble even more. Yellow vapor rose from the pot. The room filled with a fruity fragrance after she sprinkled dried jasmine and rose petals and dropped sliced apples and mashed strawberries and bananas into the brew.

Kirby gaped, captivated by SanDee's crazy concoction.

"We gotta say somethin'," SanDee said. "A poem. A spell."

"Let me get the book," said Kirby, thinking the ancient pages held just the magic words.

"No, no, no. It's gotta be special. From the heart. Whas her name?"

"Maxine Liu."

SanDee stood dazed until she snapped her fingers. "I got it," she said. "Now 'peat after me."

"Okay," said Kirby.

She lifted the saucepan and stirred it with a cinnamon stick. "Lou," she garbled, attempting a tune but tuneless.

"Liu," repeated Kirby.

"Lou."

"Liu."

"Skip to my Lou. Flies in the sugar bowl, shoo shoo shoo."

A weird feeling went through him. "Oh, my god!"

She continued singing. "A little red wagon painted blue."

"Wait a minute. Wait a minute," said Kirby, waving his arms. "That's a folk song."

"We got a luff potion, hoo hoo hoo. Skip to my Lou, my darling," she belted out.

"Stop," yelled Kirby. "SanDee, stop."

SanDee stopped. She glared at him, clearly piqued. "Wha?"

"That's not an incantation. You can't sing that."

"What are you now, a whisch or somethin'?"

"No."

"Really," she said. "Cause if you were a whisch, you'd know I *can't* sing the Beatles, who were all about luff—luff, luff, luff—the most luffed group in the world." She warbled, "All you need is luff—doo, bee, doo, bee, doo. Now, shut the fuck up and let me finish."

Irritated, Kirby held his tongue. He just wanted this crazy night to be over.

SanDee placed the pan on the kitchen table and picked up the amber oil. Her hand trembled when she unscrewed the top and shook three drops into the steaming elixir. The liquid rose to a boil. Then, reaching into her pocket, she pulled out a small crystal heart-shaped flask filled with a glowing red substance.

The bottle glistened in the light.

Kirby stared in wonder. There was something mystical about it, even hypnotic.

"What's that?" he asked.

"Liquid luff. S'magical," she said, removing the ball stopper. SanDee allowed a trickle of the liquid into the saucepan. Red steam fizzled up and the potion transformed into a bright pink broth.

"Done," slurred SanDee. She handed Kirby the pot. "Schpray it on your face like cologne 'fore you see your luffed one."

"Spray it with what?"

She sat down at the table. "Thersh a small bottle in the drawer." SanDee yawned.

Turning, Kirby opened a kitchen drawer that had plastic and paper bags. "It's not here."

"Lower," she muttered, gesturing.

He opened the lower drawer and found a small pocket sprayer. He pulled it out. "This?" he said, pivoting back to SanDee.

Too late. She appeared to be sound asleep, head on the table, snoring peacefully with a slight, gentle wheeze.

Crap, he thought, lowering his head. He didn't even know how to use the stuff. Kirby guessed you just sprayed it on and waited for the magic to happen.

The following day, dulled by drowsiness, Kirby awoke to sunlight shining through the slatted blinds in his bedroom. He stared at the ceiling, trying to remember the night before. Had he really visited SanDee, or was it just a dream? The memory of her answering the door drunk made him cringe. It all came back now. The candles. The incense. The potion. When he eyed the red-tinted pocket spray bottle on his dresser, he knew it was true.

Then he had a thought. Had Maxine left for work yet?

He glanced at the clock—6:45 a.m.

She usually left her apartment around 7:30. He smiled. The perfect time to feed Graycie, the feral cat, and strike up a conversation with Maxine while wearing the potion.

Kirby stroked his chin. Were there any holes in his logic?

Not that he could see. It seemed so simple. What could possibly go wrong?

☙

Kirby shaved, showered, and dressed by 7:20.

Inside the kitchen, he grabbed a can of Fancy Feast from a cabinet and scooped it into a small bowl. As he picked up the love potion from the kitchen table, he thought about Maxine. Should he try to impress her with his sense of humor, overwhelm her with the love potion or just be himself? Was using the potion even ethical?

Kirby thought about the lonely days, months, years when he longed for intimacy. Six long years since the mad love he'd shared with Paige in college.

He wanted to experience that feeling again.

He picked up the small bottle, tilting the red liquid, set it down. Probably wouldn't work anyway, he thought. What did he have to lose to try it?

He stared at his reflection on the toaster. Rationalization, again? Maybe, he thought. Kirby sighed. If only he could have a chance with Maxine. That would be great.

Do it!

Lifting the bottle, he spritzed the fragrance two times on his face. It misted over his skin, tingling on impact. Then he smoothed it over his cheeks and chin, making sure to spread it evenly.

He wasn't sure it would work, but he was ready.

At 7:25, Kirby exited the apartment, not sure what to expect. And like always, Graycie, the stray cat, hid near the concrete stairs, eyeing him.

"Here, Graycie," he called out. "Food."

Graycie blinked and took a few steps forward, peeking out from under the steps. She meowed.

"C'mon, Graycie." He motioned.

The cat, tentative at first, trotted toward Kirby with purpose, surprising him. She finally trusted him enough to eat her food while he was there.

Graycie wandered up and rubbed against his ankle, first with her head, followed by her flank and tail.

He smiled and bent down to pet her. She looked up at him with wide, lovesick eyes.

It must be the potion, he thought, excited. He could only imagine how it would affect Maxine.

Graycie meowed.

Across the courtyard, another cat appeared. Kirby eyed the orange tabby and wondered where she'd come from. The tabby made a beeline toward him, and then the two cats caressed his legs.

More meows. More upright tails and wide caressing gazes.

Kirby froze.

From British shorthairs to Persians and Siamese, clusters of cats appeared from every nook and cranny. In moments, Kirby estimated there were at least thirty. They yowled in heat and headed toward him.

Alarmed, Kirby took a step back. It was the potion—the goddamn potion. It was working too well.

He looked up. Cats hovered over the roofline and second-story apartment balconies.

A black cat with a white tuxedo chest jumped first. Kirby felt its claws clutch his pinstriped shirt and dig into his skin.

Howling in pain, he spun around. He pushed the black furball away, but it clung like Velcro.

The other cats, too many to count now, bolted forward. He made a mad dash to escape, but the frisky felines jumped from every direction. They landed like kamikaze pilots, latching onto him with their sharp claws, purring near his ears.

More and more cats kept coming. The musky urine smell from the clowder of cats made Kirby want to heave.

Panicked and racked with pain, he ran through the courtyard yelling and screaming, doing whatever possible to dislodge the amorous animals.

Maxine stepped outside her apartment, saw him, and stopped. "Kirby?" she called.

He sprinted by with cats hanging all over his body, followed by a herd of fast-moving felines, and disappeared down the concrete steps that led to the garage.

He regretted there was no time to talk.

After being chased for fifteen blocks, he slogged through a muddy vegetable garden in Mar Vista, detoured down a smelly flood retention basin near Marina Del Rey, and hid in a garbage bin full of spoiled food at Bristol Farms. It was an enormous effort to rid himself of the love potion smell and the animals who followed him. Finally, when it appeared safe to leave, he backtracked to his apartment, got into his car, and searched for SanDee.

Kirby arrived at the Farmers Market around one o'clock, closing time, just as the vendors were packing up. Steadfast in his focus, he rushed by departing customers on his way to No Man's Land. While doing so, it occurred to him that maybe he should have changed clothes and taken a shower before coming over. Men, women, and children—and even a few dogs—avoided him as he passed by.

He burst into No Man's Land. Julie Moreau still hawked her Scandinavian Beet Sauce and Vic Trumbo, the blind violinist, sawed his fiddle. Sure enough, SanDee was there, packing up her autographed photos and folding the card table.

She looked disheveled. Her dirty-blond hair seemed uncombed, and she wore the same black, wrinkled Adidas sweatsuit from the night before. Dark sunglasses hid her eyes.

Just seeing her made the angry knot in his stomach tighten.

"Kirby?" said SanDee, straining to see him from behind her shades. "Where were yuh today?" She gazed at him.

"Yech—" She scrunched her face. "What happened to you?"

Kirby scowled. "I used your love potion. That's what happened."

"It worked?" she asked.

"No, it didn't work." He pointed to his smelly, stained, and torn clothes. "Does this look like it worked?"

SanDee lowered her glasses and stared at him with red-rimmed eyes. "You probably didn't use it right," she said in a derisive tone, one Kirby had never heard her use before.

"You told me to spray it on like cologne."

"Did you dilute it with water?"

"You didn't tell me to dilute it with water."

She scowled. "I told you last night to weaken it by a quarter. Don't you remember?"

"You were drunk last night when I came over, SanDee. You forgot to tell me."

She stiffened. Deep lines appeared on her forehead when she furrowed her brows. "Are you calling me a drunk?"

"I have no idea if you—" he said, trying to calm her down.

"I'm not a drunk," she screamed.

Kirby took a step back. He was worried now. What if she didn't help him with the potion? Something about the formula was wrong, but it sure did lure the cats.

SanDee moved forward, fury in her eyes. She pointed at Kirby. "You're just like all of them," she shouted. "Just like all the producers who tried to keep me from becoming a star."

"I was just referring to last night," he implored, placing a hand on his chest. "We need to adjust the po—"

"Now you're saying I'm a drunk, so you can keep my love potion business from growing."

"That's not true, SanDee. You've gotta listen—"

A bundled stack of signed photos smashed him in the face and clattered to the ground.

"Asshole!" SanDee shrieked.

He regained his balance and stared at her with his cheek stinging from the blow. Maybe he ought to cut his losses and go back to traditional wooing, ineffective as it was.

His would-be matchmaker stomped by, dragging the card table under her right arm, heading across No Man's Land.

Kirby scrambled to pick up the photos. "SanDee, wait," he called. She ignored him.

"How much do I dilute the potion?" he called out. "A quarter of what?"

SanDee, moving forward, raised the middle finger of her left hand. "Fuck you, Kirby!"

"But SanDee—"

She and her knowledge were lost to him, it was clear. Defeated, he slumped against a bench, wondering what he'd done wrong. And it had all started out so well. He guessed the potion was worthless now unless he, somehow, figured out how to dilute it himself.

Kirby showed up for his job at Cinder's Deep-Water Grill in Culver City at night. He made sure there was no remnant of the love spray on his thin frame after taking three showers with Scent-A-Way Odorless Body Soap and Shampoo, a cleaning solvent used by hunters to neutralize any human body odors while hunting. He figured if it was good enough to fool wild animals, then it should work with cats.

He wasn't in the best mood when his shift started, but he had rent to pay and a shaky entertainment career to support, so he went about his business as usual.

The evening had started slow, but crowds soon packed the restaurant. They spilled out from the industrial modern-style bar to the waiting area near the front entrance.

Kirby moved expertly between the kitchen and the dining room, taking orders and delivering food. He'd forgotten about the love potion for a few minutes until Gia, the shapely red-haired hostess, led Maxine and her boyfriend Brad into his section.

They sat down at a nearby table, and he froze. He wasn't ready to explain the morning.

"Kirby?" said Maxine, motioning him over. "Are you our waiter tonight?"

He approached their table. "Lucky me," he replied. He avoided Maxine's gaze and stared at her dark gray pantsuit and black high heels instead.

She smiled. "What happened this morning?"

Kirby pulled on his collar.

Brad spoke over his date. "Yeah, yeah, look, Kirk, or whatever your name is, just bring me a Jack and Coke, okay?"

"Brad," snapped Maxine, clearly annoyed.

"And two menus," Brad added.

"Why do you have to be so rude?"

Brad shrugged his shoulders. "What'd I say?"

Jerk, thought Kirby, frowning. She was obviously dating the wrong guy.

"Well, what are you waiting for?" growled Brad.

At that moment, an idea seized Kirby, and not a good one. What if he doctored the magic potion right now? He'd brought the vial with him, hoping to experiment with diluting it at closing. If it worked, she'd be with him instead of Brad. He'd treat her with the love and respect she deserved. It seemed perfect.

"I'll bring the menus and your drink right out," he blurted.

Dashing to the kitchen, patting his pants for the spray bottle, Kirby called "Jack and Coke" to the bartender.

Once inside, he made a beeline past the sauté station, which smelled of pan juices and butter, toward an empty hand washing sink in the corner. He turned on the faucet and pulled out the bottle.

A tall, pear-shaped man wearing a black suit with a red tie, standing in the kitchen line, shouted to him over the noisy room, "Kirby, you've got tables." The man raised his wrist and pointed to a watch.

Crap, it was Lorenzo, the assistant manager. "I'll be right there," he yelled back.

Kirby eyed the potion. He had to dilute it a quarter. How difficult could that be?

He stared at the bottle. It appeared to hold four ounces. Therefore, if a cup held eight fluid ounces, the bottle was one-half cup. If he diluted the bottle by one-quarter or one ounce, that would be one-eighth of a cup. Now, a quarter of a cup is four tablespoons. So, an eighth of a cup is two tablespoons. But what if SanDee meant a teaspoon? There are three teaspoons in a tablespoon. If he diluted the potion by one-quarter of a teaspoon, he would need somebody with a fucking math degree.

"Shit!" he screamed in frustration.

Lorenzo glared at him.

"It's okay," he reassured Lorenzo with a wave.

Kirby studied the bottle again. Room lights illuminated its pinkish color.

He furrowed his brow. It had to be two tablespoons. One-quarter of a teaspoon would probably not make much difference, he concluded.

After diluting the bottle and misting his face with the magical mixture, Kirby figured he was ready.

He gazed around the hectic kitchen. No one paid attention, especially the waitresses picking up their orders at the counter line. At first, he wasn't concerned, but he soon became worried. What if he hadn't correctly diluted the potion? He'd have to fight off a swarm of women just before approaching Maxine. He winced and rubbed his chest. He was assuming a worst-case scenario.

Lorenzo glowered from the kitchen door. "Kirby!" he yelled.

"Coming, coming," said Kirby.

He hurried toward Lorenzo. No women approached him. Only a few male servers looked up and smiled as he passed by.

Kirby exhaled, relieved. There may have been no problem in the kitchen where other smells dominated, but the real test was on the other side of the swinging door.

🍃

When he bolted into the dining room, Kirby noticed at least seven women, not counting the ones in the bar area, in his vicinity. None of them made an overture, but a pit still formed in his stomach.

So far, so good, Kirby thought. He guessed the added water had reduced the potion's potency, so it only worked if you were in direct contact with a woman.

As soon as he arrived at the booth, Kirby noticed Brad's irritated mug.

"Where's my Coke and Jack?" Brad snarled. "And the menus."

"Hold on, Brad," said Maxine, touching his hand. "Let me talk with Kirby for a minute."

Kirby moved closer to the table so Maxine could breathe in the potion. He smiled.

"That was you with the cats this morning, right?" she asked, clearly concerned. "Are you okay?"

Brad leaned in. "Geeze, Maxine, why are you giving him such a hard time?"

The change in his demeanor unnerved Kirby.

Maxine turned to Brad. "I'm not giving him a hard time."

"Of course, you are," he said calmly, patting her on the wrist. "So he didn't bring the drink and menus. It's no big deal."

Maxine stared at Brad in what looked like disbelief. "What's wrong with you?"

"Nothing's wrong with me. Kirby's a nice guy, that's all. Right, Kirby?" Brad flashed his million-dollar smile and winked at him.

Kirby blanched. His heart raced. Oh, my God! Was Brad now attracted to him?

"I'll ge—get the menus." He backed away.

"Wait," said Brad, darting from the booth, grabbed his arm with a vice-like grip.

The hair raised on the nape of Kirby's neck.

"You can't leave now."

Kirby pointed to the kitchen. "My work."

"Let him go, Brad," demanded Maxine.

"C'mon," he replied, dragging Kirby back to the table. "We can't let this good-looking guy go without finding out about his problem."

One yank and he was sitting next to Brad in the black leather booth. The proximity of their legs, now pressed side-by-side, sent chills down his spine. He glanced over at Maxine. Her radiant smile had disappeared, replaced by an emerging frown.

"Kirby," said Maxine sharply. "I need to speak with Brad alone. Now."

Brad's forceful hand kept him from escaping.

"Anything you have to say to me, you can say to him. Right, buddy?" He shook Kirby's shoulders.

"I'll lose my job," said Kirby, scanning the tables and not yet spotting a manager.

Brad pulled him closer. "Stay," he said.

"Are you drunk?" accused Maxine.

"No, and you're upsetting him."

"You're upsetting me," she snapped.

"Can't you see he's stressed?" Brad massaged Kirby's shoulders. "You're so tight," he cooed, leaning in.

Kirby squirmed, but his slender build was no match for Brad's gorilla strength.

"That's it!" Maxine threw up her hands and rose from the booth. "I'm outta here."

"Maxine, wait," said Brad, loosening his grip.

Kirby took advantage of the lapse, rotated right, and broke free, power walking toward the kitchen.

"Kirby," cried out Brad. "Come back. I love you."

Brushing past customers, Kirby zigzagged through the crowded restaurant, creating a commotion. His heart pounded as if it were going to burst.

"Outta my way," bellowed Brad from behind.

Sweeping past his co-worker, Alexis, who held a food tray, Kirby slammed into the pear-shaped assistant manager, Lorenzo, who was exiting the kitchen door. They both tumbled to the ground.

"What the fuck?" shouted Lorenzo.

"No time to talk," said Kirby, scrambling to his feet.

Barreling toward him like a linebacker, Brad cut an opening through the crowd.

Kirby slammed open the kitchen door and zoomed past the bustling line cooks and grill station. He had to get to the sink and wash off the potion.

"You can't go in there," Lorenzo commanded Brad. Then there was scuffling.

"Kirby," Brad said, moaning like a buffalo in heat, "Come back! Please."

Kirby turned on the faucet. He had to act fast. Brad could push past Lorenzo any second and follow him inside. Shoving his hands into the cold sink water, he splashed it onto his face, over and over and over again.

A petite brunette waitress wearing brown tortoiseshell glasses wandered up. "Are you okay, Kirby?" Hayden asked.

He turned, and her concerned look faded. Her lips curled, and eyes narrowed.

"What's wrong?" he asked.

"Douchebag!" she screamed, flipping him the bird. Hayden stormed back to the kitchen line.

Stunned, Kirby wondered what had happened. All he'd done was wash his face.

He looked at his wet hands. *Oh, no*, he thought, *the water*. He'd diluted the potion with water, a lot more water.

Kirby peered over at the kitchen line. Hayden pointed at him and chattered with other waitresses. They all glared back, anger spreading across their faces.

A female grill chef, staring at him, raised a cooking pan and pounded it against her hand.

Waitresses standing by the kitchen line grabbed dinner plates.

Kirby tensed. This wasn't good. The watered-down formula was no longer making him attracted to men but made women hate him. He was in big trouble.

"We don't want you here," shouted Rita, a stout, frizzy-haired pastry chef.

A dish whizzed by his head and shattered against the wall.

More followed.

Kirby stumbled away, trying to avoid the barrage of airborne dishware. Pots and pans pinged. Plates and platters smashed and splintered around him.

Male chefs and servers jumped into the fray to keep the women from attacking Kirby. Employees tussled and raised their voices.

"Run, Kirby, run!" yelled Pablo Muvelli, a cigarette dangling between his lips.

Kirby scrambled across the crowded floor. If he could only get into the dining room and make a run for the exit, he might be able to escape.

The kitchen door swung open and Lorenzo stormed in. "What's going on in here?" he barked.

Once again, Kirby bowled him over. Both men tumbled to the ground, slamming onto the hard tile.

Kirby grabbed his ankle and winced. Pain radiated up his leg.

Picking himself up, he limped into the busy dining room, where frightened patrons gaped at him.

Lorenzo lifted his upper body and pointed at Kirby. "You're fired," he screamed, collapsing back onto the floor.

Kirby hobbled through the maze of tables. Women scattered in disgust.

"Get away from me, you creep," screamed one.

"You're repulsive," yelled another.

An old lady with blue hair raised her walker and shouted, "You pervert!"

Angry females gave him the finger or whacked him with their shoulder bags.

Cooked sea bass and a slice of key lime pie hit him in the head, splattering all over his shirt. Beef short ribs, smoked barbecue chicken, and other sweet sticky foods followed. He'd never seen this level of rage from a large group of women before. He knew the potion had caused their anger, but he couldn't help but take it personally.

When he passed the bar, he noticed Brad, apparently blocked by a cluster of women.

"I'm going to kick your ass!" shouted Brad, who bobbed up and down and struggled to break through the crowd.

Oh, great, thought Kirby. He'd just lost the job that paid his rent, and now Brad was back to normal and out for vengeance.

In the waiting area, he hurried on his aching ankle past the brunette hostess, Gia, who battered him on the head with a stack of heavy dinner menus. As he grunted and wobbled, pain seared down his head and neck. The force caused him to stagger, and he crashed into the glass door and lay stunned.

At the bar, Brad forcefully broke free. "Outta my way," he bellowed.

Women scattered.

Kirby, vision blurry and head throbbing, clambered to his feet, pushed open the front door, and hobbled into the cool evening air. He was a mess, both physically and emotionally. How could he ever ditch Brad?

He'd planned on running but stopped. Maxine stood at the curb, opening the back door of a black BMW sedan.

She turned. Her reddened face and scowl told him all he needed to know.

When she flounced toward him, he couldn't move, as if his shoes were rooted to the ground. Regret coiled through him.

The tap of her high heels accelerated. "Why are you here?" she shouted, meeting Kirby face-to-face. "Haven't you done enough? You ruined the whole evening and my relationship with Brad."

"I can explain," he said.

"You disgust me, now and from the moment we met. You're nothing but a despicable little jerk."

Raising her hand, she forcefully slapped him across the face.

Kirby reeled. He didn't know what hurt more, his burning cheeks or his breaking heart.

Maxine stormed back to the car.

Without warning, and before Kirby knew what had happened, Brad jerked him around and sucker-punched him in the gut. Kirby doubled over, pain exploding inside, and gasped for air. His knees buckled.

"I'm not a fucking faggot," roared Brad.

Kirby dropped to the sidewalk and fell against the restaurant building. His gorge rose.

Brad pointed. "If you tell anybody what happened, I'll kill you."

Customers exited Cinder's. Brad pushed through the curious crowd and stormed back into the eatery.

Gathering his strength, Kirby struggled to stand, leaned on the wall for balance, and lurched off into the night. He had no intention of waiting around for anything else to happen. He needed time to think, be alone, and figure out why he was such a loser.

Once again, after detouring through the flood retention basin and muddy vegetable garden to get rid of the love potion smell, Kirby finally made it back to his apartment.

Depressed, he jumped into the shower and stood motionless, hot water cascading over his head and shoulders. All he wanted was to be with Maxine. Was that too much to ask?

But Kirby knew the truth. He'd done something horrible, an act both ethically and morally wrong, which now made him feel ashamed. His chin dipped to his chest. Tears welled up. Why had he done it?

Why?

The words emotional maturity popped into his head.

Hot water pelted him.

He stifled a sob. He hadn't thought about that since college. Dr. Langford once defined it as the ability to respond to the environment in an appropriate manner.

Kirby reflected. Was using a magic potion to attract a woman he liked emotionally mature? No. What about becoming a party clown, or a failed actor for that matter? No, and no.

Why did he become a performer anyway? Was it because his girlfriend had broken up with him in college, leaving him vulnerable and craving attention? Or had he jettisoned graduate school because he was afraid to grow up? Hadn't Paige called him immature? Didn't his parents say the same thing?

He stared at the shower-tiled wall. Apparently, he'd been emotionally immature his whole life.

Were any of his decisions one an adult would make?

Kirby knew the answer. He just hadn't been listening.

He thought about Maxine again. Was there any way to attract her except by using witchcraft? Was he capable of trying? Of using his brain and creativity to woo her? As of this moment, no, he wasn't, and that hurt like hell.

He pushed his head under the water and washed away the suds.

It was time for him to grow up, get real, and make some changes.

Kirby packed the last box of clothes in his bedroom. The decision to move back with his parents while he studied for the GREs was the right one. Hopefully, with Dr. Langford's help, he could still get into the UCLA Clinical Psychology Graduate Program.

He thought about Maxine while sealing the carton with packing tape. Too bad he'd blown it with her. It hurt to think about how he'd humiliated himself in front of her and what he'd lost in losing her esteem.

Picking up the cardboard container, he carried it to the living room and stacked it near the gray couch.

There was a knock at the door. Maxine's voice called out. "Hello?"

It startled him. He wanted to ignore it; pretend he wasn't home because he was afraid to face her. But then he decided an adult would act differently and wasn't he trying to become more mature?

"Be right there," he answered reluctantly.

Kirby wondered why she even wanted to visit. Hadn't he ruined her relationship with Brad? And what if she slapped him again? He touched his cheek. Considering what he'd done, he probably deserved it.

When he opened the door, Maxine, dressed in a violet-colored sundress that flattered her figure, cradled a bouquet of white carnations that smelled peppery. Then, raising her left hand, she said, "I come in peace."

"You didn't have to."

"But I did," she said, appearing regretful. "I felt awful. Said things I didn't mean. I don't know what came over me, Kirby. I'm—I'm sorry."

Her sincerity touched him, and he eased up. "It was my fault," he said.

"I don't know why you'd say that. How could it be your fault?"

Afraid to explain, he changed the topic. "Let me find something to hold those flowers. You want to come in?"

"Sure."

Kirby headed toward the kitchen, followed by Maxine. "Are you moving?" she asked.

He pulled out a brown plastic pitcher and filled it with water.

"I plan on becoming a therapist. So, I'm moving back home with my parents to study for the GREs."

"You can't have enough of those," she said, smiling and rolling her eyes.

"I know. The whole world is crazy. Right?"

Maxine handed him the flowers. "You don't have a vase?"

"I'm a poor schnook. Who can afford one?"

Maxine chuckled. "You're a funny dude, Kirby."

"Yeah, hilarious!"

"Can I ask you something?" she inquired. "You're not leaving because of, you know, what happened at Cinder's a few weeks ago, are you?"

He gazed at her. "Absolutely not," he lied, knowing he should tell her the truth. Immaturity was a curse.

There was an awkward silence.

"Well, I should be going," she said, backing up. "You look busy, and I just wanted to apologize. That's all. Good luck with your studies."

"Yeah, thanks," he replied, watching her turn. "I like the flowers."

She walked toward the door.

Kirby sensed her disappointment. He didn't want her to leave. If Maxine left now, she'd be gone forever. He had to say something.

Anything.

"I lied," he blurted out.

Maxine stopped, looked back at him.

"I didn't think you'd wanna go out with me, so—" Kirby lowered his chin, shamefaced. "I tried to attract you by using a love potion; a spray made by this crazy Wiccan woman I know, only everything went haywire." He looked at Maxine and said apologetically, "It never worked right. I'm sorry."

She stared at him as if she were trying to grasp what he'd just said. "A love potion?" she repeated. "You mean like a real love potion? A charm?"

"Yeah, I'm a idiot."

She cocked her head, wrinkled her nose, and gazed at him until a slight smile appeared on her face. "That's the lamest thing I've ever heard," she said, bursting into laughter. "A love potion for me? Wouldn't it have been easier to just ask me out on a date?"

He winced. She was right.

"Are you okay?" asked Maxine.

"No, I'm not," said Kirby, shaking his head. "I should have asked you out when I had the chance, but I didn't because, well—" He hesitated. "You know. Listen, I don't know where we stand, but—"

Maxine raised her eyebrows, appearing interested.

He tensed, afraid she'd reject him, and began to hem and haw, "—would you like to, you know, um, get a burger or a beer or something with, uh—" His lips flattened. Why was this so hard? The worst she could say was no. "Ah shit!" he said defiantly. "Maxine, you're somebody I'd like to know better. Would you go out with me?"

She smiled. "I like you, Kirby. You're an interesting dude."

Maxine liked him. He had a chance with her!

Rifling through her navy-blue shoulder bag, she pulled out a business card. "Why don't you give me a call when you're not studying, and we can get together."

She handed him the card.

"Really?" he said.

Maxine stepped closer, her gaze mischievous. "Make it soon," she said. "I have a thing for clowns."

CHAPTER SIX

CASE NUMBER FOUR: THE ORANGE KINGS

ALLEGED VIOLATION: Intentional or negligent wrongdoing
ALLEGED VIOLATION: Failure to make the world a better place
ALLEGED VIOLATION: Failure to bring love, desire and
happiness to everyone

AUGUST 1940
VAN NUYS, CALIFORNIA

When the bickering began, we were having a quiet Sunday backyard barbecue in April with the Rosenwald's at my parent's rented, bungalow-style home in Van Nuys. Maybe the warm, unusually humid weather aggravated their tempers. But like most disputes, it involved money.

The situation had been simmering for a while.

You see, Max Rosenwald and Pop were life-long friends who'd moved from Brownsville in Brooklyn to the San Fernando Valley in 1936 to start orange juice stands. Pop settled in the East Valley, Max in the West. The trouble was the West Valley was more rural, with fewer people, and Max had trouble making a go of it.

So, after Pop mentioned his business had picked up with the spring weather, Max frowned, his eyes narrowed, and the remaining hairs on his head bristled. He raised his heavy-set body from the picnic table and pounded the tabletop with his fist. The plates jumped.

"Vy should you get da East Valley," he yelled at Pop. The two men glared at each other. "Dat's vhere all da money is. You can't make good money in da Vest Valley."

My stomach tightened. I knew this was going to be bad.

Pop stood up from the table, tight-lipped. He was two inches shorter than Max and a lot skinnier. He may have seemed mild-mannered with his bushy graying mustache and thinning white hair, but he exploded on the spot. "Vait a minute, vait a minute," he hollered with a thick Yiddish accent. His face reddened. "Vhen we moved, I gave you foist choice. I took da leftover. Vest is best, you said. Vest is best."

"Vell, now it's not. I vant more money."

"Oh, I see," said Pop, shaking his head. "You vant my family and I should starve while you take over my business?"

"And vut about my family?"

"Okay, okay, Max, now you listen to me, and you listen good." Pop pointed his index finger at him. "I started dis business in da East Valley. I voiked hard, built it up, and I ain't gonna turn it over to you."

"Is dat right?" said Max, standing his ground.

"Dat's right," said Pop, nodding his head. "And we ain't gonna talk about it no more."

And with that, Max Rosenwald stormed out of our house with his family. There were no goodbyes. This was especially bad for me because his daughter Doris was my high school sweetheart and the love of my life. Somehow, I had to figure out how to get our fathers back together again and save my relationship with Doris.

That night, things took a turn for the worst, and Pop told it to me straight. He paced on the red oriental rug in the living room like an overwrought tiger. His sleeveless T-shirt molded to his stomach while black suspenders held up his pants.

"I taught about it, Lenny, and ya can't go out wiff Doris no more."

It was a stab to the heart. I plopped on the blue cloth armchair next to the couch and reflector floor lamp and put on a long face. "But, Pop…"

"No son of mine is gonna go out wiff dat *meshugana's* daughter. Ta tink he tried to steal my business. *Gonif.* Dat's vut he is—a *gonif.*"

"But, Pop, you gotta listen," I pleaded. "I love her. And there are only six Jewish kids in the entire Junior Class."

"So, go out wiff vun of dem."

"I can't. The other four are guys."

Looking for an answer, Pop raised his hands to God.

I spent the rest of the evening in my cramped bedroom. Books, messy school paperwork, and a photo of Doris beside my trusty Brownie camera on top of the dresser filled the cluttered space. But none of that interested me as I lay on my lumpy box-spring bed, depressed and staring beyond the Hank Greenberg baseball card pinned to the wall.

I only cared about one thing. What was I going to tell Doris?

After second period on Monday, I met Doris near the school cafeteria in the grassy quad area among the scattered oak trees. Doris and I had known each other since we were kids in Brooklyn. And to be honest, it's hard sometimes to believe she likes me when I'm only five-foot-eight, weigh one hundred thirty pounds and wear glasses. But Doris says she's wild about my curly brown hair and that I resemble Hammerin' Hank Greenberg, the famed Jewish home run king of the Detroit Tigers, who is six-foot-four and weighs two hundred and ten pounds. I think she's the one who needs glasses, but no way am I going to tell her, especially since she's cute as a bug and I'm dizzy about her.

Wearing her usual school outfit: a pleated plaid skirt, a snug-fitting sweater over her pale-yellow blouse, and white bobby socks and saddle shoes, Doris was downcast, looking as sad as I felt.

I leaned against the tree trunk.

Doris brushed away a tear.

"Hi," I said, trying to show compassion. I looked into her watery eyes and almost cried myself but held it together.

A frown appeared on her face. "My Dad says we can't see each other anymore."

"Mine too."

She sobbed.

I wasn't sure how to respond. "Hey, hey, c'mon," I said, sweeping aside a strand of wavy auburn hair from her face. "We can get through this. We'll figure it out."

Doris leaned against my shoulder.

"What are we gonna do, Lenny?" she asked. "If I can't see you, I'll just die."

I was perplexed. "Maybe we can sneak around and ignore our parents," I said, grasping for straws.

She gazed up at me, her eyes widening with excitement. "Yes. Let's sneak around and ignore our parents. Just like Romeo and Juliet."

"I don't know," I said, grimacing.

"Oh, it's so romantic," she swooned. "It worked out for them."

"Yeah, everything but the death part."

"Please, Lenny, please. We're just like two star-crossed lovers."

I cleared my throat and fidgeted with my glasses until she looked at me with her innocent, lovesick peepers. My heart melted instantly. As Shakespeare said, there was "fire sparkling in lovers' eyes." So, we agreed to meet by the football stands every day after school and "sin by the lips" until it was time to go home and part with "sweet sorrow" and say goodnight "till it be morrow."

Doris and I continued our clandestine love affair for the next few weeks. It was the happiest time of my life until—four months ago.

I was helping Pop out at the orange juice stand. And if you've never seen it, the building is an eight-foot-high globe made of wood, aluminum, and plaster and painted like a big bright orange. It has a cutout counter window in front where we serve ice-cold juice from the small kitchen inside and a door in the back to enter. On the roof is a large ORANGE KING sign, big enough to be seen near the intersection of Van Nuys and Burbank boulevards.

The stand sits at the outskirts of Sherman Oaks, a more populated area than the rest of the San Fernando Valley but still basically rural. In between the small number of studio backlots and homes are miles and miles of field crops and citrus farms that seem to stretch on forever. The Valley may not be heaven, but the lazy sunshine days and sweet smells of orange blossoms make it a close second. It's hard to believe that for all its serenity, there is another world war going on in Europe. It began after the Nazis invaded Poland last September.

Anyway, Pop and I were working inside the circular kitchen, surrounded by waist-high pantry cabinets in front of the window counter. On top of the cabinets were three hand juicers and a large oval galvanized bucket holding a block of ice. In the back, boxes of Snoboy Brand oranges rose against the wall, ready to be squeezed and poured over chips of ice for our thirsty customers. And as usual, I was telling Pop about how to improve the business. I'm *always* telling Pop how to improve the business. Someday, I'm going to be a famous restauranteur.

"We gotta expand, Pop, buy some buns. Get a hot dog steamer. I've been working on this chili recipe at home, see, and we'd put it on the hot dogs and…"

"How many times do I haff to tell ya," said Pop, who stopped squeezing oranges. "Ve're in the orange juice business, not da hot dog business. If ve vas in da hot dog business ve'd be called da Hot Dog King."

"But Pop, we've gotta be different. That's how you grow."

Pop's nostrils flared, and I knew he'd hit his limit. "Enough already vit da hot dogs. I don't pay ya to tink. I pay ya to do."

"You don't pay me at all." Which, if you knew Pop, was not the right thing to say. I regretted it immediately.

His stern look made me cringe, but the low rumbling of a truck and its grinding gears distracted us. We looked outside and saw an old Ford AA Flatbed truck rumbling down Burbank Boulevard. It passed the empty lots, scattered homes, and businesses, including a Signal gas station and a pink-colored store named Aldon's Produce, known locally for their red, ripe tomatoes.

The beat-up truck screeched to a stop in front of the empty lot across the street. But what shocked us was the thing that sat on the back of the flatbed: Max Rosenwald's orange-shaped juice stand with a huge ORANGE MAX sign.

I glanced over at Pop, but he'd already hurried outside and was running across our parking lot. "Vut are you doing?" he yelled at the stocky truck driver. "Yuh can't put dat dere."

I'd never seen Pop this upset before, and it scared me.

As I ran after him, through the gravel parking lot and across Burbank Boulevard's two lanes, trying to catch up, a blue Buick Century convertible swerved around me, honked, and drove on.

Pop had reached the truck by the time I got there and was in a heated discussion.

The driver pointed to his clipboard. "Listen, Mac," the order says this is where it goes, and that's where I'm putting it."

"You don't got no right," hollered Pop, pointing to the Orange King stand. "My business is over dere."

"Calm down, Pop," I said, putting my hand on his shoulder. "We'll figure it out."

"I ain't figuring out nothin'," said Pop, shaking me off.

Max Rosenwald hopped out from the passenger side of the truck. He wore baggy blue overalls, a white T-shirt and work boots. Sweat glistened on his balding head. "So, now da shoes on the udder foot."

"You," said Pop. He rushed to Max, face-to-face. "Vut're ya trying to pull," he shrieked. "You got da Vest Valley."

"I don't got da Vest Valley no more."

"Vell, ya can't put your *fakakta* orange stand across da street from me. I got rights."

Max raised a contract. "And I got a lease, see. So vhy don't ya put dat in your pipe and smoke it."

"Hey, look," said the truck driver sharply. "You want me to unload this thing or not?"

Then Pop did something I'd never seen him do. He lunged forward and attacked Max like an over-the-hill fighter. He was no Joe Lewis. His arms flailed in wild arcs as both men punched the air and tapped soft pink flesh, neither one hurting the other.

It was the most ridiculous fight I'd ever seen until I realized Pop might actually get hurt.

"Stop it, Pop," I yelled, jumping into the fray. I dragged him away.

Max staggered to the flatbed truck, drained and puffing like a blowfish. Pop, sweating profusely, issued a warning. "I'm telling ya, Max, stay avay from my business."

"I'm...opening up, Izzy," Max wheezed out. "Even a mangy dog wouldn't be treated like this."

Pop straightened and ambled toward Max.

"Easy, Pop," I said, shadowing him.

"You started it, Maxie," he said. "After everyting ve've been through, dis is how you treat your best friend?"

"Ve ain't friends no more," said Max, hacking. "Ve ain't friends."

I looked at Pop, who seemed shocked. Blood drained from his face. "Ve ain't friends no more?" he asked.

A dog barked in the distance.

The annoyed truck driver turned to Max. "Listen, what do you want me to do with this big orange?"

Max's gaze locked on Pop's. "Unload it."

Pop looked crushed. "Take me home, Lenny. I don't feel so good."

❧

The following week was tough. Pop stayed home, depressed, shuffling around the house in his striped flannel robe that smelled of mentholated ointment and Rinso Soap, talking to himself and bemoaning his fate.

"How could he do dis to me?" he complained one day over breakfast. "I looked after him vhen ve vas kids in Brooklyn. He vas just like a brudder."

"I thought you said your brother was no good, Pop?"

"My brudder is no good," he said, raising his voice. "Dat's vhy Max is just like him." He angrily waved me off with his arm. "Ah, vat are you bothering me wiff all dese stupid questions for? Can't ya see I'm in pain here?"

And school was no better. My relationship with Doris was deteriorating.

We stood by the oak trees in the quad area before third period. I slumped against the bark, feeling the furrows and ridges.

"I'm sorry, Doris, I can't meet you again today after school. I've gotta leave at noon to run the orange stand for my Pop."

Doris lowered her gaze, her disappointment obvious. "I understand."

"You do?" I let out a huge breath. "You're a peach and a half, Doris. You know that?"

I wanted to kiss her, but spying eyes were watching, especially schoolteachers and administrators, so I stood there like a dumb cluck, hoping she noticed I cared.

"Well, what about tomorrow?" she asked.

"I don't know. It depends on whether Pop goes back to work or not."

"And Friday? You promised me we would go to Munger's Soda

Fountain after school. What about that?"

"I might have to work that day, too," I said, some tension rising in my voice. "You know what my situation is."

She looked at me in silence like something was bothering her. "What's wrong?"

"Well, I understand, Lenny, but it doesn't seem fair. Especially after what your father did to my dad."

"What?" Did the girl that I love honestly believe Pop took the best location on purpose to cheat her dad?

My blood pressure rose, and anger spilled out. "My dad did to yours?" I snapped. "I wouldn't have to work after school if your dad didn't try to put my Pop out of business."

Her eyes welled up, and once again, I knew I'd made a mistake. "I can't talk now," she sniffled, brushing past me. "I've gotta go." With her head down, she ran off toward the science building.

"Doris, wait," I called out but made no effort to chase her. I figured it was probably better to let her cool off and see how she felt in the morning.

Feeling miserable, I sat down on the grass, pulled my knees to my chest, and circled them with my arms. Now everyone was fighting, and it was out of my control like an unstable spinning top.

Doris avoided me for the rest of the week, which made the pit in my stomach grow even bigger and deeper. I was worried. Had the argument ended our relationship? I was afraid to find out.

That Saturday, Pop returned to work. We drove to the orange stand in our black 1929 Chevrolet pick-up, a used monstrosity Pop had bought on the cheap from a local farmer a few years ago.

As we drove down Van Nuys Boulevard, the truck rattled and hissed. Inside the cab, warm, dry air swirled through the open windows, causing sweat to streak down my neck. I didn't talk with Pop much, especially with Doris on my mind, so I gazed out at the shifting landscape.

In the distance, Van Nuys City Hall towered over the nine-block business district and tree-lined streets. Telephone poles and electric wires stretched past stores like J.C. Penny's, Van Nuys Stationery, and the Mode O'Day Dress Shop until they reached farmland. When brick structures became dirt lots, feed stores, and produce stands, we passed construction on a new shopping center where a small farm had been. It upset me, and I quit watching. My life, like the Valley, was changing, and I didn't like it.

It was ninety degrees and rising when we pulled up to the empty Orange King stand. The heat made me drag, and I hadn't even worked yet.

I stepped out of the truck to the constant sound of banging hammers and looked across the street at Max's new place. Handymen were raising a large rectangular wooden billboard on the dirt parking lot. The sign, almost bigger than the giant orange stand itself, proclaimed in bright red letters: HOME OF THE BIG MAX—CALIFORNIA'S MOST REFRESHING ORANGE JUICE DRINK. IT'S GOT VITALITY!

Pop, one eye cockeyed, stared at the giant advertisement.

"Vut kind of *mishegas* is dis?"

I looked over at the Orange Max stand and noticed they had one more customer than we had, which was one. "It's a sign, Pop."

"I know it's a sign. Vut's a Big Max?"

"A bigger drink?" I guessed.

Pop shrugged his shoulders. "Who knows."

127

Max's customer, a lanky farmer wearing a light gray button-down shirt, jeans, work boots, and a felt hat, mounted his chestnut-colored horse and trekked to the middle of the street.

"Hey, cowboy," Pop yelled out. "C'mere."

I lowered my head, embarrassed.

The farmer acknowledged us and trotted his horse, head bobbing and hoofs clopping on the concrete, over to our side of the road.

He pulled up to Pop near our unpaved parking lot at the edge of the curb. The horse snorted and smelled of sweat and hay.

The farmer used the right sleeve on his perspiration-stained shirt to wipe his brow. "What can I do fer you fellas?" asked the weathered-looking man.

Pop, hesitant at first, eyed the farmer. "So, uh, did you have one of dem Orange Max's?" he inquired.

"Sure, did," said the farmer. "Wet my whistle."

"Vat's in vun of dem tings?"

"Let's see," he said, cocking his head. "Orange juice and some kinda sparkly water like seltzer."

Pop pursed his lips. "A spritzer." He pounded his fist into the palm of his hand.

"Sure was tasty," said the farmer. "And refreshing, too. Just like the sign says."

"Yeah, yeah," muttered Pop. "Can I get ya a free orange juice for answering my question?"

The farmer tipped his hat. "Much appreciated, not thirsty now. But if I come back this way later today, I'll probably get another one of them Big Maxes. It was good."

My heart sank. I sighed and shook my head. If Max's new drink caught on, we were in big trouble.

❦

And I was right. That Saturday, Max got most of the business. By Sunday, word had spread across the East, and people waited in line to buy their Big Maxes.

Oh, don't get me wrong. We occasionally had a customer or two, but most of the time we stared across the street, watching Max serve his thirsty patrons.

"I don't get it," Pop complained. "It's nothin' but orange juice and seltzer vater. Vut's so special 'bout dat?"

I didn't get it either, but I knew Pop had to do something different, and fast. I just needed time to think about it. And I would have, too, except the long lines at Orange Max made me mad. Boiling mad, just like the heat. Too distracted to think up a solution.

After all, Pop was a good, hard-working man, only trying to provide for his family. And then Max invaded our territory with his stupid orange juice stand and sparkling water drink, and it threatened our livelihood.

I wiped the sweat away from my brow.

Doris must have known about that sign, I thought, pacing back-and-forth, rubbing the back of my neck. Why didn't she say something? If we'd known, we could have planned for it.

But no, she didn't, and every time another car pulled into Max's parking lot, I got more irritated.

❦

The following day, I waited in front of the Van Nuys High School concrete walkway, leading to the white brick and columned administration building. Doris and I were going to talk whether she wanted to or not.

129

As I paced the walkway, clusters of kids brushed by. "Outta the way, Jew boy," said one student.

"Kike," muttered another.

Germany and Europe weren't the only places where anti-Semitism existed.

My fists tightened, but I let it go, glaring at them instead until they disappeared into the crowd.

It made no sense to fight every kid who made remarks like that in passing, especially at this school, where almost everyone felt the same way except the six of us. It didn't mean I wasn't angry; no, even more so. I'd heard those taunts since I was little and hated it. At that moment, I vowed that someday, when the right time came, I was going to get even with every single one of those sons of bitches.

And then Doris surprised me from behind. She was smiling and wearing her usual pleated skirt, white blouse, and saddle shoes.

"Hi, Romeo."

"Hey," I growled.

Her eyebrows rose. "What are you mad at?"

"Why didn't you tell me?"

"Tell me what?" she replied, clearly confused. "Are you alright?"

I stepped forward, pointing my finger. "About the sign. The sign at your dad's place."

Her gaze hardened. "Why did I need to tell you? It's just a sign."

She wasn't getting it, which frustrated me more. "It's not just a sign. It's putting us out of business."

Students gathered around.

"What do you want me to do about it?" she asked. "It's his business. He can do what he wants."

"He's a crook," I roared. "A *gonif.* Your father is underhanded."

The crowd oohed.

Tears welled up in her eyes.

When I saw her pain, I stopped. I'd gone too far.

"How could you say that?" she choked. "You're certainly not the boy I thought you were, Leonard King. Maybe my father was right. Maybe we shouldn't be together."

I winced. "Don't say that." My heart palpitated. "You know I didn't mean it. Honest. We're made for each other. Like two star-crossed lovers."

"I can't do this anymore."

I moved in to hold her, but she backed away.

"Stay away from me," she said. "I mean it. Don't ever call me again."

She dashed away before I could stop her, whisking through the crowd.

"Hymie gets the air," hooted a tall boy with a haircut so tight it made him look like a circus geek.

"Shut up," I shouted. But no one paid attention. They had dispersed, laughing, on their way to class.

After second period, I feigned an illness and came home. When I arrived, the house was empty. Pop was at work, my sister Bev was at school, and Mom was playing Mah-Jongg at the Levy's home.

Being alone allowed me the freedom to wallow in self-pity while I poured my heart out to the Hank Greenberg baseball card pinned to the wall in my bedroom. I knew he couldn't talk, but I needed someone to listen, even if it was a cheap piece of colored cardboard that smelled like stale bubblegum. I certainly couldn't tell Pop about things, especially after he'd forbidden me to see Doris.

Around dinnertime, before I could tell Mom I wasn't feeling well, Pop barged into my messy room.

"Ve need to do somethin' about da business. Somethin' new."

I turned away and wiped my eyes, making sure he didn't see I'd been crying. "What about hot dogs, Pop," I reminded him. "Let's get some buns. Bring in some hot dog steamers and..."

"Enough already vit de hot dogs," barked Pop. "If I vanted to sell hot dogs, I'd build a baseball park. Ve need a drink. Somethin' to compete wiff dat *furshlugginer* Big Max."

I sat down on my lumpy bed. "I don't know, Pop. I have to think about it."

"Ve don't haff time to tink. Ve need action." He cocked his head. "Vut's dat popular drink dey sells in downtown Los Angeles? You know, it's cold and creamy and has kind of a vanilla taste."

"Orange Swirlee, Pop."

"Dat's da drink."

"What about Orange Swirlee?"

"Listen to dis. Vut if we made one." He finger-framed the room. "Ve'll call it—da Orange Izzy."

"After your first name?"

"Exactly." He sat down on the bed next to me. "So, how do ve make vun?"

"I don't know, Pop. This doesn't sound like such a good idea. It's probably a trade secret."

"Vait a minute, vait a minute." He snapped his fingers. "I got an idea."

❦

Pop's scheme was to take the day off and hang out at the Orange Swirlee stand in downtown Los Angeles. We would take turns watching them prepare the drink while the other one would snoop around, searching for information about the ingredients they used.

It wasn't the most ingenious plan, but it made me happy because I got the day off from school and didn't have to face Doris.

After spending a few hours poking through the garbage, watching the Orange Swirlee staff, and observing the delivery trucks, we figured out what to do. All we needed were fresh oranges, granulated sugar, powdered eggs, crushed ice, milk, and vanilla flavoring. We were never going to learn what secret powder they used, so we decided to use cornstarch.

When we got home, Pop hijacked mom's blender. For the rest of the day, we acted like mad scientists, mixing and matching ingredients and adjusting measurements, until by midnight, we'd created something that almost tasted like the original.

Pop was so excited he couldn't sleep. Before I woke up in the morning, he'd already placed an ad in the *Van Nuys News* proclaiming the Orange Izzy as the Valley's answer to the Big Max and the Orange Swirlee.

That Saturday, before we drove to work, Pop bought a cheap secondhand Delco-Light Plant from one of the local farmers because we now needed electricity for the business.

The machine, a single-cylinder vertical engine, had seen better days. Every time we switched on the motor, it wobbled up to speed like a lackadaisical hamster on a wheel before settling into a rapid, ear-splitting putt-putt-puttering.

After setting up the Light Plant outside the stand and raising a hand-drawn banner advertising the Orange Izzy, we were open for business. Pop had me bring my Brownie camera to document the occasion.

Within one hour, our first customer arrived. He was a middle-aged man wearing a brown-vested suit, matching fedora, and holding a copy of the *Van Nuys News*. I snapped his picture as he approached the counter, then hid my camera back in a cabinet.

"Vut can I do for you?" asked Pop over the sound of the noisy Delco generator.

The man took off his hat, revealing black hair well-groomed into a single wave and polished with oil. "I'll have one of those Orange Izzy's," said the man.

"Vun Orange Izzy coming up."

"What?" I said, struggling to hear him.

Pop frowned and raised his voice. "Vun drink."

Taking an orange, I sliced it up, added the proper ingredients into the blender, and toggled on the machine. When it whirled into a light-colored orange drink with foamy bubbles, I turned off the appliance and handed the glass container to Pop.

He poured the liquid into a seven-ounce cup and turned to the customer. "Dattle be ten cents."

The businessman slammed a dime on the counter and grabbed the drink. He took a swig, and a smile crossed his face. "Hey, this is pretty good. Just like an Orange Swirlee."

"Vell, dat's da point."

"What'd you do. Steal the recipe?" the man guffawed.

I tensed and turned toward Pop.

"Confidentially, ve just copied it a little." Pop raised his finger to his mouth. "Shhhh! Don't tell nobody."

I glanced at the ground, wondering why Pop had admitted the subterfuge.

"Well, you did a good job—first-rate. When I saw your ad in the newspaper, I didn't believe you. But I was wrong. This tastes just like the original."

"Tanks." Pop grinned. He bounced lightly in place.

The man put on his hat and turned toward his white-wheeled, maroon Pontiac Silver Streak.

"Hope to see you again," yelled out Pop.

"Oh, I'll be back," said the man.

Pop took the dime, flipped it into his palm, and said, "Lenny, it's going to be a good day."

And Pop was right. All morning business boomed. I felt pretty upbeat and happy about it until I spied Doris and her dad watching customers enter our unpaved parking lot. Max had his arms folded, and Doris frowned, looking like she didn't want to be there at all.

I took a deep, pained breath, wishing I could change our argument and its aftermath. But I knew that wasn't possible. I was so depressed, I kept quiet, sliced oranges, and prepared Pop's Orange Izzies all morning. Every once in a while, Pop glanced at me as if he wanted to talk, but we didn't.

Sometime before noon, after filling a box full of orange peels, I lifted the carton and headed outside toward the rackety generator and metal trashcan.

As soon as the door behind me slammed shut, I stopped. My eyes widened. Marked on the stand's side—big enough to see— was a *swastika* the size of a dump truck tire. The orange paint highlighted its black ugliness.

A shiver ran down my spine. I lost my grip on the box, which smashed to the ground, scattering peels. "Who did this?" I yelled. "Who?"

Pivoting, I ran into the middle of the parking lot out front and scanned the area. There was no one except a small child with his parents ordering a drink from Pop.

My heart hammered with adrenalin. They didn't do it, I thought, and there's nobody else here who could have. Maybe somebody from school? It could've been anyone.

"Vut're you doing in the parking lot?" hollered Pop. "Ve've got customers here."

"Be right there," I called back.

I was getting tired of the hatred. The next time, I would get even, and I planned to have my Hammerin' Hank Greenberg baseball bat with me for the job.

☙

I didn't tell Pop about the incident. There was no point in upsetting him, but I made sure to cover up that revolting symbol with some flattened Snoboy boxes until I could paint over it.

That afternoon, when work eased up, I saw the maroon Pontiac Silver Streak pull into the parking lot.

The brown-suited man with the fedora stepped out of the car. He was heading to the counter, shoes crunching on gravel. There was no smile on his face.

I wiped my hands on my apron, fearing bad news.

"Are you Isadore King?" he asked Pop.

"I am. You vant another Orange Izzy today?"

He reached into his coat pocket and pulled out an envelope. He handed it to Pop. "I think you should read this."

Pop grabbed the envelope, ripped it open, and pulled out the folded letter. I peeked over his shoulder and noticed it had a law firm letterhead.

"Vut is dis?"

"It's a cease-and-desist letter. Chase, Gorelick and Zachary represent the interests of the Orange Swirlee Company. Your drink, as good as it is, infringes on the trade secrets and intellectual property created by Simon Atwood, Hank Gaines, and the Orange Swirlee Company."

"I don't understand. Ve just made an orange drink. Dat's all."

"I don't think you can sell the Orange Izzy anymore, Pop."

Pop angered. "You keep out of dis. Dat's not vut da man said."

The man placed his hat on the counter. "I'm afraid your son is right, Mr. King. Orange Swirlee is telling you to quit selling your drink."

"You can't do dat. And vut if I don't?"

"Orange Swirlee is a growing corporation. They have over seventy-five stands in the U.S. and are very protective of their intellectual property. I'm afraid if you fail to stop selling your beverage, they will sue you, seek damages, and put you out of business."

My stomach churned.

"May I call you Izzy?" the man asked Pop.

"Yes, sure," said Pop.

"Listen, Izzy. You seem like an honorable man. Hard-working. Industrious. You don't want to put your family through more financial hardship, do you? Times are still tough."

Pop frowned, nodded.

"So, we can trust you to stop selling the drink and not take this matter any further?"

"Yes," said Pop, soft-spoken. "Ve'll take down de signs. Der von't be no more Izzy."

Upset, I lowered my gaze. I couldn't stand to see Pop so disheartened and sad.

☙

The next day, Pop and I drove to the orange stand in silence. More desert-like weather had been forecast, and dry air whistled through the cab as we sped down Van Nuys Boulevard.

"Hey, Pop," I said. "What if we changed some ingredients in the drink?"

"Ve ain't gonna change nothin'. Ve're in enough trouble. I don't vant to talk about it no more."

So, I didn't.

At Burbank Boulevard, we pulled into the empty gravel parking lot and got to work yanking down the banner proclaiming the Orange Izzy. While I turned on the generator and spent five minutes painting over the *swastika*, Pop waited for an ice delivery, which came a few minutes later. I returned inside the giant orange, used an ice pick to make some ice chips, and moved a box of oranges to the counter. We were all set for business.

By four-fifteen, Pop decided to go home. We'd only had five customers all day as compared to Max's thriving business across the street. I begged him to stay, assuring Pop more people would show up, but the fire had vanished from his eyes. Since the Orange Swirlee attorney had visited, Pop looked as if he'd aged ten years. He stood stoop-shouldered and resigned. His fragile appearance worried me, and I agreed to close the stand on my own.

And then we heard an automobile roar down Burbank Boulevard, its loud pistons rumbling at high gear.

Startled, I looked through the counter opening.

An eighteen-foot burgundy-colored Duesenberg convertible swerved into the parking lot and skidded to a stop on the gravel. Its motor reverberated like a powerful airplane, white exhaust billowing and puttering from the rear until the driver shut off the engine.

"Vut is dis?" asked Pop.

I stared at the car. It shone in the daylight, illuminating the extended hood and winged hood ornament. The chrome side pipe exhausts jutted out from the engine like caterpillar legs, and the magnificent-looking radiator grille and round headlights gleamed in the sun's rays.

The driver's door popped open. A six-foot man with a rugged jawline and mussed-up brown hair staggered out of the car. He wore a pale blue work shirt, jeans, and cowboy boots and held a silver flask.

He strolled toward us and looked familiar. It wasn't until he got closer that I knew who he was.

Excited, I grabbed Pop's arm. "Pop, Pop," I said, pulling him away from the counter.

"Vut're you doing? Ve got a customer."

"I know who that guy is," I said, practically bouncing up and down. "It's the King."

Pop looked confused. "King. Vut're you talkin', King? Ve live in America. Dere is no King."

"No, Pop, listen. *Marauders across the Prairie. Sagebrush Serenade. It Happened One Day.*"

"Vut happened one Day? Did somethin' happen?"

"Pop," I said sharply. "It's Chuck Lombard. Majestic Pictures. King of the Singing Cowboys."

He raised his eyebrows. "Oh, da King."

Lombard slapped an impatient palm on the counter. "Say, what does a guy have to do around here to get a drink?"

"Okay, okay," murmured Pop. "Hold your horses." He approached Lombard, and I followed. "Now, vhat'll it be?"

"Gimme a drink," he bellowed. "I came here 'cause your sign says you're a King."

He pointed with a thumb to his chest. "And I'm a King."

His boozy breath made me recoil. Lombard was stewed.

"Ve don't sell liquor here. Maybe you should go."

"What're ya talking about?" slurred Lombard. "I brought my own booze. See?" He lifted the flask. "My wife Kitty, I mean Kate, says I drink too much and flirt with every broad I see. But that old cowgirl has got a lot of nerve callin' me a flirt when she's been makin' eyes with that foreign bohunk on the set. I oughta punch that guy right in the nose."

Pop looked around. "Vut guy?"

"You gonna serve me that drink or not?"

"We'll serve you, Mister Lombard," I said.

"Thanks, kid." He leaned on the counter and swayed. "That's more like it."

While I squeezed oranges, Pop made small talk with the King. Then I spotted my Brownie camera and wondered, what if I took a picture of Chuck Lombard and Pop standing outside the stand. We could place a framed copy of it on the counter and then advertise the business as the place where Chuck Lombard, King of the Singing Cowboys, buys his orange juice. That might save Pop's business.

My adrenaline rushed. "Oh, boy!" I said.

"Vhere's da juice," yelled Pop.

"Right here."

I handed him the glass container, and he poured it into a cup.

"Dattle be ten cents."

Lombard grabbed the cup and held the flask over it. "Now you're talking," he said. "This here—this gin's gonna make me an Orange Blossom."

I raised my palms. "Stop!" I shouted.

140

"Say, what is this?" Lombard snarled.

"Vut are you doing?" Pop yelled. "Let da man have his drink."

"Let me take a picture first," I said. "You and Pop."

"Wha' for?"

"Cause..." I thought for a second. "I'm a fan."

Lombard appeared flummoxed, evidently struggling to think straight. "Okay, but no liquor in it, okay? 'Cause I don't want Kate or the studio to see I been drinkin'."

"We'll be right out." I pushed Pop toward the back door. "C'mon, Pop."

"I don't vant my picture taken."

"Trust me. We can tell people the King of the Singing Cowboys came here."

Pop shrugged. "Dis is crazy."

I grabbed my camera and hustled outside to the front counter.

Lombard could barely stand up, and he leaned against the counter for balance. "Hey, you better not be makin' a sucker outta me, or I'll sock you inna nose."

I maneuvered Pop next to the King, took three steps back, and raised my camera. Neither Pop nor Lombard looked too happy, so I said, "Smile and say oranges."

Just as I clicked the shutter, Lombard flashed his famous choppers and lifted the silver flask into the shot.

"Uh oh," I said.

"Vut?"

"I need to take another picture. The flask got in the way."

Lombard's smiled disappeared. He glared at me, his face darkening with rage. "Are you takin' me for a buggy ride?" he roared. "You said one shot." His hands clenched and unclenched.

I was shocked at how easily riled he was. I stumbled over my words. "But you didn't want any…"

He stepped toward me.

Pop grabbed his arm, stopping him.

Lombard bared his teeth and bucked to get free, but Pop had more strength than I realized. Lucky for us, the King was intoxicated.

"Leave him alone," Pop yelled. "He's just a kid. He only vanted a picture."

"Yeah, a picture," Lombard sneered. He broke free of Pop's grip. "My fans," he said cynically.

Lombard drank from the flask and wiped his mouth with his sleeve. "I gotta get outta this joint," he said. "This place gives me the jitters."

He pushed aside Pop and lurched toward his Duesenberg.

I rushed over to make sure Pop was okay. "You all right?"

Lombard's car engine rumbled to life. The ground vibrated underneath our feet.

"Let him go," said Pop.

We watched as the Duesenberg roared out of the parking lot. It disappeared onto Van Nuys Boulevard, leaving a trail of smoke behind.

Pop looked at me with worried eyes. "Dat photo better be verth it."

The next week, I had the picture developed at DePauk Photography and placed an ad in the local newspaper featuring the photo. In between, I attended school and avoided Doris. That is, until Thursday morning during the twenty-minute break before my third-period class.

I had been en route to meet Jerry Burke, the editor of the school yearbook. When I turned a corner in the bustling hallway, a group of students and cheerleaders raised a long rectangular banner announcing the Moonlight in Paradise Spring Dance in two weeks.

The sign made me heartsick. Doris and I had planned on attending together, our first dance as a real couple. Now, I figured, I'd be spending the evening at home, staring at the ceiling, wondering why the love I felt was meant for someone I couldn't have.

"Lenny..." called out a familiar, screechy voice.

I turned and stared into Louis Eigner's squinty eyes. Louis, one of the five other Jewish kids in school, wore tan pants that fit high on his waist and a red and blue plaid shirt with a wide, unbuttoned collar. His slicked back, curly hair shone with Brylcreem.

"Hi, Louis," I said, not wanting to talk.

"I heard about you and Doris. Is it true?"

I sighed, lowering my gaze. "Yeah, I guess so."

"Geez, that's too bad. You sure made a swell couple. Well, as long as you're not going together anymore, do you mind if I ask her to the dance next week?" He squinted. "She's the nicest girl in school."

My blood pressure exploded. "Do what you want," I barked. "You think I care?"

"What're you getting so sore about, Lenny? It's not like you've got dibs on her or anything."

"Oh, go suck an egg."

I bolted past him through the crowded hallway.

I knew getting mad at a nice guy like Louis seemed wrong, but the mere thought of Doris dating him, or anybody else, made me burn.

When I reached the school yearbook office, I jerked open the door and entered.

Inside was a large green chalkboard, a bulky teachers' desk, and twenty wooden school desks divided into five rows. The back wall had clippings from the *Van Nuys Mirror* newspaper and a photo collage called JOURNALISM AND YOU.

Jerry Burke, dressed in his usual neatly pressed clothes, sat on the teacher's desk, arms crossed against his chest. I noticed his shiny black oxfords, polished as always.

"Thanks for coming, King," he said. "Have a seat."

I sat in one of the front row desks.

He unfolded his arms and leaned forward. "So, I heard you broke up with your girlfriend. What's her name? Doris?"

I pursed my lips. I wasn't sure I liked where this was going. "Rosenwald. Doris Rosenwald."

"Right."

There was an awkward silence.

"You wanted to see me?" I asked, forcing a smile.

"Right. I was thinking," he said. "Since you don't have a date anymore for the dance, we want you to show up and take pictures for the yearbook." He gave me a pointed look. "After all, you are one of the staff photographers."

I lowered my chin and grimaced, realizing I'd probably have to take pictures of Doris at the dance.

Burke's forehead wrinkled. "What's wrong? Jews don't worship on Saturday night, do they?"

Once again, more stupid Jewish remarks.

"Not my family," I said sharply.

He slapped his hands together. "Good. Then you can do it?"

144

I wanted to decline. Tell him that it hurt too much to attend, but I didn't. If I failed to help out, I'd only get blamed for not fitting in. It was already hard enough to be Jewish at this school without adding fuel to the fire.

"I'll do it," I said, resigned.

Burke smiled. "Thanks, King. You're royalty."

I didn't say anything.

He put his arm around my shoulder. "You know," he said, appearing surprised. "I was wrong about you. For a Jew, you're not pushy or obnoxious at all."

That was the last straw. I scrambled from the room before I could punch him in the face, only to witness, in the hallway, Louis Eigner asking Doris out to the dance.

She said yes—looking at me while she said it.

There were no words. I stood deflated. It wasn't even ten-thirty, and my day was already a disaster.

After school, I jumped on my bike and peddled over to help Pop clean up the stand. I just wanted to forget about the day. But when I arrived, Pop was already outside in an animated discussion with a businessman.

The man, wearing a blue tweed suit and holding a straw fedora hat, appeared calm.

Pop rubbed his chin. "I don't understand vut you vant me to do. Dat picture belongs to my son."

I stopped by the giant orange, kicked the bike stand, and rushed over to them.

I frowned. I couldn't understand why the Orange Swirlee people wouldn't leave Pop alone.

"Is this your son?" asked the man, acknowledging my presence.

"Vut's it to you?"

The man stuck out his hand. "Charles Seaforth. Majestic Pictures publicity."

"You mean you're not with Orange Swirlee?" I asked.

He laughed. "Afraid not, kid. Orange Swirlee's may sing with flavor, but nobody can croon like Chuck Lombard, King of the Westerns."

Relieved, I shook his hand. "Leonard King. What's going on?"

Pop complained. "Da man says he vonts da picture."

"My Lombard picture?"

Seaforth stepped forward. "Maybe I can explain," he said, evidently trying to appear sincere. "A few days ago, Mr. Lombard came here after a horrible, horrible argument with his wife." He shook his head. "I know, we've all been there. But then he did something unthinkable. He picked up a bottle of the devil's mouthwash and got drunk."

"*Fershnickered* is more like it," said Pop.

"Anyway," Seaforth said, clearing his throat. "Mr. Lombard believes the picture was taken while he was under the influence of alcohol. Now, I know you just wanted a picture with the King of the Singing Cowboys, but Chuck Lombard is a world-renowned star and a hero to boys and girls all over this country. So, you wouldn't want Mr. Lombard to be perceived as something he's not, a boozer, would you? Especially after arguing over a personal matter with his wife?"

Pop lowered his gaze. "I guess not."

"What about you, son?" said Seaforth, smiling. "Think you can help out the King?"

I knew what he wanted, but I didn't care. We needed that picture to save Pop's business. "But it's my photo," I argued.

Seaforth snapped his fingers. "Say, I have an idea. What if I got you a hand-signed autographed photo of Chuck Lombard instead? You can hang that on a wall."

I shook my head. "It's not the same. Anybody can get one of those. You just write the studio for a picture."

Seaforth seemed taken aback.

"My photo proves something," I continued. "That Chuck Lombard was a customer and came to our business."

Pop looked weary. "Just give da man da photo."

I turned to him, adamant. "No, Pop. I won't."

"Hold on there," said Seaforth. He didn't seem quite so calm now. "What if we paid you for the picture? I'm sure you and your father could use the money."

I glanced across the street to Max's busy place. "Never!" I said.

"Vait a minute." Pop held up his hand. "Let me talk to my son."

Pop pulled me aside. His eyes looked tired. "Let it go, Lenny. Tings are tough for us right now. Ve could use da money."

"But—"

He interrupted. "You're a good boy, Lenny. I know vut you're trying to do, but let's talk to da man."

So, once again, I obeyed and followed him back to Charles Seaforth, who was leaning against our orange juice stand. I wasn't happy about it, but Pop had a responsibility to our family and needed the cash.

"Vut kind of money vas you talking about?"

The publicity man beamed. "Well, seeing as how you two have been real gentlemen about this whole thing, I'm going to give you my very best offer, straight from the studio. Two thousand dollars for the picture and negative."

Pop and I stood stunned. That was more than two year's income.

"Everything okay?" asked Seaforth.

"It's very generous. Dat's all."

"Of course, it is," he laughed. "What didja think I was gonna do? Jew you down on the price or something?"

Pop's demeanor changed and his face reddened. "Vut did you say?"

I tensed. All the anti-Semitic comments I'd seen and heard bubbled up. I was tired of it, and I was tired of stupid men like Charles Seaforth, who felt they could say anything derogatory about the Jews.

"Get out," I screamed.

"What's wrong?" said Seaforth looking dumbfounded. "What about our deal?"

"Dere ain't no deal," said Pop.

Enraged, I ran inside the stand and grabbed the Hank Greenberg baseball bat leaning against the wall.

"I'm sure we can work this out," said Seaforth to Pop.

When the publicity man eyed me, running toward him brandishing Hammerin' Hank's bat over my head, he made a beeline for his red Hudson convertible. He jumped in and turned on the engine. It roared to life.

"We had a deal," he protested. "The studio's not going to be very happy about this. I'd watch myself if I were you."

I swung and missed the white-walled car just as it screeched back, stopped, and peeled out of the parking lot onto Burbank Boulevard.

Pop trudged up. We both stared as it zoomed away.

"Hank Greenberg, you ain't," said Pop, shaking his head.

After the incident, we worried something terrible would happen, but it never did. Pop worked, Bev and I went to school, and Mom kept losing at Mah-jongg. Pretty soon, before we knew it, two weeks had passed, Saturday night arrived, and the Moonlight in Paradise dance loomed large before me.

I still didn't want to go, but I'd given my word even though it pained me.

When I stepped into the living room wearing my light gray slacks, a white dress shirt, and a red grid-patterned tie, *Gang Busters* was playing on the radio. Pop seemed more concerned than usual. He stopped me before I could put the Brownie camera strap over my shoulder.

"I vant you to take the truck tonight."

"It's okay, Pop. I'll walk."

"Valk nothing. You take da truck. Suppose somethin' happens."

I gave him a skeptical look. "Really, Pop? It's Saturday night."

"Okay, smart guy," he said, challenging me. "Suppose John Dillinger and Baby Face Nelson ambush you at da school dance tonight and bring out dere Tommy guns. *Rat-a-tat-tat.* Vut are you gonna do den?"

I tried to keep from laughing. "First of all, Pop, Hoover and the FBI killed Baby Face Nelson and John Dillinger six years ago, so they're dead. Second of all, they wouldn't be anywhere near the school dance because they lived in the Midwest and aren't high school students. And third, why don't you listen to *Your Hit Parade* on NBC instead of *Gang Busters*? It's driving you crazy. You worry too much, Pop."

"Okay, okay. Maybe you're right." He placed his hand on my shoulder. "But I still vant you to take da truck. I vorry. Dat's all."

I knew what Pop meant, and I loved him, too. "Okay, Pop," I said. "I'll take the truck."

"Good boy."

He handed me the keys, and I hugged Pop and left.

Once outside, I opened the squeaky truck door. The Hank Greenberg bat rested on the front passenger seat. Pop had left it in the pickup for protection ever since our run-in with Seaforth.

After hopping in, I turned on the lights, jiggled the ignition key, and the old rattletrap sputtered to life. It took five minutes to drive to school and park, another five to reach the boys' gymnasium.

Some kids milled outside the lighted entrance. Crickets chirped over the melodic, big band trombone solo playing inside. At the door, I exhaled and walked into the dance.

The decorations were stunning. Twinkling lights dangled from the ceiling like stars, and a gigantic papier-mâché moon hung in the corner. Its cherubic face smiled down on all the hoofers, jitterbuggers, and cement mixers that danced on the shiny gym floor. Red, gray, and white balloons with curly streamers hung under a net for release later in the evening. And standing on a riser in between cardboard palm trees was a swing band with three saxophonists, a trombone player, two trumpet players, an overtaxed drummer, and a male singer wearing a white sport coat.

Even though I promised myself I wouldn't do it, I immediately searched the dance floor looking for Doris, hoping she wasn't there.

No such luck. I found her wearing a teal green dress with a sweetheart bodice that caught my attention, and dancing so close to Louis Eigner that it made me want to weep. She looked beautiful. I sighed, knowing it should have been me dancing with her instead.

But what could I do? I was there to take photos, which I did, spending the next forty-five minutes snapping pictures and staging portraits for the good old Crimson and Gray Yearbook.

While I worked, I periodically peeked at Doris. Kids jumped and twirled and cut loose on the dance floor, but she had stopped dancing. She stood at the edge of the flooring, not talking, looking sad. Louis Eigner seemed oblivious to her moods; he grinned at everyone.

It bothered me. I still loved her and didn't want to see her so unhappy. I debated whether to say hello, cheer her up, or even ask her to dance if she'd let me.

And then she looked over and smiled.

My heart raced.

Her smile wasn't big, more like a slight one that quickly disappeared after she wiped away a tear. It touched my heart. When she turned for the exit, I knew what I had to do.

"Hey, can you take our picture?" said Bob Brust, combing his slicked-back hair. He stood with Betty Willett, who towered over him like a skyscraper.

The gym door slammed shut.

"No!" I snapped, dashing away.

"Thanks a lot, King," yelled Brust.

I hit the double-metal doors and raced outside, past the cafeteria, and into the quad area. Swing band music echoed through the empty pathways and buildings.

Biting my lip, I scanned for Doris on the warm summer night. She seemed to have disappeared into the darkness—until I saw a figure silhouetted by moonlight on the library steps.

"Doris," I called out. She didn't respond, and I moved closer.

Finally, when I neared the stairs, she turned and looked down.

"Who's there?" she asked.

I don't know what possessed me, but just seeing her delicate features in the light made my heart swoon, and I said, remembering she loved Shakespeare, "But, soft! What light through yonder window breaks? It is the east, and Doris is the sun? Arise fair sun, and kill the envious moon."

"Leonard?"

"It is I, Leonard, my fair lady. And you are my love."

Doris giggled. "O Leonard, Leonard, wherefore art thou, Leonard?"

"I am down-eth here, my sweet maiden, hoping we can talk-eth," I said, cringing. "I am not thy enemy. You are a Rosenwald, and I am only a King. Leonard King, son of a humble orange juice salesman."

"Tis but thy name that is my enemy; thou art thyself, though not a King. What's a King? That which we call a rose by any other name would smell as sweet."

I jumped on the steps and touched the balustrade. "An orange can be just as sweet," I said and winced. "And it is sold by both Rosenwald and King. So, why can we not be together, my love? You need but two oranges and chipped ice to make an orange drink."

Doris appeared to cringe. "Oh, dear Leonard, your Shakespeare is painful to my ears, but the sentiment is music to my heart."

She drew closer as I walked up to her. "With love's light wings do I perch these stairs. My love is deep, and I ask for thy forgiveness. By yonder blessed moon, I swear my love is true and that I have been heartbroken ever since our breaketh-up."

"And so have I," she said. "Tis why I cried after seeing you in the gym this evening."

"Then can we work-eth it out and find a way to tell our *meshugana* parents we are but one?"

"Yes," she said, grinning. "We are but two star-crossed lovers."

I stared into her eyes. Then, when Doris squeezed my hand, I leaned in and kissed her gently on the lips, and she draped her arms around my neck and kissed back.

"Hey, you kids, stop that!" yelled a male voice.

We both turned. Barreling toward us, and holding what looked like a lit cigarette, was Mr. Brewster, the Boys Vice-Principal. He'd been a chaperone at the dance, and now he was looking to make an example of someone.

"Is that you, King?" I heard Mr. Brewster shout.

"C'mon," I said, pulling Doris with me.

We rushed down the steps and headed into the building shadows, away from the school.

"Where we going?" she giggled.

We were going to the only spot I knew where we could be alone and talk, and neck, and gaze at the stars; millions of them that sparkled and twinkled in the night. A place that wasn't near prying eyes at school or in a beat-up old truck. But somewhere we both knew well.

"We're going to my Pop's orange juice stand," I said.

And then we ran into the darkness.

We sped down Van Nuys Boulevard in Pop's old truck. Doris leaned against my shoulder; I had a smile on my face. It was the happiest I'd felt in weeks. Doris and I were finally together again, and not even our parents' feud or my family's money problems could change that.

And then something terrible happened.

When we were one block from Pop's stand, a fireball of violent red and yellow flames burst upward from the side of the building.

Doris screamed. I slammed on the brakes, and the truck screeched to a halt.

My heart pounded. Everything flashed before my eyes. Pop's business ruined, everything destroyed. We needed help, and we needed it now.

"Get out," I said, raising my voice.

"No," she cried.

"Run for help. Call the fire department. I've gotta put out that fire."

"No, Lenny. Please."

"Now, Doris!" I screamed, "Run."

She opened the door and charged out, bawling.

I jammed the accelerator. The old truck lurched forward.

Flames engulfed the giant orange now. Clouds of smoke billowed sky high. My photo of Chuck Lombard was surely ashes.

Backing out of our gravel parking lot was a black Dodge sedan with no license plate.

Did they start the fire? I didn't know or care. I was going to stop that car from leaving no matter what.

I violently jerked the wheel to the left. The truck jumped the curb. It headed straight for the black car. When I swung into a semi-spin, the flatbed of the pick-up plowed into the rear of the moving vehicle.

I slammed into the dash on impact.

Both cars stopped.

Blood trickled down my face. My ribs hurt, and I moaned.

Outside, the Dodge's wheels screeched and spun, but the car was stuck, attached to the old truck like a speared animal.

The orange stand was burning like a blazing globe, deep red and amber flames licking upward from the fiery structure.

I grabbed the Hank Greenberg bat and opened the squeaky driver's door. After tumbling out, I limped toward the other car. I clenched my teeth. Somebody was going to pay for burning down Pop's business.

Smoke burned my lungs. My eyes watered while I made my way to the Dodge.

"Get outta that car," I croaked, gripping the weapon.

There was no answer.

"Get out," I repeated.

When I reached the driver's side, I swung the bat once, twice, and then the window shattered. The car door swung open, banging my ribs.

A heavy-set, middle-aged man wearing a sleeveless T-shirt and pants rushed out, holding his injured arm.

"Don't hit me," he screamed, running away. "Don't hit me."

I stumbled after him, racing through the parking lot. "Come back here," I yelled.

In the distance, shrill fire engine sirens blared in the Valley.

"Stay away from me," he shrieked until he slipped on the gravel and fell.

Standing over him, I frowned, my hands tightening on the bat. I raised the weapon over my head. Was he sent from the studio or just another Jew-hater? One wrong word and I would bash his skull in. I hauled back, my face hot, my blood rushing.

The brightness of the flames lit up the man's face. He appeared frightened, staring back at me with wide, fearful eyes.

"Did you start that fire?" I shouted, wiggling the bat. My muscles and veins strained. I wanted vengeance.

"Yes," he whimpered.

"Who sent you?"

"I can't say," he said, choking up and crying. He covered his face with his arms. "Don't."

I wanted to hammer him. Pound in his head with a crushing blow, but I didn't. I stared down at him instead and thought about myself.

I was breathing hard now.

I'd vowed once when the right time came, I was going to get even with every single one of those sons of bitches who'd hurt my family and me. But then I wondered if I followed through, wouldn't that make me just as bad as them?

Beads of sweat rolled down my cheeks.

Did it matter who started the fire that destroyed Pop's business? Did I really want to maim or kill someone to find out?

In front of the raging blaze and the remnants of Pop's stand, I lowered the bat. I thought about the last few weeks and how I had reacted to the insults and slurs, and about Hank Greenberg, who had played baseball to the highest level with dignity amidst all the anti-Semitic remarks.

And then I realized something I could never articulate before: true power comes from defining your own destiny. There were other ways in life to defeat the haters in the world without reacting impulsively or violently. The best way was to choose my path, make my choices and achieve success.

I looked down at the arsonist. I may not have been Hank Greenberg, but I knew when not to swing.

After the firemen came and the police arrested the arsonist, Mom and Pop showed up. Doris and her parents soon followed.

We all waited in the parking lot. The Rosenwald's stood near the policeman. We were closer to the firemen who hosed down the embers.

Pop was inconsolable. "Vhy did dis happen?" he said, "Vhy?"

I tried to comfort him even though I was feeling sad myself. "Don't worry, Pop. We'll make it through this," I said. "I know we will."

He looked at me with regret. "It vas dat damn photo," he said, shaking his head. "Dat damn Chuck Lombard photo. Vut am I gonna do now?"

A dark shadow enlarged as it got closer and covered us over.

"Izzy," said Max Rosenwald.

I looked up, and Max stood with his family. His expression was contrite.

Pop appeared to eye Max with distrust. "Vut d'ya vant, Max?

Doris pushed her father closer.

"Vell," said Max, "I vas sorry to hear about your business."

"You tink dis is somethin'? Dis is nothin'," said Pop. "Ya tink you're gonna beat me in the East Valley?"

"Pop," I said, raising my voice.

He backed down. "Tanks, Max. I 'preciate it."

"So vut are you gonna do now?"

Pop shrugged. "I don't know. Start over, I guess."

"Vell, I was tinking. I don't see vhy the East Valley can't be big enough for da both of us. Vhy don't you come in wit me? Ve'll run da business together."

"Vut? And make dat *farkakta* Big Max?" asked Pop, standing up.

I sighed. The feud was never going to end.

"It's better den dat stupid Orange Izzy," retorted Max.

"Vut are you calling stupid?"

And once again the two men stood face-to-face, eye-to-eye, anger in their voices, just like at the backyard barbeque months ago.

"So, ve gonna be partners?" snapped Max.

"Is dat vut you want?" snapped Pop.

"Dat's vut I vant."

"Den dat's vut I vant, too," said Pop, softening. He wiped away a tear. "You're my best friend, Max. Ve grew up together. Just like brudders. Let's not forget."

And just like that, the war was over. The two men hugged and broke into smiles.

Relieved, I limped over to Doris and held her hand. As far as we were concerned, everything was back to normal, except that it wasn't.

Oh, not in a bad way, of course, but for the better.

Apparently, the arsonist told the police to call "Jimmie." And they talked with their supervisor, who then called Majestic Pictures, and later that evening, in the middle of the night, a tired man named Jimmie Wilcox, wearing a black suit, showed up at our house and said he was a fixer—he fixed problems.

Wilcox explained to Pop that the studio wanted to keep news of the fire out of the papers. For his silence, they would buy him a brand-new restaurant on Ventura Boulevard near the RKO backlot in Encino.

Pop wouldn't do it without Max, and so Max was summoned over at three in the morning, wearing only his pajamas, and they bought his business, too.

That summer, after the fire was mysteriously credited to the old Delco light plant generator Pop bought and not an arsonist, Izzy and Max's Grill opened up on Ventura Boulevard, selling hamburgers, hot dogs, and Big Max's to great success. Or, at least, more success than the two juice stands they'd left behind.

And me? I'm working at the Grill after school, still inventing that special chili recipe for hot dogs, and dating Doris. Someday, I'm going to marry that girl. And when I do, we're going to open our own restaurant and hang celebrity photos on the wall.

You know, you can't be successful if you don't hang the photos.

CHAPTER SEVEN

CASE NUMBER FIVE: FROGGYLAND

ALLEGED VIOLATION: Emotional Distress
ALLEGED VIOLATION: Failure to do my best for the people
I am helping
ALLEGED VIOLATION: Failure to bring love, desire and
happiness to everyone

MAY 2019
BUENA PARK, CALIFORNIA

L arry Taylor nudged the accelerator, and his car inched forward
into the overflowing parking lot.

He grimaced. It was so damn frustrating. Everything should
have been perfect on this, the most important day of his life—and
the delay wasn't helping. After all, Larry knew today wasn't just
any ordinary day. He was taking his girlfriend, Amber, to

Froggyland, the third largest and least known amusement park in Orange County, California, for the best date ever.

He'd planned it for weeks. After a fun-filled day of entertainment and rides, he'd kneel on his right knee and propose to her in the middle of the flower-lined walkthrough at the Froggyland Castle, popularly known as the most romantic spot in the park. The place "Where every Toad becomes a Prince."

Larry couldn't wait to surprise her.

He eyed Amber sitting in the front passenger seat. She was the girl of his dreams. The pretty, long-legged, blond-haired art major from Denver had charmed him ever since they'd met at the UCLA Research Library two years ago. She was his first real girlfriend and the only girl in college who'd taken an interest in him. So, of course, he was going to love her.

But what if she said no? His neck stiffened, and he rubbed his face.

Amber gazed at Larry. "What's wrong?"

"Nothing."

"You look worried."

"I'm not," he said, reacting defensively.

"You've got that stupid look on your face again." She imitated him by wrinkling her brow, clearly thinking it was funny. It wasn't.

"No, I don't," said Larry, wishing she'd let it go.

"Fine," she said tersely. Amber turned and folded her arms across her chest.

Oh, great. Now she was mad. How could he tell her he was worried? They were both graduating from UCLA soon, and the fear that she might take a job or move back home to Denver was almost too much for his lovesick heart to bear. That's why they had to get married. If he lost her, he'd lose everything. Right?

The Chevy Suburban in front rolled forward then slammed on its brakes.

Larry did the same. "Damn it!" he snapped.

Amber glared at him. She was clearly not happy.

"Sorry," he apologized.

"You know I don't like you cursing, Larry."

He didn't like her speaking to him like that, but she was so *freaking* beautiful!

"I know, I know," he said.

And he did know. Amber didn't like him to lose his temper, either. Actually, when they'd first met, Amber didn't like a lot of things about him, but he'd changed for her. Better clothes, different friends. He'd even lost touch with his childhood friend and former neighbor, Molly, who loved Froggyland so much she once worked at the Hot Frog Stand in the park. He really missed her sometimes. They'd known each other since first grade. All part of growing up and being an adult, he guessed.

It took another twenty minutes for Larry to get his car near the front of the line. He tried hard to hide his irritation from Amber by politely smiling and asking trivial Froggyland questions. Simple ones, like did she know Uncle Del Smiley, the creator of Philly Frog, had had his head cryogenically frozen after he died, or whether she knew that Froggyland had an underground tunnel system beneath the theme park?

When she failed to respond and seemed pouty, his heart sank.

"Are you alright?" he asked.

"Yes," she answered with enough frost to ice the windows.

His smile dropped. Was she going to act like this all day?

The car in front moved up to the parking attendant, and Larry inched his vehicle forward.

After the Suburban hurried off, the parking attendant raised the palm of his hand. A second attendant dragged out a folding PARKING LOT IS FULL floor sign, painted with a cartoon head of Philly Frog, and blocked his lane.

"What?" screamed Larry, forgetting Amber was in the car.

The college-aged attendant, wearing a lime-green vest, walked over to the driver's window. "Sorry, sir, lot's closed. There's more parking over at the Felix Fly lot off Froggyland Avenue."

"But that's on the other side of the park," said Larry, sighing heavily.

"Just follow the exit signs, sir."

"You mean you're going to make me wait in another line?"

"Just go, Larry," said Amber, clearly impatient.

Larry looked at her, realized he didn't want an argument, and reluctantly drove toward the Felix Fly lot. He felt his shoulders inching toward his ears.

After parking his car, they boarded a crowded tram and sat next to four screaming babies and two loud middle-schoolers. When they arrived at the park entrance, they, once again, stood in a lengthy security line where Amber and he cooled their heels in another long queue, one of eight, to enter "The Hoppy-est Place on Earth."

He gazed around, focusing on the curved, hunter green Froggyland entryway. Mounted at the top was a large, buggy-eyed Philly Frog wearing a backward baseball cap. The creature greeted people with a wide toothless grin.

The sign always made Larry smile. He'd been visiting Froggyland since he was a kid and loved every inch of it. He'd even taken his younger sister Alison here for her birthday year-after-year until she got into high school and then thought the place was for dorks. Larry couldn't understand it. Who wouldn't love this place? He surmised not everyone had a passion for it like him, and his old friend Molly.

The hot sun beat down, and he was starting to sweat underneath his pale-yellow T-shirt and blue Levi's. Larry felt his right eye burn and closed it to keep from hurting. His contacts. *Crap!* He should have worn his glasses.

Amber rubbed his back. "You okay, babe?" she asked, apparently over the snit.

"Yeah, I'm okay," he said, not wanting to tell her about his contact lens, especially since she'd convinced him to buy the damn things in the first place, changing his natural honey-brown eyes to granny-apple green. "Just got something in my eye. That's all."

He stared at her with his one good peeper. His girlfriend was spectacular. She wore a black low-cut racerback tank top that revealed her ample cleavage, white short shorts, and matching tennis shoes that accentuated her slender and perfectly toned legs. When she turned, her wavy golden hair cascaded over her slender tanned shoulders. And her smile, when she smiled, made his heart melt. Not bad for a guy majoring in history who, two years before, was fifty pounds heavier and made people wonder whether he was Seth Rogen's paunchy brother.

Amber placed her arms around his neck and leaned in.

Her breasts pressed against his chest, making him want to cover her smooth skin in kisses. He could smell the strawberry scent in her hair.

"Coming here has really made me happy, baby," she cooed.

"Really?" said Larry, beaming.

"Really," she said, kissing him gently on the cheek.

Larry touched his pant pocket. The engagement ring he'd put there would be going to the right woman.

"You know what would also make me happy," she said, kissing him again.

"What?" Larry pecked her on the lips.

"You take that real estate exam like we talked about."

He flinched. "What?"

"Oh, come on, Larry, my dad says salesmen make the most money. Don't you want to make money?"

"Course I do, but a salesman? I'm a history major. You know I was thinking about teaching."

Amber pulled away, plainly annoyed. "For god's sake, Larry, history is just about old things and dead people. Who cares about that? It's like wearing last year's fashions. How many times have I told you? You've got to think about your career and everything else in life like it's art." She rubbed an imaginary bowl. "Something you can mold."

He touched the back of his neck. "I don't know, Amber…"

"Think about us." She pouted. "Our future."

His eyes widened. *Our future.* Amber had never said that before. Did she mean our future like she'd marry him? Holy Crap, he wanted to jump with joy. He'd better not blow this.

"Well?" Amber demanded.

"Okay." He hesitated. "Maybe."

A wide smile crossed her face, and she squeezed him, almost knocking him over. "You're the best, baby." She smothered him with fervent kisses, ending up pecking him on the face and neck. "You won't regret this."

His broadening grin made his cheeks ache. He was in heaven, enjoying every moment of his well-earned rapture.

"And then you know, honey, you'll go on TV."

"I'll what?"

"We'll produce and star in our own real estate show, *Fix and Dump*."

Suddenly, heaven wasn't so grand.

Once inside the park, Larry held Amber's hand as they edged past the flagpole in Frogtown, USA, a Victorian-style street, the main gateway to the amusement venue. The themed street led to Ribbet Park and the other lands, which fanned out like spokes on a wheel.

At the end of the street, directly past Ribbet Park, the Froggyland Castle rose over the entrance to the always amazing Enchanted Forest. On either side of Ribbet Park were the rip-roaring Calaveras County, the gold rush town, and the most fun land in the park, Froggy's Future Faire, where you could visit the world of tomorrow—today.

"Come on, slowpoke," Amber giggled, once again in a happy mood. They hurried past the crowded Frogtown shops with their hobbit-sized doorways, which led to restaurants and stores like Tadpole Tavern, Lilly's Pad, and Froggy's Ye Olde Souvenir Emporium.

Larry lagged behind and worried. The whole time he'd waited outside with Amber, she'd told him all about *Fix and Dump*. Larry had never seen her so bubbly and animated before. He tried to be supportive and be the best boyfriend he could possibly be, but if she continued to mention that stupid program again on this day, the most important day of his entire life, he was going to scream. His smile felt strained.

"Larry!" she demanded.

"Coming," he said, huffing and puffing. He finally caught up to her in the middle of Ribbet Park, next to the famous Philly Frog and Uncle Del Smiley statue.

Larry eyed the shiny bronze monument dedicated to the thin-haired, scowling Uncle Del Smiley, a stogie protruding from the corner of his mouth under his bushy metal mustache; he held a tiny Philly Frog in the palm of his hand. Below, on the concrete pedestal, was a copper plaque that read: *It all started with a friggin' frog.* Based on the way the statue frowned, Larry wasn't sure Uncle Del Smiley was all that "hoppy."

"Don't forget to remind me to take my vitamins at noon," said Amber. "I have to take them exactly at that time—in a restaurant. Okay?"

"Wouldn't it be faster to drink bottled water in line while we waited?"

Amber's eyes hardened.

Realizing he'd upset her, Larry backed down. "Okay. We'll go to a restaurant."

"That's all I ask," she said, clearly irked. She pulled out her iPhone and touched the screen. "My app says Froggy's Pirate Adventure has a two-hour wait."

"Maybe we should get a LeapFrog pass and reserve a time."

"I don't want to wait, Larry," she whined. "I want to go on something now."

Larry watched a human-sized Philly Frog sign autographs across the Plaza, next to a green popcorn cart. "What has the shortest wait then?" he asked.

Amber looked at her smartphone.

He continued to eye the costumed creature. When the bigheaded frog spied Larry, it froze like a statue. Its bulging eyes stared right at him and bored straight into his skull.

"What about It's a Small Pond?" Amber asked.

The tall figure stepped forward to obtain a better look at Larry, then raised its arm and pointed at him.

It unnerved him. Larry felt a chill run down his spine. What the fuck was that frog staring at?

"Larry," Amber snapped.

"Okay, okay, let's go," he said. He grabbed Amber's hand and pulled her toward The Enchanted Forest behind the Froggyland Castle. He didn't want to be anywhere near that creepy croaker.

Twenty minutes later, Larry eyed his wristwatch, sighed, and took one step forward. The line to It's a Small Pond, crowded with angry adults and bawling babies, spilled out of the rainforest-decorated queue and onto the concrete walkway outside. The wait felt like he was standing in slow-moving molasses.

Amber wasn't helping the situation. She prattled on and on about *Fix and Dump* as if he were actually interested in that ridiculous program.

"Now listen, Larry, when we get the show sold, we'll have to change your look," she said, peering at his head.

"What do you mean?"

Amber stared at him with a keen eye. "I mean, we'll need to change your clothes, mold you into something more exotic. And you'll have to grow a man bun. Yes, that's what we need—a man bun."

"How can I grow a man bun? Male pattern baldness runs in my family."

"We can solve that."

"What're you gonna do? Glue a ball of hair on my head? I'll look like a samurai sushi chef."

Amber folded her arms. Her eyes narrowed. Yep. Angry again. "You're just not taking this idea seriously," she grumbled.

"I am," he said. "I just don't want a hair transplant."

"Don't you get it?" she explained. "We need to have an image for the show. I get to be the beautiful interior decorator, and you get to be the geeky real estate agent who acts as a general contractor."

Her assessment stung, but he defended himself anyway. "But I don't know anything about home repair."

"How difficult can it be? Pound a few nails, screw a few screws."

"Listen to me, Amber," he pleaded. "I'm no good with tools. I failed woodshop in seventh grade. Don't make me relive that experience."

"Don't be ridiculous."

Amber presented her back and ignored him. The line inched forward.

"Oh, c'mon, Amber." But her silent treatment only made his stomach tighten.

He glared at the congested walkway and feared the worst. What would he do if she stayed mad?

Then, in the distance, he spied a large green head bobbing up and down behind a family pushing a black umbrella stroller. The costumed creature appeared to prowl the area, intently scanning people, determined to find someone. Anyone.

Him.

The frog was looking for him.

Shit! His heart raced. He wanted to hide. All because a big and ridiculous-looking lumbering frog was stalking him. Why?

He crouched down behind Amber and her flowing golden locks.

"What are you doing, Larry?" she said sharply.

"Quiet."

"Are you trying to embarrass me?"

"No, no," he said. "It's that frog."

Philly Frog ambled in front of the It's a Small Pond queue and goggled its wide-open plastic eyes into the crowd, clearly searching for him.

Amber turned to look at Larry, but he scrambled behind her to stay hidden. Kids in line giggled. Larry's mind raced. Had he done anything to piss off whoever was in that outfit?

"Quit playing around," Amber ordered. "I mean it."

"I can't."

"What's wrong with you?"

He didn't answer. When the creature trudged on, Larry stood up, relieved. He smiled, which was more than Amber was doing.

"Is this how you're going to act on our television show?" she snapped.

"No, no, of course not," he said, holding his palms up. "I wouldn't."

Amber paused. Panic washed over her face. "What time is it?"

He looked at his watch and cringed. "12:05."

"You were supposed to tell me about my pills," she said, raising her voice. "I'm supposed to take my pills."

"We're only a few minutes late," he said, patting her shoulder to try and calm her down.

She jerked away. "Don't you understand? I take my pills at the same time every day with food. I have to take my Prozac with food."

"Prozac?" His mouth fell open. "How long have you been on that? You told me they were vitamins. You're always taking vitamins."

"It is a vitamin, Larry," she snapped. Amber pointed to her head. "It's a vitamin for my brain."

"It's an antidepressant."

"Oh, don't be so dramatic. I've only been committed twice. That's all."

"Committed? Twice? But that's more than once."

Amber grabbed his arm and jerked him out of line. "It was years ago before we even met. C'mon, let's go."

"But the line."

"Forget the line. I need to take my vitamins now."

Amber power-walked through the noisy crowd and headed toward the Froggyland Castle. Unfortunately, people kept stepping in front of Larry, making him dodge, slowing him down—adding to his anxiety.

Should he be worried about her?

"Amber," he called out, "Wait for me." But she continued to widen the gap.

Once through the castle, she headed toward the drawbridge. Larry sped up and bolted past an Asian family holding a cluster of green Philly Frog balloons.

His legs and feet ached, but he kept moving, always thinking about Amber. Did it make a difference if she took medications? Antidepressants were advertised on TV all the time. And plenty of people went to therapy, too. All that mattered was that he loved her, and she loved him. She'd even said so after that Bruno Mars concert last summer at the Greek Theater. He couldn't give up on her now.

Amber was waiting for him when he caught up to her at the Victorian entrance to Lilly's Pad restaurant in Froggyland, USA.

She looked sad.

His hated to see her upset, but what could he do?

Amber put her arms around his neck and seemed to melt into his body. "Are you mad at me, baby?" she asked.

Larry petted her hair and lied, "I can never be mad at you."

"I'm sorry I didn't tell you." she said. "I just didn't want to be—" she paused. "—judged."

"I won't judge you. Let's make sure you take that pill." He affectionately rubbed his nose with hers. "Hold my hand."

Amber squeezed his palm and snuggled close. Her love encompassed him, and he knew that after this, whatever happened, everything would be okay.

Turning, Larry took a step forward and squarely smacked his forehead hard on the low-rise metal awning hanging over the hobbit-sized door to Lilly's Pad. He dropped to his knees in pain. Before he passed out, he looked at Amber and thought the ringing in his ears sounded like wedding bells.

When he woke up, his head throbbed. Gazing down, Larry realized he was sitting inside Lilly's Pad restaurant at a small, circular, wrought iron table with a white countertop.

Amber sat in the chair next to him, motioning for someone to come to the table. "You okay, baby?" she asked.

"I think so," he said, shaking his head to clear it.

He eyed the room. On the painted walls were colorful trees and bushes, and the expanse of the floor had green-tiled lily pads scattered throughout the room. Nearby, people chatted at wrought iron tables and chairs, competing with the piped-in cricket and frog croaking sounds from the speakers overhead.

At the family-style, greasy-smelling cafeteria lines, people flocked past the self-service displays pushing trays of Froggy Fritters, Big Bullfrogger burgers, and Amphibian fries toward the cash registers.

A hunky-looking, six-foot-two guy, who seemed their age, placed a cup of water in front of Amber. He wore a man-bun and a green Lilly's Pad apron.

"For you, *mademoiselle*," the waiter said in a flowing French accent. He appeared to grin at her, and she smiled back.

Larry didn't like how he was making eyes at his girlfriend.

"Who are you?" he asked brusquely.

"I helped you up after you hit your head on the door, *monsieur*."

"That's all right, Raoul," said Amber. "I'll explain everything."

The flirty waiter backed away, eyeing Amber as he left.

She appeared to blush.

"Amber?" said Larry, snapping his fingers to get her attention. He felt his blood pressure rising.

"Don't you just love his man-bun?" she said, practically swooning. "And that French accent. Oh, my. Why he could even be on *Fix and Dump* if you weren't the co-host."

"Are you listening to me?"

She lifted two small, oval-shaped pills to her lips.

Two chubby kids, a boy, and a girl, wearing green Philly Frog T-shirts, giggled and ran around a table. The girl brushed by Larry, almost bumping him.

"I didn't like the way that guy was looking at you," he said.

"Why? Are you jealous?" Her eyes narrowed. "You know I don't like that."

The boy slammed into Amber's shoulder, and she dropped her pills. She immediately gazed at the floor. Her eyes widened. "Oh, no, my pills. I dropped my pills." She pointed to the boy. "No thanks to that little shit!" she screamed.

Larry raised his palms. "Okay, okay. I'll find them. Just calm down."

"Hurry, Larry. Hurry."

Larry dropped to his knees, hitting the green tile. He leaned forward and placed his hands on the smooth, cool floor. Then, moving ahead, he slowly crawled around, looking for the two white pills.

The kids, out of control, rushed past him.

"It might be over here, Larry," said Amber, pointing to the floor.

"It's a frog!" yelled the young boy.

"Yay! A frog!" screamed the little girl.

Before Larry could react, the two chunky kids jumped on his back, straddled him like a horse, and kicked him in the ribs. The increased weight strained his back, and he buckled.

"Get off me," he shouted. He tried to raise his body, but the kids were too heavy.

"Go, Philly, go!" laughed the boy, bouncing up and down. "Go, Philly, go!"

The little girl giggled.

"Larry," demanded Amber. "Come up here this instant and quit playing around."

"Help me," pleaded Larry. The boy kicked him in the nether regions with his Stride Rite sandals. Sharp pain exploded like a white-hot knife stabbing him, and he collapsed to the hard tile, moaning. He squeezed his eyes tight to hold back the agony. His eyes welled.

The kids were jerked off his back. "Don't make me spank you again," yelled a man. He heard the kids dragged away, screaming and crying.

While his pain subsided, Larry lay still until he opened his eyes and the world appeared fuzzy.

"Are you alright?" he heard Amber ask.

He tried to focus but couldn't see anything except a bright, blurry haze. He was blind as a bat.

Terror gripped him---*his contacts*. He'd lost his granny apple green contacts somewhere on the floor. And not just any floor, but a vast, green-colored lily pond restaurant-themed one.

He needed those lenses. He had no backup.

Spouting profanities, Larry frantically patted the ground around him, running his palms over a stray French fry and loose grit.

"What are you doing?" Amber asked.

"I lost my damned contacts," he said, distraught. "Help me."

"Are you trying to get me mad?"

"Would you just help?" said Larry, raising his voice.

Amber looked down at her tank top. "I found them," she said, grinning.

"My lenses?" said Larry.

"No, my pills."

She placed the two ovals in her mouth and took a sip of water.

Larry scooted across the floor, the green tiles spreading out before him. Unfocused shapes walked around.

Nearby, a blurry boy said. "Look, mommy, somebody lost their eyes."

"Watch out, baby, your ice cream," said a nasally voiced woman.

"My contacts!" yelled Larry, jerking toward the kid.

The boy screamed, and a mound of ice cream splattered on the floor. His wailing drowned out the entire room.

Larry saw a hazy woman jump into his view. "What's wrong with you?" she shrieked at Larry. "He's just a little boy."

The kid convulsed with uncontrollable sobs.

Amber, clearly enraged, charged the mother. "You can't talk to my boyfriend that way," she snapped. "He just wanted to find his contacts, which are now under that fucking ice cream cone. No thanks to your brat."

Larry felt his stomach flutter.

The angry mother slammed her foot on the frozen lump with her flip-flop, grinding it into the smooth green tile until the melting mess smeared the floor. "Fuck you, bitch!" she yelled.

Some of the nearby customers gasped.

Dragging the bawling child away, the mother gazed back at Amber and shrieked, "Bitch!"

Larry frantically rubbed his fingers through the dirty ice cream-covered floor, looking for his contacts. The cold chilled his fingers.

Amber bent down and glared at him. "Are you going to let her talk to me that way?" she said, raising her voice.

"I can't see," said Larry.

Reaching down, Amber picked the contacts out of the sticky soup. Chocolate goo dripped from the lenses. "Here," she said, handing them to Larry.

He pinched the lenses between his fingers and made a face.

"I can't wear these," he said, frowning. "They're ripped and sticky."

"Just rinse them off."

"Damn it, Amber. Don't you understand?" he said, raising his voice. "They'll hurt my eyes."

He struggled to see Amber's face through his blurry vision.

"You know I don't like that, Larry," she snapped.

"Don't be mad, Amber." He reached out to her. "I'm sorry."

She pushed him aside. "Don't touch me. I mean it."

He could see Amber stand up and back away. "Where are you going?" he asked.

"Away—from you."

Larry lunged forward to stop her but slipped on a splotch of ice cream. He crashed onto the hard, cold tile, crushing what remained of his damaged contact lenses. Scrambling to his feet, he scanned the ill-defined room and saw someone he thought was Amber leave through the front door.

"Amber!" he cried out.

Bolting after her, he stumbled into a wrought iron chair, banging his right knee against the metal. Pain radiated down his leg. While hobbling in haste toward the restaurant entrance, he barreled into a family of five, almost knocking them down, before staggering out onto the crowded sidewalk. Fuzzy and colorful shapes wandered the street.

Larry gazed around Frogtown, USA, looking for anything that resembled Amber. Then, in the distance, he spied something that could be a curvy and voluptuous blonde, stopped in the middle of the cobblestone street.

"Amber," he yelled, but the piped-in music and noisy crowd drowned out his voice.

He left the sidewalk and ran toward her, wanting to apologize and tell her he loved her, say anything he could to get the day back on track.

"Amber," he screamed, waving his arm, but she appeared to be talking with someone else.

He squinted to see better, but it didn't help. A tall, indistinct green thing stood next to her. Was it that same stupid frog that had been stalking him all day? Frowning, he quickened his pace.

Larry pushed between a teenage couple holding hands.

"Amber," he called again.

The closer he got, the less fuzzy she seemed. Standing next to her wasn't the frog.

It was a man in a green golf shirt with a man bun on top of his head. Anger surged through him. The French waiter from the Lilly Pad restaurant.

He barreled into the tall green-shirted figure. "Stay away from my girlfriend," he yelled, pushing violently. The man fell to the street like a sack of potatoes and howled.

"What are you doing?" snapped Amber.

"Saving you from that French waiter," he said. "Nobody's going to pick up my girlfriend."

"You jerk!" she yelled. "That's an old man."

"My leg." A senior citizen writhed on the cobblestone street. "I can't get up."

Amber squatted down to help the gray-haired codger. "Are you all right?" she asked.

"But what about the man bun?" asked Larry. "Where's his man bun?"

The old fellow moaned louder.

Amber handed Larry a round, black, flat-crowned hat with a pompom on top. "It's a beret, Larry," she said, clearly disgusted.

His heart sank. He'd mistakenly struck an old man, injuring him, and probably lost Amber to boot. "I'm sorry," he said to the old-timer, feeling lower than dirt. "I couldn't see." He turned to Amber. "You know I didn't mean it."

"I'm gonna sue," cried the elderly man.

Two security guards, one thin and the other fat, wearing light brown pants and hunter green polo shirts, grabbed Larry by his arms and dragged him to the side of the cobblestoned street. Their grips hurt like hell.

"Hey!" said Larry.

The thin guard spoke first in a stern manner. "Move forward and don't resist."

"You're hurting my arms," protested Larry.

"Shut up, kid," said the fat guard. "You're in big trouble."

Amber watched the two guards pull him away.

Panicked, he yelled, "Amber, please don't leave. Just meet me at the castle tonight at 5:30. I've got a big surprise for you tonight, I promise. Please."

The two guards laughed.

"The only people you're gonna meet tonight is at the Buena Park Police department," said the fat guard.

"But I've got to propose to my girlfriend," whimpered Larry.

"You should have thought about that before you decked the old guy with the beret," said the thin guard.

The two men led him to the end of Frogtown, USA, and made a left toward Calaveras County, the western-themed land.

Beads of sweat formed on his lip. Larry had never been so scared in his life. Without Amber, and facing a potential lawsuit and a criminal charge on his record, what hope would there be for his future?

"Where you taking me?" he asked.

"No talking," barked the thin guard.

They crossed under a carved arch of frogs posing in cowboy hats.

Larry stared into the fuzzy landscape of Calaveras County, a themed land based on Angel's Camp, the old California gold prospecting town, and the San Andreas Fault.

He knew the place well, even if he couldn't see it. To his left was the Rush'in River, and across its barrel bridge was Prospectors

Island, where Gabby Gator and Wally Woodchuck helped park-goers pan for gold and hunt for treasure.

The guards turned to the right. Squeals came from the Calaveras County Jumping Frog pit and the Rootin' Tootin' Shootin' gallery.

"Almost there," said the heavyset guard.

When they marched past the rumbling and vibrating Shake-in-a-Quake restaurant, they crossed the Calaveras County Twain Station rails and entered a door in the painted Angel's Camp backdrop. The entrance led to a concrete stairwell. Larry strained to see inside the unclear, dim space.

The guards escorted him down the metal stairwell and stopped mid-descent. Below, in the darkness, someone struck a match, and a flame ignited. Larry heard three puffs. A smoky cedar smell wafted upward.

"Bring him to my office," croaked a man's gravelly voice.

The guards finished guiding Larry down the stairs into a busy utility tunnel underneath the park. On the ceiling, fluorescent lights brightened the dull gray walls where large, blurry green arrows pointed toward the different-themed lands. Rock music blasted through the underground passage.

The eerie setting made his heart pound.

An electric utility vehicle whooshed down the corridor, carrying what Larry suspected were uniformed maintenance workers and costumed characters.

Frightened, Larry felt his legs wobble when they neared a door that read SECURITY. The thin guard opened the doorway and ushered him into a small gray and sparsely decorated waiting room that had what looked like an empty bookcase, two chairs, and a picture of Philly Frog hanging on the wall.

The heavyset guard stood by the door. "Wait here until further directed." He pointed to a Philly Frog painting. "If you leave, we'll know. The frog has eyes."

"You mean like a camera?" asked Larry, concerned.

"Let's go," said the thin guard to the heavy one.

The guards exited, and the door locked. Larry sat down in a chair and heard a low, mechanical whine come from the painting.

What seemed like hours later, afraid to move, Larry sat glued to the chair, his imagination running wild. Why hadn't the security guards come back? Were they preparing paperwork for the Buena Park Police Department? He squirmed in his seat. And what about Amber? Was she still at Froggyland, or had she left with the French waiter from Lilly's Pad?

Were they kissing?

When he couldn't handle the stress anymore, he bolted for the door, determined to escape. He had to find Amber before it was too late. But before he reached the door handle, the security guards burst into the room and grabbed him by the arms.

"Where do you think you're going?" said the thin guard.

"Lemme go!" screamed Larry.

"Let him go," cracked an old man's gravelly voice—the same one from the staircase.

The two guards loosened their grip, and Larry slipped from their grasp.

"What's the matter?" said the codger. "Problem with your girl?"

Larry turned toward the familiar voice. Standing near him was a man in blurry outline, hunched over a cane. He wore what looked like a Hawaiian shirt, red golfing pants, and brown canvas sneakers. Larry squinted and noticed the older man's hair and mustache were winter white. A smelly cigar stuck out of his mouth.

"Frog got your tongue?" demanded the old coot. "Well?" he said impatiently, tapping the cane on the tiled floor.

"Who are you?" asked Larry.

The man reached into his pocket and pulled out a pair of black-framed glasses. He thrust them forward. "Here, wear these," he said. "They're for reading. They might help."

Grabbing the specs, Larry placed them over his eyes, and his world refocused. His sight wasn't perfect, but at least he could see again, especially the open bookcase door that led into a larger room.

He took another look at the elderly man, finally recognizing him. His jaw dropped. "You're Uncle Dell Smiley," he said. "I thought you were dead."

Uncle Dell Smiley hobbled toward the open bookcase. "C'mon, I don't have all day."

Larry mindlessly followed him into the hidden room. Inside was the most luxurious office he'd ever seen. Thick avocado green carpet sprouted across the floor, weathered wood paneling rose up every wall, and an expensive hand-carved executive desk with gold trim drew his eye. Copper pendant lighting globes floated overhead. An Oscar® stood on the corner of the desk, and a plaster figurine of Philly Frog who stood bent over, pants down, mooning anyone who entered the room, took pride-of-place. Larry almost laughed but kept his mouth shut. He was in enough trouble.

Uncle Dell Smiley climbed into his honey-colored leather chair behind the executive desk. It squeaked when he sat.

Since there were no other chairs, Larry stood in front of the desk.

A console behind Uncle Dell had twenty video screens broadcasting from all parts of the park.

"You wanna know why I didn't croak? Bite the big one?" asked Uncle Dell. "Why my head isn't cryogenically frozen, or that I'm not an animatronic robot?

"Sure," said Larry, eyeing the old man.

"Well, it's none of your goddamn business. That's why," he snapped.

"But I heard—"

"Frogwash! It's all frogwash. Are you as stupid as you look?"

Larry frowned. The day was too awful, and now this.

"What're you gonna do, cry?"

"No," Larry said, lifting his eyeglasses to wipe away a tear.

Uncle Dell Smiley leaned forward in his chair. "I could have you locked up, kid, and maybe I will."

Larry felt his heart sink.

"You know why I didn't? I've been watching you all day long. Right on those goddamn TVs. Pathetic. Chasing after your girlfriend like she was some kind of goddess. You must love her, don't you?"

Larry nodded.

"I loved somebody like that once." He placed his hand on the Philly Frog figurine. "Created him in my garage. Made him come to life, drawing after drawing. He could sing and dance and made me laugh. He was the best part of me." He picked up the statue. "Oh, I loved this frog, but so did the audience. They loved him even more."

Larry watched Uncle Dell Smiley pause for a moment, sadness in his eyes.

"I'm a simple man, kid. The more popular the frog got, the more I had to change. People thought I was some kind of genius or somethin' like Walt Disney or Steve Jobs, who were master showmen. All I wanted to be was an artist, not some corporate symbol on display all the time. I don't even like kids. Pretty soon, it was just easier to disappear and fake my own death so I could be in control. Sometimes, kid, not every relationship in life is worth it."

Larry pursed his lips. Jesus, was he trying to give him some advice?

Turning his head, he gazed at a wall clock near the TVs.

It was 5:10 p.m.

His eyes widened. His heart jumped. Had he been underground that long? He jerked his head around, looking for a way out. He had to meet Amber at the castle.

"Why are you fidgeting?" snarled Uncle Dell.

"I've got to meet my girlfriend," he said, desperate to leave. "My whole life depends on it."

The old man leaned back in his chair like he had all the time in the world. He pulled the cigar out of his mouth. "Let me tell you a story."

"Oh, man," Larry moaned. "Really?"

"Shut your fly-snapper, kid, and listen."

He tensed.

"Philly Frog and Gabby Gator were hiking in a large vegetable patch, looking for a midday snack, until they wandered up to a rabbit hole in the middle of a garden. A pink bunny hopped up, saw the gigantic opening, jumped in, and said, 'Wheee!'"

Confused, Larry tilted his head. He didn't understand. "What?"

"A hole, kid. He jumped into a hole. Are you stupid?"

"That's uncalled for."

"Huh?" Uncle Del Smiley relit his cigar. "So, while Philly Frog and Gabby Gator were still standing by the hole, another bunny hopped up, saw the opening, jumped in, and said, 'Wheee!' Uncle Dell took a long, savoring puff. "Finally, a third bunny bounded into view, saw the huge hole, leaped in, and yelled, 'Carrots!' A smoke ring floated out of his mouth. "And that's the story, kid."

"What kind of stupid story is that?" said Larry. "It makes absolutely no sense."

"Just like you and your girlfriend, kid."

The comment annoyed Larry, and he pointed at the parkland icon. The anger that had been building all day long surged up and exploded. "You take that back. You don't know what you're talking about. She's perfect for me."

"Get the hell out of here," growled the old geezer. "Go find your sweetie. Make your mistake. What do I care? If I need a good laugh, I'll watch you on the TV."

So, he knew about *Fix and Dump*, too.

Turning, Larry made for the bookcase door, where the two guards stood. They grabbed him before he could exit.

"Let him go," bellowed Uncle Dell. "He'll learn."

Larry broke free and made a beeline for the utility corridor. Once the security door slammed shut behind him, he never looked back.

He sprinted down the busy passageway to Froggy's Future Faire, the land with the closest exit to the Froggyland Castle.

Reaching an underground stairwell, Larry zipped up the metal steps and exited at the back of Asteroid Burgers. Able to see because of the borrowed glasses, he then raced past a frog-shaped rocket ship that sold soft drinks and Aunt Polliwog's Pies, the rotating

Carousel of Frogress show, and the multicolored, neon-striped, Captain Space Toad's Cosmic Orbiter Bounce-a-Tron ride.

When he exited Froggy's Future Faire, Larry could see the Froggyland Castle on his right. He sprinted past the Philly Frog and Uncle Dell Smiley statue in the middle of Ribbet Park and headed toward the towering fairytale structure.

At the drawbridge, a large crowd clogged the entryway. Larry pushed through crying kids and bawling babies. He tried not to think about being late, but his fear bubbled up anyway.

When he reached the front of the crowd, a human-sized Felix Fly was wearing a police uniform. The fascistic fly raised his right hand to halt.

"Oh, c'mon," screamed Larry.

The creature pointed to an A-framed sign blocking the entrance that read:

THE CASTLE IS CLOSED FOR THE 7:00 PM PARADE.
PLEASE DETOUR TO CALAVERAS COUNTY, PARDNER!

He scowled at the costumed insect. "The parade's not for an hour," he argued, raising his voice. "I've gotta meet my girlfriend."

Felix Fly shrugged, and his plastic wings fluttered.

Larry took a step forward. "Let me through," he warned the irritating insect.

The bossy bug shook his head and pointed his furry finger at Larry.

"Are you threatening me?" demanded Larry.

"I'll call security," said a muffled voice inside the large fly head.

Larry eyed the castle and saw a blonde with a black razorback tank top disappear inside the palace gates. Was that Amber? He didn't know.

His heartbeat raced. "You've got to let me go," he pleaded.

"My girlfriend's up there."

Felix Fly pulled out a small, handheld 2-way radio.

Larry lost patience, "Oh, screw it!" He shoved aside the pushy pest.

The fly stumbled backward. The crowd erupted in applause.

Dashing across the wood plank bridge, he reached the grand arched entry and entered the flower-draped walls and mosaic-tiled walkway. Larry paid scant attention to the colorful decorations. He was too busy scanning the foyer looking for Amber, who wasn't there.

Her absence annoyed him. Why hadn't she shown up? He would have waited for her.

He paced the concrete floor, resentment building with each step.

Where was she? Oh, that would be just like Amber, he thought, getting angrier. He turned and walked back. Always doing what she wants without any thought about me. How many times had she run roughshod over his emotions? How many times? Sometimes, she could be so damned selfish. Beautiful, but selfish.

There, he'd said it. She was inconsiderate and self-absorbed. And he'd say it to her face, too, if she ever showed up. He'd look her right in the eyes and—

"Larry," he heard Amber say above the noisy crowd.

He stopped and spun around. Could it really be her? "Amber!" he cried out. His heart swelled. All anger melted away.

She stood across from him, frowning, her well-toned arms folded across her chest.

"Amber, I knew you'd come," he said, eyeing her face. Wasn't she happy to see him?

She responded coldly, "I almost left. I don't even know why I bothered to stay after the way you acted. Maybe it's because you said you had some kind of surprise or something."

"Yes, a surprise," said Larry, mindlessly patting his pants.

The ring was gone. He touched his back pockets. Did he lose it in the park? Sweat broke out on his forehead.

"Well?" demanded Amber.

He dropped to his right knee without the ring. It was just another fucking screw-up. What else could go wrong? The day just wasn't going the way he'd planned.

Amber took a step closer, appearing surprised at his actions. Her icy demeanor softened.

Larry looked up at her beautiful face and slender body. She seemed to be expecting him to say something, but he was at a loss for words.

He didn't understand it. Wasn't this the moment he'd been waiting for? An awkward silence lingered.

"Larry?" Amber said.

He shifted his knee and cleared his throat. Wasn't this supposed to be the happiest day of his life? She was supposedly the woman of his dreams, and all he felt was his stomach tense.

Was Amber the right one?

He'd never questioned that before, and it scared him. He loved her, but she was always trying to change him. Make him into something he wasn't. And that *Fix and Dump*, the stupid TV show she wanted to sell. Was he really going to do that? Would she make the same sacrifice for him?

"Oh, for god's sake, Larry," she said, hands on her hips. "Hurry it up."

He ignored her and stared through the castle. What did Uncle Dell Smiley say? Sometimes not every relationship in life is worth it? Was Amber worth it? Is that what he'd meant? He tried to think straight but wondered whether there would be anything left of poor old Larry Taylor, flawed as he was, after marrying her. Would he be unhappy?

Larry stared at Amber, his resentment building.

"Are you going to say anything?" she demanded.

He said nothing.

"Look, let's just get this over with," she barked. Amber narrowed her eyes. "Go ahead and propose, or do whatever you were going to do, so we can make up and plan *Fix and Dump*."

Her last statement pissed him off, and he grimaced. "Amber?"

"Yes?"

"I..." He cleared his throat. "I..."

"You want to marry me?" said Amber smugly.

"No!" he snapped. "I wanna break up with you."

Dazed, Larry climbed to his feet. The pit in his belly had disappeared. He'd actually broken up with Amber. For the first time in ages, he felt good.

He looked at his now ex-girlfriend. Her stunned face made him feel awful. She looked as if she was about to cry.

Larry was suddenly stricken with remorse. He hadn't meant to hurt her. He didn't like hurting anyone.

"You wanna break up with me," she said, swallowing back tears. "You wanna break up—with me?"

"Uh...well..." he muttered, starting to regret his decision.

"Nobody breaks up with me. I break up with them."

Larry winced.

She pointed her index finger at him. "I fix them, and I dump them. And that's what I just did with you, asshole. I fixed you, and now I'm dumping you. Fix and Dump! Fuck you, Larry. And by the way, you were nothing but a pity fuck to me."

He pulled back. Her hurtful words had pierced his heart.

Larry touched his chest. The pain was building. How could someone he'd once loved so much be that mean? Did she ever really like him at all?

Amber turned and stormed out of the castle.

"Way to go, bud," shouted a passing jerk.

Larry didn't even bother chasing her. He was too crushed inside to care.

Sitting alone on a bench in Ribbet Park, staring at his shoes, Larry felt miserable.

Two hours had passed since he'd broken up with Amber. While everyone else in Froggyland seemed to be having a great time, enjoying the rides, laughing, eating, and generally getting caught up in the magic, he was still in his head, sifting through the rubble of his shattered life.

Amber had been his first true love, or at least he'd thought she'd been. Now he wondered if he'd ever fall in love again. He remembered those lonely days before he'd met her and was not anxious to revisit that limitless void.

The string lights hanging above flickered on, pushing back the encroaching darkness.

He raised his head. Philly Frog, the human-sized amphibian that had stalked him all morning, barreled toward him.

He sighed. *Oh, crap!* Weren't things bad enough?

Larry analyzed the situation and decided he was in no mood to fight. Defeated and tired from the day, he waited for the confrontation.

The frog ran up to Larry and stopped. It said nothing.

Larry looked up at the frog.

"Hey, I don't know what your problem is, but if you're gonna hit me, or yell at me, or kick me out of the park, just get it over with, okay? I'm depressed enough already."

"Larry?" said a muffled female voice behind the heavy frog head. "It's me, Molly. I haven't seen you since forever."

He stood up. "Molly?"

"Yeah, I'm working today. I saw you before with some girl." She reached into her Froggy pant pocket and pulled out some green passes, raising them for him to see. "I've been trying to find you all day. I thought you might like these LeapFrog passes for the lines." She elbowed Larry. "You know, to impress your date."

"She was my girlfriend," sighed Larry.

"She's gorgeous." Molly looked around. "Where'd she go?"

He wiped his teary eyes. "We broke up," he said, trying to control his cracking voice.

"Are you okay?"

The dam broke, and he made hoarse wet sounds.

Molly pulled the Froggy head off, revealing a pleasant young woman with brown eyes, short brunette hair, and a wholesome-looking face. "I could get fired for this."

"Don't...get...fired..." Larry hiccupped.

She helped him to the park bench, and they sat down. She rubbed his back with her felt frog hand. "It'll be alright," she said. "I know it hurts."

"I'm sorry we lost touch, Molly," he said, wiping his eyes. "I wasn't a very good friend."

"It's okay, Larry." She placed her hand in his. "We can talk about it later."

He sniffled. "Thanks."

"Let's just sit here and relax and enjoy the park until you calm down, okay?"

"Okay."

"Because that's what good friends do. Right?"

Molly smiled at him, and he loosened up.

They sat silently on the bench. Green lights illuminated the castle. The Future Faire rides were all lit up and blinking and flashing like the fourth of July.

He took a deep breath and eyed the castle. An aged sanitation worker with a bushy white mustache and cigar protruding from his mouth, pushing a metal trashcan on wheels, gave him a thumbs up when he passed Ribbet Park. Larry thought there was something familiar about the guy until he realized it was Uncle Dell Smiley, in the flesh. The old fella had done him a solid, after all.

"This is nice," Molly said. "Nothing like Froggyland to cheer a person up."

"Yeah," he said, knowing he was sitting with a good friend. For the first time in a long time, life made sense.

She touched his hand.

He smiled. It was comforting to know that someone liked him for just being good old Larry Taylor.

CHAPTER EIGHT

CUPID-1637, PART THREE

JUNE 2063
PARADISE CITY, HEAVEN

After reviewing the last three cases, Pixel rubbed his temples. Cupid-1637's handling of these matters seemed to be getting worse. His client, on the other hand, seemed blasé.

Pixel thought about each incident.

At Froggyland, Dean had broken up a couple, Larry and Amber, instead of lighting a match for a true love get together; Larry and Molly were still only friends. It was pointless. The break-up only caused Larry Taylor emotional distress and pain. Pixel anticipated the panel hammering his client hard on the alleged violation of failing to do his best for the people he had helped. He wondered if the argument of incompatibility would save Dean on this one.

There were similar problems in the Orange Kings case. Dean had busted up the relationship between Leonard King and Doris Rosenwald. Why? From all known information, they were a happy couple. Yet, to separate them, Dean had to damage their parents' lifelong friendship, cause financial hardship for Leonard King's family, and subject the kid to underlying anti-Semitic taunts. He'd done these acts so Leonard and Doris could get back together. The case was a disaster from any angle you looked at it. *But was it really?* Didn't it provide them with a more solid bond forged by difficulties?

Finally, in the love potion matter, his client had allowed Kirby Briggs to intentionally use an illicit drug in an attempt to manipulate the feelings of a woman. Not only were Kirby's actions most likely illegal under State and Federal law on Earth, but it was a violation of both his intended and third-party victims' free will.

Free will. The concept was as old as Adam and Eve. And truth be told, with all the different religions and gods and goddesses in heaven, no one could agree on what it meant. Roman Catholics thought it encompassed one thing, Orthodox Christianity another. It was the same for Judaism, Hinduism, and Islamism. And then there were cults of all stripes as well as the Church of Jesus Christ of Latter-Day Saints, the New Church, and all the numerous denominations of Christianity. Not to mention all the religions he'd failed to think of, including those already vanished or died out, present and imaginary. One utterance of the topic during the hearing and the panel would be in session for the next hundred years debating it. Somehow, he'd have to skirt the issue of free will.

"Everything okay?" asked Dean.

"We need a break," said Pixel, standing up.

He then led Dean outdoors for some fresh air.

☙

Once outside the big, multi-storied, modern office building, Pixel and Cupid-1637 walked down the concrete steps. Before them lay the Paradise City Plaza, a rectangular park with massive flowing fountains, well-manicured lawns, and flagstone walkways. Surrounding the park were similar administrative buildings.

As angels and angels-in-training traveled through the plaza in a business-like manner, walking, running, strolling, and flying to their appointments, white doves descended from the skies and peacefully glided above the concrete utopia.

Standing at the bottom of the steps, Pixel looked up and a bird dropping splattered near his feet. He shook his head, pulled out a pack of cigarettes, and thought the whole thing was the most perfectly ironic symbol of heaven. It looked nice and pretty on the surface, but underneath all the saintly veneer, the entire place was a bureaucratic mess. At least the air smelled clean.

Pixel placed a cigarette between his lips. He was still bothered by the seemingly hopeless cases the gods had given him to handle. He wasn't sure anything could be done to save Dean.

More negative thoughts. Pixel shook his head to clear it but couldn't. There was something odd about Dean's case. Almost like it had too many violations. Why was that? Just one or two would have made the same point.

Don't go there!

And why such overwhelming evidence? Was someone trying to keep the panel from listening to dissenting arguments?

Stop it!

The panel would give his client a fair hearing; they'd listen. Heaven had always been that way. To think otherwise was both dangerous and absurd.

He gazed at the ground. Why was he thinking these things? Was there something going on that he didn't know about?

"You okay?" asked Dean. "You look distracted."

Pixel looked at his client. "No, I'm fine. Really." he said, even though he wasn't.

"That your vice?" The romance agent pointed to Pixel's cigarette.

"Yeah, I smoked a lot on Earth."

"That how you died?"

"Lung cancer. Two years after my wife left me. Fun times!"

Dean had an empathetic look on his face. "That's too bad, man. You had it tough."

Pixel shrugged. "That's life, right?" He lit the cigarette with a match, took a relaxing puff, and exhaled smoke.

"Yeah, I wanted to be married once," said Dean. "Have a kid, too."

Pixel furrowed his brows. He made a mental note of this revealing remark.

Carrie Lansdale exited the building and slinked down the steps. A goatee-bearded man accompanied her. He wore sandals and a robe and held a lyre in his arms.

The Cupid's assistant elbowed Pixel in the arm. "Hey, look."

Pixel gazed over and saw her. Once again, his heart skipped a beat. He couldn't take his eyes off her. The woman was more beautiful in the daylight than when he'd first seen her in the doorway.

"Carrie," shouted Dean.

Pixel shot his client the stink-eye.

The new social worker stopped and turned toward them. Recognition washed over her face, and she beamed. "Pixel."

He said nothing at first, shuffled his feet, nodded, and raised his right palm to acknowledge her greeting.

"Hi."

"I wish I could talk," she said. "I've got to take my client Apollo—"

"Apollo's assistant," grumbled the goateed man.

"I'm sorry," she said and repeated back to her client, evidently embarrassed, "Apollo's assistant." Then, turning to Pixel, Carrie volunteered, "When I worked in the Pre-Columbian American Division we didn't have assistants. Quetzalcoatl, the Aztec god of life, the light and wisdom and ruler of the West, didn't need any help." She looked at her watch. "I've gotta go." As she started walking away, she called out, "I'll try to drop by your hearing later today. Maybe I can learn a few things. Some people in the office said you were the best at it."

"Best at what?" asked a surprised Pixel.

Carrie and her client melted into the crowd around the plaza.

"Go talk to her," said Dean, pushing him gently. "She wants you to follow her."

Pixel shook his head. "I don't think so."

"Why not? I told you, she likes you."

"I don't know. We've got your case, and our time is tight. And besides, she's out of my league."

Dean rolled his eyes. "What is wrong with you? Where's your self-confidence?"

The Cupid's assistant paced in front of Pixel, growing more agitated by the second. "I can't believe you're going to defend me. Is this how you'd act in front of the panel? If you can't even talk to a dead chick, how are you going to represent me properly? Oh, this is great, man. Just great."

Folding his arms, Pixel checked his anger. "Don't worry about me. I can handle myself at the hearing. The way I act around women doesn't concern you."

Dean said, his face reddening, "Poor parenting. That's what it is. If I were your parent, I would've taught you differently—"

"Taught me what?"

"I said *if* I was your parent—"

Parenting. Pixel's eyes widened. "Quiet!"

"What'd you say?" said Dean, clearly annoyed.

Pixel, deep in thought, put up a hand. "I'm thinking about something you said earlier."

The Cupid's assistant unclenched his fists.

"I have a question for you," said Pixel. "Why did you say you wanted to have kids since we know you'd gotten your girlfriend pregnant? You were already a father, but you ran away."

"Hey, man, I wanted to have that kid, be its dad, but I got killed before it was born."

"Were you scared?" asked Pixel.

"Yeah, wouldn't you be?" Dean's eyes welled up. "I felt pretty guilty about it, too, Pops. I didn't want to be the kind of dad my father was. I wanted to get involved in their lives, tell them things I'd learned, so they wouldn't make the same mistakes I'd made."

"And yet, you left everyone in a lurch." Then, nonchalantly, Pixel flicked his unfinished cigarette into an empty waste can.

"What do you want from me, man? And what does this have to do with my cases, anyway?"

"Why did you break up Larry Taylor's relationship at Froggyland?"

"Because that kid was a dope. He was with the wrong girl and needed to grow a pair." Dean bit his lip. "As a matter of fact, all those kids required my help. Immature, every single one of them." He counted on his fingers. "Kirby Briggs and his stupid love potion; Leonard King living in a world of baseball cards, Shakespeare, and hot dog recipes."

"C'mon," said Pixel. "Everyone is immature growing up."

"Not these guys. Bad parenting, that's what it was. None of those kids had anybody to set them straight. And I was the only one who could do it. I helped break up Larry Taylor's romance, so he'd learn not to be a doormat. I forced Leonard King to deal with pain, hardship, and anti-Semitic remarks so he'd become mentally stronger. And I humiliated Kirby Briggs with that love potion, so he'd friggin' grow up. I mean, geez, the guy was twenty-seven years old."

"Do you think you exceeded your authority on any of those assignments?"

"How would I know? Nobody trained me. The Cupid's Oath says I have to do my best for the gods and the people I am helping, and implied I could get involved in their lives. And that's what I did. They all ended up with the possibility of love. So, I did my job."

Pixel cocked his head, stared at Dean. "*Hmmm*," he said. "Maybe there's something else involved here."

"Like what?"

"Well, it's just a thought, but what if you tried to help those particular kids because you wanted to become the father you never were."

Dean stood dumbfounded as if realizing something about himself for the first time. He chuckled and pointed at Pixel. "Hey, man, you're good. I thought I was a psycho or a badass or something," he chirped. "Who knew I was just mentally screwed up?"

Pixel grinned, a rare public display of emotions. He was pretty proud of himself. "That may be true, Dean," Pixel said. "I think we have something to build on for your defense."

On top of a nearby building, a carillon played the melody to "All You Need is Love," a song made famous by the Beatles. The group, now surprisingly, performed as the house band at

Olidammaras, a swanky underground nightclub located in the deity neighborhood of the Dungeons and Dragons sector. Pixel really liked the place.

When the bell chimed to announce the time, Pixel looked at his watch: 1:00 p.m.

Only three hours left before the hearing, and they still had more cases to review.

Unfortunately for Pixel, as positive as he felt about the new arguments defending Dean, the questions he'd had about the volume of violations and the upcoming hearing continued to linger.

CHAPTER NINE

CASE NUMBER SIX: THE THEATER

ALLEGED VIOLATION: Intentional or negligent wrongdoing
ALLEGED VIOLATION: Failure to do my best for the people
I am helping

SEPTEMBER 2006
LOS ANGELES, CALIFORNIA

His face lined with age, Leonard Brown, thin and frail-looking, stood in front of a white, two-story building with faded red trim. The old theater was a study in neglect: the black-and-white SILENT MOVIES sign bleached out, the façade cracked and ugly, and the stucco pocked where it had fallen away, revealing rusted chicken wire. It saddened him to see graffiti and obscenities spray-painted on the box office and large mural, obliterating the faces of Chaplin, Theda Bara, and Charlie Chase.

A police car sped by. Sirens wailed in the distance. Homeless men loitered near the corner. The neighborhood had really deteriorated since he'd left.

"Bye Bye Love" by the Everly Brothers crooned from his coat pocket. He pulled out the cell phone and recognized the number—his fiancé, Vicky.

"Hello, honey," he said, and then he listened to her talk about all the new furniture she wanted to buy. He loved her, but sometimes when she harped on about a topic, his energy seemed to ebb away. "I know, I know," he piped in, "but I'm here right now. I promise I won't be that long."

She continued to bend his ear.

"Yes, I know, but I can't do that. I need to complete the walk-through before I can sign the closing papers. Just give me a few hours, okay?" Leonard eyed the battery icon on his phone. "I'm almost out of power, hon. I'll meet you at the realtors at four." He paused. "I love you, too. Bye."

He stuffed the phone into his tan windbreaker and hoped she didn't call again. He needed time to say goodbye to the place.

Across the street, one of the homeless men moved closer and scowled.

Unnerved, Leonard unlocked the galvanized steel accordion gate. Coffee cups, fast food wrappers, broken glass, and yellowed newspapers choked the expanders, making sliding the collapsible barrier difficult. As he pulled on the metal, he knew it would be the last time he'd ever enter the old place.

It felt bittersweet. He and Claire had inherited the building in 1965. Now he was selling it to buy a Winnebago and marry Vicky in Las Vegas. That wasn't how he'd envisioned his old age. Leonard thought he would be with Claire forever.

Pulling out another key, he opened the battered and vomit-stained front door, releasing a stale, musty odor.

Once inside, he relocked the entrance and flicked on the lights. Dust flittered in the soft glow of an ill-lit crystal chandelier. Some wood paneling had separated from the walls. The lobby was more worn than he'd remembered.

Leonard eyed the red threadbare art deco carpet. A soiled blue blanket and a child's wooden toy horse, two items that shouldn't have been there, crowded a corner. He tensed.

Was somebody living in the building?

"Hello?" he called out, his voice sounding unnaturally loud in the stillness.

No one answered.

He scanned the room. On his left were the faded oak doors that led to the movie theater. Dusty framed pictures of silent movie stars and movie posters for *Wings* and *The Gold Rush* hung on the wood-paneled walls, all the way to the stairwell that led to the second-floor apartment.

On his right stood the empty glass-cased candy counter and an old Cretors and Company Ambassador popcorn machine, now opaque with dirt and grime.

He grinned. Claire had always fluttered around the place like a butterfly, dispensing snacks and soda. Sometimes, when he wasn't busy, he'd sneak down from the projection booth and watch her captivate the customers with her smile.

How he loved that smile.

Cautiously, he walked to the stairs and prayed no squatters lived in the building.

As he unclipped the velvet rope on the stairway, he wondered whether he should have come back at all. It had been painful to live here without Claire. They'd spent their lives together in this theater, caring for an art form most people had forgotten. They hadn't made much money, but the movies had made them laugh and cry and even saved their marriage during its darkest hour.

He shut his eyes. Too many memories. That's why he'd closed the theater down—that's why he'd agreed to sell it—and now he had returned the one place that was sure to make him relive his sadness.

He reached the top of the stairs and turned toward the apartment. Inside were three connected rooms: the kitchen, the master bedroom, and overlooking the alley—the room that would have been their Katie's.

He didn't want to think about that either.

Leonard pushed open the apartment door and stared into the kitchen, empty except for storage cabinets and pale green walls.

Then he gazed at the floor. Something odd caught his eye.

A tin film canister lay in the middle of the room, a round container that hadn't been there when he'd left three years ago. He scanned it carefully. Its surface had no dust, and someone had written the words OPEN ME across the top in black marker.

Snatching up the metal receptacle, he pried open the lid. His eyes widened. Inside he found a washed-out Polaroid photo taken at the hospital: Claire snuggling Katie in her arms the day she was born. The picture had disappeared long ago.

Heat flushed through him. "Is this some kind of a sick joke?" he yelled out.

A familiar sound echoed up.

Pop-pop...pop-pop-pop....

Leonard tensed again. "Who's there?" he cried out. "This is a private building."

Pop-pop...pop-pa-pop-pop....

He rushed to the stairwell and spied the candy counter. A yellow glow emanated from the popcorn machine. The smell of toasted corn wafted through the air.

His heart rattled faster. He was an old man and didn't want to die or get mugged. Not by some intruder in a run-down building.

He pulled out his cell phone to call the police.

Dead. No juice. Why hadn't he charged it the night before? Stupid, stupid, stupid.

Pop, pop…pop, pop, pop….

He struggled to think. He needed to get outside. Call the police from a neighboring business or the liquor store across the street. That's what he'd do.

Leonard fled down the stairs. When he reached the candy counter, the popcorn machine abruptly shut off and fell silent. He stopped and looked. The popcorn maker had nothing inside.

His hair lifted on the nape of his neck.

A child giggled, and he turned.

The oak doors leading to the movie theater slowly opened. Ragtime music flowed into the lobby.

"I don't know who you are," he cried out, voice shaky. "But you're trespassing."

The music segued into "This Magic Moment" by the Drifters. It stunned him, and he froze. The song had been his and Claire's favorite since before they were married. Tears welled while he listened and imagined them dancing, her moving in his arms.

"Claire?" he called out, knowing it was irrational. Rushing to the theater doors, he entered the auditorium.

He made his way past the aisles on the sloped floor of the rectangular movie house. There were gaps in the rows of frayed velvet theater seats. Whatever hadn't been removed appeared broken, too stained, or damaged to use. Paint peeled from the beige and gold-trimmed walls, and the portraits he'd painted on the ceiling of famous silent movie star faces had faded away. At the bottom of the slope sat an elevated stage with tattered curtains, pulled back, and a wrinkled movie screen. And below, by a side wall, was an Aeolian player piano. Leonard stopped walking when it switched back to ragtime music.

White light beamed out of the projection booth onto the screen.

I don't think this is very funny, he wanted to yell but watched agape instead. The only noise heard was the whirring of a movie projector and a bouncy syncopated score that filled the room.

A scratchy image flickered onto the screen. The opening title card read: HAPPY TRAILS PRODUCTIONS.

Leonard stared at the movie. He'd never heard of that studio before, and he knew them all.

The title card dissolves to a 1920's Craftsman-style home, just like the one he and Claire had always wanted to buy. Superimposed over the house is a title: A GAL FOR ME. In the movie, Oliver Hardy, dressed like a mail carrier, skips into the frame munching a half-eaten banana. Before he opens the curbside mailbox, Hardy throws the peel onto the sidewalk. Buster Keaton, strolling by, tips his porkpie hat, steps on the skin, and double flips backward until he lands on his rear. Frantic, Hardy tosses the mail into the air and runs to Buster.

Leonard watched, fascinated—Keaton and Hardy had never worked together. The movie continued:

A dazzling young woman in her early twenties with light bobbed hair and a radiant smile exits the house onto the porch. She wears a white apron over her knee-length flapper day dress. She waves and calls out to Hardy and Keaton in the title card:

"ARE YOU BOYS ALRIGHT?"

"Claire," said Leonard, staring in disbelief. "Is that you?" He staggered down the aisle to get a better look. "Claire," he whispered.

The woman on the screen looked out toward him and grinned.

"HELLO, DARLING," the title card read.

Blood drained from Leonard's face. Light-headed, he lurched forward, knees buckling, until, smothered in darkness, he crashed to the floor.

As he regained consciousness, Leonard heard voices.

A man's baritone voice said, "A guy like me can take a fall like that, but not someone like him. I've been doin' it my whole life."

Leonard glanced up and saw a skinny man wearing a porkpie hat leaning over him. He looked a lot like Buster Keaton.

"Aw, anybody can fall on his ass," said a voice from the crowd.

"You don't know beans about falling," said Keaton. "It takes practice. A lot of practice."

"I'll take care of this," said a female's sweet familiar voice. "Leonard, darling, it's Claire."

His heart soared. Had that really been Claire on the screen—and now crouching beside him? He'd longed to touch her, kiss her again.

He blinked a few times to refocus. Clustered around him were Charlie Chaplin, Buster Keaton, Oliver Hardy, Colleen Moore, Stan Laurel, Clara Bow, John Gilbert, and a roomful of lesser-known silent film actors—and Claire. She looked as youthful now as when they'd first met—like a young June Allyson—and smelled of honeysuckle perfume. Her favorite.

"Claire," he said, reaching out.

She helped him rise to his feet.

Standing near her, he wrapped her close and they kissed, his lips touching her soft, fresh skin. Oh, how he'd missed her.

And then he stopped, pulled back. A feeling of dread came over him.

"What is it, darling?" she asked.

"Am I—am I—dead?"

"No, baby, you're not." Claire squeezed his hand. "We're—I guess you might say we're memories."

"That's right," piped in Keaton. "Memories."

Charlie Chaplin, the little tramp, moved front and center. He twirled his cane, stopped, and adjusted his fingerless gloves. "Let me explain," he said with a British accent. "We exist somewhere beyond the screen. A world and a place where we're still young and free and remembered—"

"This is a dream," said Leonard. "I hit my head when I fell—" He touched his forehead—it was sore—and pulled back bloody fingertips. "You see," he said, showing them.

"I assure you, sir," said Chaplin, clearly indignant. "I am *not* a dream. I am a star!"

"Leonard, dear," said Claire. "These stars—they exist because people like us remembered them. Cared for their movies. We kept them alive in our hearts."

"I don't understand," he moaned. A tear rolled down his cheek. "I saw you die, Claire. Right upstairs in our bedroom—from cancer. And now you're young and beautiful and living in their world, and you're not even a movie star like them. I—I don't even know what you are."

Claire touched his face with a gentle reassurance he remembered. "When I died," she began, "a bright light pulled me upward. I followed it and landed in the little house, surrounded by these lovely people." She glanced around at their faces. "They wanted to help me. Images from the movies we'd loved and had spent our lives preserving. They wanted to keep my memory alive in their world."

"This doesn't make any sense," said Leonard, shaking his head.

"Of course, it does. Don't you see, darling," she said. "We can—"

"Forget it, Claire," butted in the great John Barrymore, dressed like he'd just performed in *Don Juan*. "He's not worthy."

"Yeah, why should he be given special consideration?" chirped in baby-faced comedian Harry Langdon. "He doesn't even care about us. Just look at this place—it's a goddamn mess!"

The silent stars grumbled. Their dissatisfaction spread across the room.

Leonard's stomach tightened.

"Please, please," implored Claire, raising her hands. "He cares about you. He cares about all of you. Don't you remember?"

"Let *me* explain," said Chaplin.

"Oh, Jesus and Mary!" moaned screen idol John Gilbert, wearing his doughboy outfit from *The Big Parade*. "Charlie, you are insufferable!"

"If it weren't for Leonard," continued Chaplin, "new audiences wouldn't even know who we are. Remember that little girl with the Barbie doll who would come to the theater every Saturday? Leonard would spend all afternoon talking about our movies with her, and now she's writing a thesis on why silent films matter. And what about that bratty kid with the Fonzie T-shirt? He's now showing us to his children on YouTube. We don't know how many people he's influenced. Maybe that's why our films get sold on Blu-ray or streamed through the Internet!"

"Those aren't legitimate forms of exhibition," said John Gilbert, rolling his eyes.

"You would say that Squeaky." snapped Chaplin. "Your voice almost killed talkies."

Gilbert sneered and clenched his fists, seemingly ready to punch Chaplin in the face.

Claire intervened. "Boys, boys," she said. "Control yourselves. We're here to talk about Leonard."

"Pardon us," said Oliver Hardy, shyly twiddling his tie. "But my associate and I think Leonard has left a legacy of love and appreciation. Don't we, Stanley?"

"We most certainly do," said Stan Laurel, nodding his head to Hardy.

The other stars murmured in agreement.

"Then it's settled," exclaimed Chaplin. "Leonard is deemed worthy."

"Fine, he's worthy!" snapped John Barrymore. "Why not just let everybody in?"

"What are you talking about?" said Leonard, throwing his hands up.

"To join them. Us," Claire said. "Don't you want that? We can live together in the little house forever."

Leonard looked away. He'd never loved anyone as much as he'd loved Claire, but now he was afraid of what she was asking. His heart hammered frantically, and he broke into a cold sweat. What would he do about Vicky?

"What's wrong, dear?" she asked.

"When you died," he said, lips trembling. "Life was too painful. I couldn't stand to live here without you. I prayed to God that, somehow, he'd made a mistake, and you'd walk back into my life like nothing had ever changed. But that never happened."

"I'm here now," she said.

"I know, but since that time, I've met another woman, someone who cares for me and has tried to heal my heart. She's helped me, Claire, and I love her."

One look at Claire told him everything. He could see the sadness in her eyes.

"As much as you love me?" she asked.

Leonard paused, knowing the truth, something he'd tried to deny and could never tell Vicky. "No," he said. "Not as much as you."

"Oh, Leonard." She hugged him. "We're going to be so happy."

"I can't go with you, Claire," he told her. "I want to, but I made a promise. To Vicky."

"You don't know beans about romance," groused Buster Keaton.

"I tink it's romantic in a sad sawht of way," said Clara Bow.

Her Brooklyn accent made Bessie Love and Harold Lloyd cringe.

"Why are we even bothering?" quipped Barrymore. "I told you he wasn't worthy."

"No, he's doing the right thing," said Claire, teary-eyed. "The honorable thing."

Leonard felt helpless. "Claire, please don't cry," he said, knowing he'd lost her a second time. The pain in his heart threatened to overwhelm him.

The movie stars began to fade away.

Claire turned translucent. "You're a good man," she said. "I'll always love you." She blew Leonard a kiss.

"Stay here, Claire. Please!" Leonard bolted forward to stop her until a little girl clasped his legs.

"Daddy, daddy, come with us," she sobbed. "Don't leave me again."

He gazed down at the child with blond curls, who was disappearing before his eyes. Could it be Katie? The daughter they'd lost at birth? She looked just like Claire.

Emotion bubbled up, and he bent down to hug her. "Oh, my Katie, Katie, Katie," he said. "Is it really you?"

She squeezed his legs tighter.

The silent movie stars reappeared and surrounded them. Claire stepped forward, tears in her eyes.

Hugging Claire and Katie, Leonard basked in their warmth. He knew what he had to do next.

When Vicky saw Leonard lying on the theater floor, she rushed past Kip Davies, the gray-haired realtor, and cradled her dead fiancé close to her overweight body. She couldn't bear the thought of being alone again without anyone to support her. "This can't be happening," she cried. "No—"

Davies placed his knotty hand on her shoulder. "I need to call the police. Can you—can you stay with him while I make the call?"

"Alright," she said, tears streaking down her face.

She watched Davies trudge up the aisle, his shoes clip-clopping on the hard concrete floor until he exited out the theater door. Vicky turned back toward Leonard.

Dead. Lifeless. Leonard.

She scowled. A new feeling welled up inside. "How could you?" she screamed, violently shaking his body. "You promised me a wedding and a Winnebago and a life where I would be taken care of. Now, get up! Get up! Talk to me." She slapped his face, then pushed him away. His head hit the floor with a dull thud.

White light beamed out of the projection booth. The brightness distracted her, and she squinted. "Who's there?" she yelled. Ragtime music played on the empty piano.

A silent movie projected onto the screen.

In it, a strong, strapping man in his early twenties, his golden-haired wife, and their little, curly-haired daughter stand in front of a beautiful 1920's Craftsman-style home, waving. The woman gives him a smile and a loving kiss.

Vicky stared at the film and pursed her lips, confused, wondering why the actor in the movie looked so familiar.

"Leonard?"

CHAPTER TEN

CASE NUMBER SEVEN: THE DATING BUREAU

ALLEGED VIOLATION: Failure to respect authority
ALLEGED VIOLATION: Failure to make the world a better
place and help people at all times

MAY 2062
NEW HOLLYWOOD, CALIFORNIA

Gilby Ford felt annoyed. After arguing with the Intergalactic Bank of New Hollywood about the missing credits in his savings account, he rode the Underground to his boring job as Senior Fieldmelder for the Chronoscope Filmwerks Company. It wasn't that he didn't like his vocation; he just didn't understand what he did or how it worked. Yet, somehow, he'd been promoted twice. Go figure. There was always good employment for experienced fieldmelders.

When his workday ended, he said goodbye to his boss and rushed back to the Underground.

It was imperative he got home as soon as possible to check his holophone. He was getting married over the weekend and expected to receive the final certified paperwork for his pre-birth arranged marriage to Phaedra Singh, coordinated twenty-eight years ago by his parents and the government. He'd never met Phaedra before, but he'd seen her holopix many times, and they'd matched DNA perfectly.

Gilby smiled, feeling like a lovesick schoolboy. It was a genetic union made in heaven—the perfect marriage for both of them. Something like this could only happen in a truly free and democratic society.

He couldn't wait to get married. According to Federal law, it was his time to procreate.

Boarding a slick-lined maglev train, Gilby pushed and shoved his way through chattering robots and people to an empty seat by a large liquid-molecule, touch-enabled window. Above him, running continuously on an electronic display were rolling video ads for new homes and lives on Dagron-5, a trendy off-world colony and housing development. A place he had no desire to ever visit. He was pretty happy with life on Earth, thank you, and the free and democratic society he lived in. They provided everything he needed. He wasn't going to move for anyone.

As soon as he sat down, the train car filtered air around him that smelled like body odor and a hyper blend of vaped smoke and pot.

He scrunched his face, tears filling his eyes. He hated the foul-smelling aroma the Transit Authority circulated in every train, but the government had determined people felt more comfortable around fragrances that reminded them of a simpler, less modern time.

The doors closed, and the train lights dimmed.

The maglev train lifted and jerked forward, speeding on a journey through the subway tube. Standing passengers held onto pole straps and swayed with the ride.

A middle-aged man with gray-peppered hair and a wrinkled Stay-Fresh™ black suit dashed through the packed car and sat next to Gilby, invading his space. He inched away while the man studied him through dark aviator-style sunglasses.

"How'd you like to make some extra credits?" asked the man.

The question took Gilby aback. "Are you talking to me?"

"What other fieldmelder am I talking to?"

"How'd you know I was a fieldmelder?"

The man took off his glasses. "Oh, please. Most fieldmelders are five-foot-eight to five-foot-ten. Have brown hair and blue eyes and are a bit average—looking——kind of scruffy. You fit the mark, kid. Lucky guess."

"Whatever you're selling," Gilby said indignantly, "I'm not interested."

"I'm not selling anything." The man pulled out a business card and handed it to him. "Frank Popper, Attorney-at-Law."

Gilby studied the card. It blinked on-and-off like a neon sign.

"Hey, most fieldmelders can use some extra credits. It's the nature of the profession. The job is dependent on guys like you. It just doesn't pay squat."

"That's true," said Gilby.

"You're getting married soon, right? Pre-arranged marriage?"

His eyes narrowed. "How'd you know?"

"Lucky guess. Statistics."

Gilby crossed his arms. "Leave me alone."

"C'mon, kid. All you have to do is fall on the floor and pretend you were run over by that big robot over there." Popper pointed to a two-ton boxer model with a punch-drunk head. "Don't let his looks fool you. He works for me. We can probably settle with the Transit Authority for fifty-thousand credits."

"I think you'd better go," said Gilby. "I have no intention of defrauding anyone. And besides, the government would know right away."

The maglev slowed to crawling speed and glided toward the station. A tiled loading area came into view outside as robots and people shuffled near the train door.

Popper stood up and took a step toward the crowded exit. "Don't fool yourself, kid. The government makes mistakes all the time."

"No, they don't," said Gilby.

The train stopped.

"Why don't you keep my card. You never know when you might need it."

Moving to his right, Popper dashed through the open doors and disappeared into the teeming crowd.

"Fat chance," Gilby shouted over his shoulder.

When Gilby entered his high-rise apartment, a red light blinked on his holophone in the corner.

The confirmation about his marriage, he hoped.

Crossing through the sterile winter-white living room filled with hovering chairs, a couch, and a coffee table, Gilby pressed the flashing button.

A light beamed out onto a small quarter-stage area. An official government notice, with an appropriate government seal, floated in the air. A low stern voice said:

"Attention. Attention, Gilby Ford. Important notice from the Department of the Dating Bureau. You are hereby ordered for induction into the Dating Bureau of the United States of America. Report to the Dating Bureau office located in New Hollywood, California, on Monday, May 15th, 2062."

Gilby gaped. That was this coming Monday, after his marriage to Phaedra Singh. His heart raced. Somebody had made a huge mistake.

"Your prior pre-birth arranged marriage has now been formally terminated," beamed the holophone. "All involved subjects are now released from their respective genetic obligations. For further information, this message will be turned over to General Skinner."

A General with three stars on his helmet appeared and sat behind an organized mahogany desk. His grey mustache and weathered face indicated he'd seen a planetary war or two.

"At ease, Ford," said the General. "You're being inducted into the Dating Bureau. Do you have any questions?"

"This is all a big mistake," he blabbered, "I'm supposed to be married this weekend, and—"

"The government doesn't make mistakes, Ford. You're being inducted."

"But can't you do something? I don't even know why they canceled my marriage."

The general looked at him with disgust. "Let me check the files." He rifled through a folder, then looked back at Gilby. "Says here there are some irregularities in your record."

"What does that mean?"

"I can't tell you, Ford. It's top secret. And besides, you're a fieldmelder. Everybody knows fieldmelders can't be trusted."

"What are you talking about?"

"You may appeal the decision. However, if you appeal, you can only do so on the date of your induction."

"Wait a minute. Wait a minute. What does the Dating Bureau do?"

"My God, man. Don't you read your weekly government bulletins?" snapped General Skinner, furrowing his brow. "The Dating Bureau is a government-sanctioned dating service for those with no pre-birth arranged marriages. Failure to find a mate within one-year subjects you to a large fine or death."

Gilby felt lightheaded. "Death?"

"Yes, Ford. It's your patriotic duty to get married no matter how undesirable you are. Just another benefit of being a citizen in a free and democratic society."

The General blipped out. The holophone shut off.

Gilby covered his face with his hands. What would he do now? He didn't even know how to get in touch with Phaedra Singh. They were to have met for the first time at the altar. This was a complete disaster.

After careful consideration, Gilby determined he had no other choice but to show up at the Dating Bureau on Monday and appeal.

After the weekend, Gilby arrived at the Department of the Dating Bureau, located in a federal building off Garbo Boulevard in New Hollywood. Like almost all government offices, the building was situated in an old, outdated vertical mall that once housed Kidney's R' Us, Rapid Robot Repairz, and Clone City.

Upon entering the pedestrian concourse, he immediately landed in a jam-packed walkway. It teemed with homeless tents;

public preachers proselytizing on long, narrow upholstered benches; robots hawking food and services in front of empty gift shops and stores; and human lawyers selling legal advice near the busy courthouse gateway.

Gilby zigzagged through the bustling crowd, stepping over litter on the floor. He paid no attention to the cacophony of sounds overpowering the piped-in Muzak that filled the big building.

When he reached the doors to the Dating Bureau, a robot panhandler with one wheel begged for credits. Gilby ignored him and entered the department.

Inside, the Bureau was quiet. People, primarily males, stood patiently in twelve long lines that moved forward like molasses streams in late January.

Gilby took his place in a queue. He stared at the faded Artificial Annie's Candies and Mock-Donald's Hamburger signs hanging on the wall above the unused and dilapidated kitchen equipment that prior tenants had left behind.

A bulky man with wisps of hair turned to Gilby.

"First time at the Bureau?" asked the man.

"Yes," said Gilby. "And you?"

"Second time. Hope the last time is the charm."

"What do you mean?"

"You only get two dates. If no marriage by then, it's poof…."

Gilby turned pale. "You mean death," he said, thinking of the abrupt finality.

"Yeah, I know, but what can you do? It's the law."

"But General Skinner said I had up to one year."

"You mean the guy on the holophone?"

"Yes," said Gilby. "The general who talked with me."

The man laughed. "You can't believe him. He's not even a real general. I thought everybody knew that from the weekly government bulletins. He's just a paid actor they hired for authenticity. The actual Dating Bureau law was written on the Induction Notice in small print."

"How small?"

"Microscopic."

Worried, Gilby rubbed his face, wondering what else he didn't know that was important.

By the time Gilby could speak with a caseworker, it was afternoon. Tired and bored, he waited in front of the line for sour-faced Yeffeth Cross to motion him over.

Cross, wearing a light brown sweater with a white shirt collar peaking above the crewneck, stamped some paperwork, took a bite from a smelly salami sandwich, and frowned. "Next," he called out.

Gilby approached the counter.

"Name and date of birth?" asked Cross.

"Gilby Ford, March 27, 2036."

Cross typed on an invisible keyboard. A computer screen popped up and floated in front of him. "New inductee?"

"That's what I wanted to talk to you about," said Gilby, "You see—"

"You're not new," said Cross. "Says you're here for a second date. First date with a Phaedra Singh."

"Wait a minute. You've got it all wrong," he protested. "She wasn't a date. She was my pre-birth arranged fiancé."

Cross glared at him. "I don't care. The government is never wrong."

"Hey," said Gilby, his blood pressure rising. "I should never have been inducted into the Dating Bureau in the first place, and now you're telling me I went on a date that never even occurred. What about my rights? I want an appeal."

"Listen," said Cross, annoyed, "it's been a long day. And I don't get paid enough credits in my grade to be yelled at by the likes of you. If you have a problem, take it up with General Skinner."

"He's not even a real general," said Gilby, raising his voice. "He's just an actor."

"Well, that's not my fault."

"This is outrageous." Gilby craned his neck, searching for someone. "Where's your supervisor?"

A P-40 ElectroSim BSwift Administrative Robot rolled up behind Yeffeth Cross and idled. The machine did not look human. It had a thick round torso with multicolored buttons that rapidly blinked when it calculated information. There was no neck, only an oval cylinder head made of metal with mechanical lips and eyes bolted to its face. Any effort to make the P-40 look friendly resided in the details: the thick black eyeglasses it wore and the white visor hat on its head that read SUPERVISOR.

"What seems to be…the trouble, Cross," said the P-40 in stilted English.

Cross rolled his eyes. "This guy says there's a mistake."

"Let…me see."

The P-40 reached over with its mechanical claws and speedily typed on the invisible keyboard.

The robot's lights blinked and buzzed while it worked. Gilby stared in awe.

The mechanical supervisor turned toward him. "There is no mistake…Mr.… Gilby…F. Ford."

"That's not my name." Gilby frowned. "It's Gilby D. Ford—D for David. It's Gilby David Ford."

"Let…me check." Then, turning back to the computer, the P-40 sped up. Its blinking lights and quivering body calculated so fast that Gilby thought it would overheat and explode.

Appearing indifferent, Yeffeth Cross casually ate his sandwich.

The mechanical machine abruptly stopped. It stared at Gilby. "Something…is…not right," said the robot. "There are eight…Gilby…Ford's…in the database."

Gilby brightened. "So, the information is incorrect?"

"Wrong…Mr.…Gilby…David Ford. The government never…makes mistakes." The P-40 swiveled toward Cross. "Assign him his second date…while I…manually investigate."

"You're the boss," said Cross.

"You can't do this," pleaded Gilby. "How long will your investigation take?"

"Up to…six months."

"But I could be dead by then."

"I…will…keep…in touch."

The P-40 rolled away, leaving Gilby and Yeffeth Cross alone.

Cross glanced at the robot and grimaced. "Dumb bucket of bolts," he complained. "Think they can replace humans in supervisory roles just cause they're less emotional."

"Listen, I don't care about your stupid problems. My life is in danger and—"

Reaching under the counter, Cross pulled up a holopix.

"Who do you pick? You have three choices."

"There's only one holopix."

"That's because the government picks your date for you."

"Then why did you ask?"

"I don't question," said Cross. "That's the benefit of living in a free and democratic society."

Gilby pursed his lips and stewed, wondering how he'd ended up in this nightmare.

Cross turned on the holopix, and a photogenic blond with olive skin, green eyes, and a slender body appeared. "Her name's Lavina Zimberg. Your date's tomorrow night at a government-sponsored restaurant. Her holonumber and restaurant address have already been sent to your holophone."

"Thanks," said Gilby, growling his displeasure.

"And don't forget."

"Forget what?" he snapped.

"You need permits to buy government-approved candy and flowers."

"Oh, good lord."

"Should take the rest of the day." Cross took another bite of his stinky sandwich. "Have a nice date."

It took five hours, but Gilby successfully obtained the permits to buy government-approved candy and flowers before his scheduled date with Lavina Zimberg on Tuesday night. When the licenses were issued, the S-20 robot clerk warned him that the state-approved warehouse closed at four o'clock daily. So, now he had that problem to worry about before the date. He only hoped there would be no fieldmelding emergencies brewing at work to make him late.

Stepping into the mall concourse, Gilby passed by the courthouse and attorney Frank Popper chatted with an old, bearded man and his broken-down droid.

Gilby lowered his head, not wanting to be recognized. Popper immediately acknowledged him.

"Did you think about my proposition yet?" shouted out Popper.

"No."

"We could make a lot of credits." Popper eyed him. "Where'd you come from? Dating Bureau?"

"That's none of your business," he replied brusquely.

"It's written all over your face, kid. Just a guess, but I'd say you're on your second date."

The bearded man and his droid snickered.

"It's all a mistake," said Gilby, stopping. He rubbed the back of his neck. "They'll clear it up."

"Yeah, sure they will," said Popper, rolling his eyes. "You still got my card?"

"Not that I'll ever need it."

"If you do, just press the flashing neon holonumber, and I'll be there within seconds. Of course, it'll cost you extra by then."

"Whatever," said Gilby, wishing the conversation would end.

Popper tilted his head, studying him some more. "You ever been to Dagron-5 before, kid?"

"You mean that horrible, off-world colony they advertise on the train? Why would I wanna go there?"

"No reason," said Popper, smiling as if he knew something Gilby didn't. "Just asking."

On the train ride home, Gilby stared at the brand new Dagron-5 relocation ads and fumed. They were pretty and poetic in their puffery. Dagron-5 had three moons; state of the art limestone homes with PortaPak Breatheasy Detoxifiers; bubbling sludge-filled lakes surrounded by crimson wetlands; and the Devil's Hole subterranean golf course with its flower-ringed, lavender-smelling acid pit. The commercial described it as a planetary paradise.

The more Gilby thought about it, the angrier he got. How dare Frank Popper ask him if he'd ever been to that planet.

He'd heard the rumors. It was a horrible place: unlivable, unruly, and full of sin; lawless; subject to chaotic and constant civil unrest; an uncontrolled free market; and self-governed societies. And those were just the homeowners' associations. Heaven only knew what the actual government was like.

He folded his arms and leaned back in his seat. He wanted no part of ever visiting Dagron-5. It just wasn't something he was interested in, even if they did have a shortage of fieldmelders.

When Gilby arrived home to his sterile-looking apartment, there were two messages on his holophone. The first came from Yeffeth Cross, letting him know his date with Lavina Zimberg was scheduled for Tuesday night at 6:00 at the Chez Luna Restaurant in New Hollywood—a government-sponsored eatery that served authentic fancy Faux-rench flavored food.

The second message was more important. After Gilby pressed the blinking holophone button, a human-looking but mechanical robot with a camera lens in the middle of its forehead popped onto the quarter-stage area.

When the robot talked, the camera lens lit up ruby red. "Are you Gilby—D for David—Ford?" asked the grinning automated head.

"I am," said Gilby, confused. "Who are you?"

"Let me introduce myself, Mr. Gilby—D for David—Ford."

"Just call me Gilby."

"Yes, right, Mr. Gilby. My name is Sheckley, the spy assigned to observe your date tomorrow night."

"Wait a minute," said Gilby, his eyes narrowing. "What do you mean, spy?"

"Oh, it's all completely normal. The Dating Bureau has spies monitor all second dates to prevent fraud and date misrepresentation. I'm telling you to be transparent. Just part of being in a free and democratic society."

"Well, that doesn't sound so democratic to me."

The red lens on Sheckley's forehead abruptly shut off. "Please, Mr. Gilby, watch yourself," said the robot, taken aback. "I will erase that last comment so as not to create any suspicion on your behalf. You're lucky I'm not officially working on your case until the date starts. Otherwise, I'd have to report you to the Bureau. And you know what would happen then."

Gilby blanched. "I'm…I'm sorry," he said, realizing he'd talked too much.

"You should be, Mr. Gilby. It's a good thing for your sake I'm programmed to respect the boundaries of my mission: to report back any abnormalities or crimes that occur during the date, not beforehand."

"You don't have to worry about me," said Gilby, raising his palms.

"I should hope not," said Sheckley, frowning. The red light flicked back on his forehead, blinding Gilby. "And when the date happens tomorrow night, Mr. Gilby—D for David—Ford, trust me, I'm going to keep my eye on you, real close. You, sir, are not to be trusted."

"But—"

Sheckley ignored him and blipped out.

That night, Gilby couldn't sleep. He tossed and turned, worried about the date. What if it didn't go well? Lavina looked beautiful.

What would she want with a fieldmelder like him? Would they really kill him if it didn't work out?

In the morning, things were no better.

After getting stuck in the turbolift at his apartment building, he missed the 7:45 Underground and arrived at work thirty minutes late. He was immediately met by his roly-poly manager, Erdrich Santoli, who berated him about his overdue fieldmelding reports. Gilby was ordered to finish them by noon.

Stressed, he retreated to his glass-encased office, where he answered a holophone call from the Intergalactic Bank of New Hollywood. There was a problem with his bank account. His credits were missing—again.

"What do you mean?" said Gilby, his hair stiffening on the back of his neck. "I had this same discussion with Mr. Ferdner in Finance on Friday. My credits were placed in the wrong account."

A mousy-haired woman stared back. "That's not what our system shows," she said in a high-pitched, nasal voice. "Our records indicate you're overdrawn. Unless you satisfy the overdraft amount immediately, we will be forced to suspend your account."

"Where's Ferdner? Let me speak with him."

"I'm sorry. Mr. Ferdner is unavailable. Perhaps you'd like to speak with Mr. Angers in Accounting."

"Can he help?"

"Probably not. His first day at work is next Monday."

Gilby's headache intensified. Over the next three hours, he spoke with eight different bank employees until his problem was finally resolved by Mr. Beitelspacher, the Bank Manager, who said they'd transfer the missing credits back by noon.

Relieved, he sank into his levitating chair. But before he could relax, his boss, beet red and seething, burst through the glass door.

"What the hell are you doing about this fieldmelding problem, Ford?"

"What fieldmelding problem?" he stammered.

"The one that started in the collider room fifteen minutes ago and spread to the kitchenette."

He lowered his gaze and stared at the desk. A bead of sweat appeared on his upper lip.

"Well?" demanded Santoni.

Raising his head, looking his supervisor in the eyes, Gilby said the only thing he could say under the circumstances: "I'll get on it right away."

"You'd better," complained Santoni. "The last fieldmelding disaster we had lasted three days, and the company was forced to lock down the building.

Hours later, after checking all the obvious fixes like loose membolators in the rotating laser coil billets or burned-out multiwinding flexortubes and sensor diodes, Gilby was stumped. He didn't know anything about his job. How was he expected to solve a burgeoning fieldmelding catastrophe?

He sat zombie-like at his desk in front of the invisible computer, staring out past the translucent walls, agonizing about his problems. It was almost 3:45. What if he missed the date?

His heart hammered. The Dating Bureau would never believe him. A fieldmelding mishap would mean nothing to them. They'd sacrifice him in a minute if it cleared up their induction numbers.

A loud horn blared, rattling glass walls. Bright yellow lights flashed on and off in the office.

Gilby's eyes snapped open. Widened. It was his worst fear ever. Lockdown!

He swiveled his chair to watch the havoc outside his office. People yelled and screamed, attacked each other. Ran around and overturned and destroyed furniture. Someone threw a wastebasket that smashed into his glass walls, cracking them on impact.

Hyperventilating, Gilby turned toward his computer. He couldn't think.

Erdrich Santoni burst into his office. His terror-stricken eyes told Gilby everything he needed to know about the situation. "We need an answer now," his boss yelled. "They've gone crazy out there."

He said nothing.

"Gilby?" Santoni barked.

Gilby stared blankly ahead, trying to focus, but all he could think about was the date he'd miss with Lavina. They'd probably kill him for that. He didn't know what to do. He tugged at his shirt collar, feeling hot, lightheaded. He struggled to breathe. When the room began to swirl and spin like a merry-go-round, his eyes glazed over and light became darkness.

"Gilby!" screamed his boss.

Pitching forward, he passed out and face-planted onto the invisible keyboard.

On impact, he computer screen lit up with thousands of numbers, whirring and pinging, clicking and clacking, faster and faster, writing code no one had ever seen before, until the entire visual display turned pure white, went nova, and shut off.

The office fell silent. Lights flicked on. Then the room burst into celebration. People hugged, laughed, danced, sang, and made fools of themselves. Shredded paper floated down and littered the office like streamers at a party.

The next thing Gilby knew, Erdrich Santoni was shaking his shoulder. "Gilby, wake up. Gilby."

He slowly opened his eyes. "Wha, what happened?" he asked, dazed. "Why're they cheering?"

"You saved the company. The fieldmelding disaster is over. You're a hero."

"I am?"

"You'll be promoted for this."

"Again?" he said, wondering what he'd done.

"Might even be management this time."

"What time is it?" said Gilby, rubbing his eyes.

Santoni looked at his watch. "3:54. Why?"

Gilby bolted to attention like a man on a mission. "I've got to go. Dating Bureau. Flowers and Candy."

"Wait. You've still gotta write those reports."

Grabbing his coat, Gilby lurched toward the glass door. "I'll write them tomorrow."

Riding in the Underground, Gilby fidgeted. He worried that he'd be late to pick up his government-approved flowers and candy. Was there a penalty for not bringing them on the date? He shook his head. Once again, he should have read those government-issued bulletins.

After exiting the train at Laurel Station, he leapt onto the florescent-lit platform, pushed past pedestrians, police officers, and peddlers, and sprinted up the concrete stairs to the city streets above.

Turning right, he dashed into the busy sidewalk and zigzagged his way through the bustling crowd until he reached a solar lamppost at the end of the block. Attached was a Government Candy and Flower Depository sign pointing into a dim, narrow alleyway.

Gilby rushed into the empty, brick-walled laneway; splashed through foul-smelling puddles; and prayed the warehouse was still open.

But no such luck. When he arrived, there were Krillian hyperchromium and steel padlocks, the hardest manufactured alloy in the universe, attached to the doors. A pulsating red sign indicated the depository was closed.

He lowered his chin to his chest. Now, what would he do?

"*Psst!*" said a smarmy male voice. "C'mere."

Gilby raised his head. Standing to his left were two men. The tall slender one wore a white Panama hat and vanilla ice-cream-colored zoot suit. A toothpick protruded from the corner of his mouth.

His plump partner had dressed in baggy black suit pants, a wrinkled white shirt with a gaping collar, and tie knotted loosely.

He tensed. "Who are you?" asked Gilby.

The Toothpick Man took a step forward. His cologne smelled like burnt toast and bacon. "We're here to help."

"Yeah, help," repeated Baggy Suit in a raspy voice.

"I don't need any help." Gilby eyed the alleyway, looking for an escape.

"Of course you do," said the man, wiggling his toothpick. "You need flowers and candy for your date, don't cha?"

"Yes, but—"

"Then we're your guys, pussycat."

"Your guys," said Baggy.

"I don't even know who you are."

"Tell him, Rolo," said Toothpick Man.

The fat man palmed a titanium-plated Markey 3200 pulsed-ruby laser pistol. "I'm Rolo," he said.

He nodded to Toothpick Man. "And this here's Griffin. Any more questions?"

Gilby would have answered, but a chill ran down his spine. He only managed a weak smile.

"We're not bad guys," said Griffin, tipping his Panama. "Just honest businessmen."

"Yeah, businessmen," Rolo scraped out.

"What do you want?"

Griffin stepped closer. He furtively looked around to see if anyone else was there. "We've got bootleg flowers and candy."

"Straight from Dagron-5," added Rolo.

"Can't even tell the difference between the government-sponsored brand and the fake," said Griffin knowingly. "And just between you and me and the laser post, the candy has thirty percent more pheromonal-delics to help you achieve a more passionate evening if you catch my drift."

"I think I'll just go on my date without them," said Gilby inching away. "Thanks."

Griffin grabbed him by the shoulder. "Don't be a sap. You wanna die?"

"No!"

"Don't you read your weekly government bulletins?" He spoke as if Gilby was an idiot. "It's not enough to just go on a date. The government spies keep track of what you do all night by counting points. If you don't have enough at the end of the evening, even if the date's a success…SHOOF…."

"SHOOF?" Gilby said, fearing the worst.

"You know." Griffin pointed to his own Markey 3200 laser gun protruding from his right pant pocket. "SHOOF."

"Yeah, just like my dearly departed brudder," Rolo rasped. He wiped his teary eyes.

"I need to sit down," said Gilby, his legs turning to jelly.

Rolo and Griffin propped him up.

Griffin bent so close the coffee-and-bacon scent tightened Gilby's throat. "Don't worry, pussycat. We only use 'em if we get stiffed. You wouldn't stiff two honest businessmen now, wouldja?"

"No," he said, nodding.

"I knew you were a smart guy," said Rolo.

Griffin pulled out a flimsy black business card-sized machine from his coat pocket. "That'll be one-hundred credits for the flowers and candy."

"That seems like a lot."

"Who asked you," barked Rolo. "Punch in your access code."

Gilby pressed some flat digits on the small device. It lit up to register the sale.

"You made a wise choice, pussycat." Griffin spit out his toothpick, pulled another one from his breast pocket, and inserted it into his mouth. "Rolo, get the man his flowers and candy."

The gruff response came back, "Okay, boss."

Within seconds, Rolo returned holding a gold-covered candy box and a bouquet of pink and red roses. He shoved them at Gilby. "Here."

Clutching the items, Gilby backed away.

Griffin waved. "Don't forget to tell your friends about us for all their flower and candy needs."

"Yeah, gardenias are our specialty," added Rolo.

"On second thought," said Griffin, "Don't tell your friends. We'll find them."

Rolo brandished his laser blaster and croaked, "Then we'll find you. Now, scram."

His heart hammering, Gilby stumbled away and made a beeline for the alley exit. When he reached the street, he heard Griffin's laughter echoing behind him.

☙

Twenty minutes later, Gilby reached the hunter green and white-bricked Chez Luna restaurant building. It had been a trying day, but now he needed his luck to change.

Glancing up at the fading sunset, he made a quick prayer for a successful evening. He desperately needed Lavina Zimberg to like him and vice versa. His life, and probably hers, depended on it.

When he reached for the door handle, an image of Sheckley popped up and floated in front of him.

Gilby gasped.

"Do not be frightened, Mr. Gilby—D for David—Ford. I am Sheckley, your government-appointed spy for the evening."

"I know," said Gilby, annoyed. "You're early."

"I came to wish you good luck on your date. But unfortunately, circumstances have changed, and I will not be joining you for the evening like I normally would."

Gilby couldn't believe his luck. He smiled. "Oh, that's too bad," he said insincerely. "The government must have finally realized this isn't my second date."

"Oh, no, Mr. Gilby, far from the truth. The other robot spy, Jenkins, charged with this district, had a self-induced programming meltdown, and I've been assigned to watch four other dates tonight, including yours. I will periodically pop in during the dinner and calculate how you're doing."

Gilby's smile waned. "Great."

"I must say, Mr. Gilby, you're off to a wonderful start, point-wise, that is. Flowers and Candy." Sheckley turned on his red lens and shined it at the gifts. "Are those government-approved?" he snapped, appearing irritated. "They don't look government-approved."

"Of course they are," Gilby lied. He laughed nervously. "Now, where would I get fake flowers and candy?"

Sheckley's red lens studied his face, making him uneasy. His stomach knotted into a shape he didn't even know existed.

A shrill buzz sounded.

Sheckley snapped off the lens. "Something's happening on one of my other assignments," he said, clearly alarmed. "I must go, Mr. Gilby. And if I were you, I'd watch myself. As I've said before," —he leaned in— "you're not to be trusted."

The image faded, and Sheckley disappeared.

Sagging against the door, Gilby tried to control his shaking hands. It would be a miracle if he survived the evening.

Gathering his courage, Gilby made his way into the glitzy restaurant. Large chandeliers hung throughout the eatery, rimmed with mini pendant lights. Scattered around the room stood tables for two, set with white tablecloths, black napkins, expensive-looking silverware, and pink taper candles lit for ambiance.

He was greeted by a doe-eyed hostess with shoulder-length brunette hair, standing behind a podium next to a white-washed brick pillar.

"Bonjour, *monsieur*," she said in a honeyed French accent. "I am Yvette. May I assist you?"

"I'm here to meet Lavina Zimberg. Has she arrived yet?"

"Oui, *Monsieur*." She checked the register. "Are you Gilby—D for David—Ford?"

"Yes."

"We have a wonderful table for the both of you." She snapped her fingers, and a Relco RP-15 robot waiter rolled near them. The human-like droid wore a beige long-sleeved shirt, black bow tie, and matching vest. A white cloth napkin hung over his right mechanical arm. His face, although plain, had been designed with a needle-thin mustache and a condescending sneer.

"Follow me," said the robot with enough disdain in his voice that Gilby actually thought he *was* in France.

Snaking through the busy dining room, past hard-working android servers carrying food and drink on silver platters, Gilby smelled the floral and honey aroma of Faux-rench tomato bouillabaisse and chicken coq au vin. They were the most famous synthetic French dishes ever made from protein-flavored Octobeans, mashed Fungal slabs, and Solarian Groteen cubes. His mouth watered. The secret was clearly in the broth.

When they approached the table, Gilby recognized Lavina. His heart quickened. She was more beautiful than the holopix he'd seen. Her luscious blond hair perfectly framed her delicate features. A warm smile filled her face.

Approaching, he murmured, "I'm Gilby."

She stood up. *Oh my*. She wore a close-fitting, blue floral dress that accentuated her slender figure.

"Lavina," she said, reaching out to greet him.

"Hi." He shook her soft hand.

There was no magic when they touched, which worried him. Wasn't he supposed to have felt something? He didn't know. He'd never been on a date before. "I got these for you," he added and handed her the flowers and candy.

"They're beautiful." She sniffed the roses. "But you didn't have to."

Gilby shyly nodded.

"Have a seat, *monsieur*," said the robot waiter.

Lavina placed her gifts on the table.

Sitting down, Gilby smiled at her, but worrisome thoughts lingered. He tensed and clutched his own hands on the table. His chest tightened. What if there was no chemistry between them? He didn't want to die. He was too young. Gilby gazed at the nearby tables. Other couples seemed to be at ease, leaning close to one another and talking, which only added more pressure.

"Did you have trouble finding the restaurant?" he asked, rubbing the back of his neck.

"No, it was near my office. You?"

"Not really." He paused and drank from his water glass. He had an urge to keep drinking.

Lavina smiled at him.

He fidgeted, feeling the importance of the meeting. *Life or death.* He took another sip.

"What do you do for a living?" she asked.

"I'm a fieldmelder."

Her face brightened. "Me too. You like it?"

"I guess." He took a deep breath to relax. Tried to think of something else to say but couldn't.

Lavina leaned in, touched his hand. "Are you nervous?"

"Yes."

"I am too."

"You sure don't look it."

"What's the point," she said. "We might as well acknowledge the elephant in the room. We're both on our second dates. Can't do anything about that. So, we might as well have some fun and enjoy the evening. What else can we do?"

"But if it doesn't work—"

She interrupted him. "We can't worry about it."

"I guess you have it all figured out, right?" he said.

"I'm just trying to relax, that's all. Like you should."

Gilby exhaled. "You made me feel better."

"Good." She brushed aside a sweep of beautiful blond hair.

The gesture intrigued him, but he had to be honest. "This dating stuff is hard," he said. He wiped his brow. "And I thought fieldmelding was tough."

"Do you really like fieldmelding?" she asked, leaning forward.

No time for cat-and-mouse. "No. Do you?"

"Of course not," she said, appearing surprised he'd even ask such a ridiculous question.

He grinned. There was something genuine and refreshing about her which he decided he liked, surprising himself. "I don't even know what I'm doing most of the time," he admitted. "It's a complete mystery to me."

"Me too."

And they both laughed.

"Wine?" he asked, lifting a bottle of Synthen-del.

"Please," she said sweetly.

The two talked intently throughout the evening, from where they grew up, to what schools they attended. He told her about his weird parents. She chatted about her friends and her desire to travel. Did he know she wanted to be a counselor once, but the government outsourced those jobs to robots? In college, Gilby studied to be an astronomer. But when he checked the classifieds, there were no jobs, just plenty of work for fieldmelders—whatever those were. Her pre-arranged husband died before they could marry. Gilby complained to Lavina about the government mix-up that canceled his engagement.

When he reached out to clasp her hand, she laced her fingers through his. Her touch warmed his heart and soothed his soul. Then, looking up, their eyes met. Time slowed down as if no one else existed, and they basked in endless pleasure. Whether this feeling was cosmic or serendipitous, he didn't know, but there was definitely something going on between them, and he wondered if Lavina was "the one."

In the glow of candlelight, she looked at him, head tilting, with ever brightening eyes—until the temperature around them suddenly dropped, and she rubbed her bare shoulders. "Is it cold in here?" she asked.

Before Gilby could answer, the plates and silverware on their table rattled. The air sucked in around them, bending light into a small collapsing vortex that rumbled to a stop near Lavina. Sheckley stepped out of the rotating quantum tunnel. Then the teleportation hole he used closed up and disappeared. "Oh, my," he said. "Things seem to be going swimmingly around here. More points for the both of you."

Gilby frowned. "It's you again."

"Yes, Mr. Gilby—D for David—Ford. It's me. I'm just doing my job, as you well know."

"Bad timing," grumbled Gilby.

The android spy eyed him with disdain.

"Hello, Sheckley," said Lavina.

"Hello, Ms. Lavina Zimberg," he said politely. "You, I trust."

A Relco R-15 robot waiter with the pencil-thin mustache rolled up to the table and presented Gilby with a digital bill on a black business card-sized machine. "Your check, *monsieur*. I assume you can pay it?"

"Of course I can pay it," said Gilby, surprised at the question. But then, again, it was a French robot.

"Just punch in your access code, and I'll bring you *ze* receipt."

Sheckley glared at the flowers and candy.

While Gilby punched in his numbers, Sheckley's red lens flicked on. The light shrouded the table.

"What're you doing?" asked Gilby.

"Are you sure these are government-issued flowers and candy?" said Sheckley sharply.

Gilby crossed his arms. His stomach tightened. "Why wouldn't they be?"

"Because government-approved merchandise has infinitesimal sensors in each flower and piece of candy. And I'm not picking up their signals."

"Oh," said Gilby, his voice trailing off.

"They look real to me," said Lavina.

Gilby stared at her, surprised she would risk her own life to defend him.

"Well, they are not, Ms. Zimberg," said Sheckley. "I assure you."

"Maybe the sensors are broken, or even you," she said, her smile stretching a bit too falsely.

"That is absurd. One demerit for you, Ms. Zimberg, and may I say you *had* a perfect score."

Across the room, rushing straight for the table, was a stubby, overweight man in a black suit. The Relco R-15 sneering French waiter followed closely.

Gilby stood up, puzzled.

"Halt!" yelled Black Suit, clearly infuriated. "Stop him."

"What did you do?" demanded Sheckley.

"I didn't do anything," said Gilby, lifting his arms in confusion.

Panting, stumpy Black Suit arrived at the table. "You, sir," he said, poking his finger at Gilby, "need to pay your bill."

"I did pay."

"The bank says you're out of credits. Need I remind you, this is a government-owned facility. It is illegal to eat food or steal goods without monetary payment."

"I see," said Sheckley, his lips pursed, nodding.

"Wait a minute," said Gilby, shaking his head. "I didn't steal anything." He could feel his life slipping away. "The bank. They made a mistake. I spoke with Mr. Ferdner in Finance on Friday and Mr. Beitelspacher, the Bank Manager, this morning. He said they'd fix it this afternoon. They promised."

"Listen," said Black Suit, thrusting the invoice at Gilby. "I don't care if you spoke with Mr. Jaggers, the janitor on Jupiter. Who's going to pay this bill?"

Gilby turned to Lavina. "You believe me. Don't you?"

She grabbed his hand and held it. "I believe you," she said.

"See," he said to Black Suit.

The overweight man's face reddened. He looked like he was about to explode.

Sheckley confronted Gilby, the red lens burning into his eyes.

He struggled to see.

"So, do you admit to committing a crime, Mr. Gilby—D for David—Ford?"

Gilby used his arm to shield the brightness. "No! I do not."

At the front of the restaurant, there was a high-pitched whine, three deafening *SHOOFS*, and a burst of arching flashes that lit up the room like sheet lightning. When an overhead chandelier crashed to the floor, people screamed.

Gilby veered toward the commotion. Standing in the entryway by the frightened doe-eyed hostess were Rolo and Griffin. They each brandished a smoking Markey 3200 laser gun.

"Shut up, all of youse!" yelled Rolo, his voice sand-paper raw. "Griffin has somethin' to say."

The room quieted. Griffin took a step forward. Shattered glass crunched under his shoes.

Concerned, Gilby dropped to the floor under the table, dragging Lavina with him.

Her fingers clutched his arm. "What's going on?" she asked.

"I know those guys. They kill people."

"You definitely lead an interesting life," she said. Her eyes glowed with evident admiration.

Gilby's heart tumbled. He peaked beneath the tablecloth.

Pulling a toothpick out of his mouth, Griffin glowered at the terrified, cowering crowd. "We got no beef with you people," he said apologetically. "We're just honest businessmen trying to make a simple buck." A vein on his neck twitched. "But when someone pays with no credits and stiffs us, well, we take care of business in our own way."

Rolo waived his gun. "Yeah, business."

Griffin jerked his head. "C'mon, let's search this joint." They advanced into the crowded dining room.

Sheckley bent down under the table and narrowed his gaze at Gilby and Lavina. "Get up this instant," he ordered. "This is most embarrassing. You two are still on a date."

"Quiet!" hushed Gilby.

"Come out, come out, wherever you are, pussycat," sang Griffin.

"Pussycat," repeated Rolo.

"He's over there," yelled the heavyset manager, pointing to Gilby's table.

Gilby felt the hairs lift on the back of his arms and neck. "No!" he shrieked.

The thugs bolted through the crowded restaurant, pushing aside customers to get to Gilby. En route, they stumbled over a waiter and thudded to the floor. Flashing laser shots brightened the room.

Gilby turned to Sheckley. Beads of sweat appeared on his forehead. "Help us?"

"You teleport, don't you?" Lavina asked the spy.

"I am only an observer," said Sheckley.

"But you beam in and out of here all the time," said Gilby. He watched Griffin and Rolo stand up. "Take us with you?" he begged.

"I can only transport you if you have committed an illegal act or are in the process of committing an illegal act. That is the law. Have you committed a crime?"

Rolo and Griffin rushed toward the table. They raised their guns. "I see you, pussycat," Griffin taunted. "Be prepared to get blasted."

Gilby grabbed Sheckley's round and cold metallic shoulders. "You're right," he said. "The flowers and candy are fakes. They're not government approved. I admit it. I committed a crime. I did it."

"I knew it," exclaimed Sheckley. The collapsing vortex opened up behind him. The air around him sucked in.

244

"And Lavina helped," added Gilby.

"What?" she said, surprised.

Aiming, Rolo and Griffin stared down Gilby in his lair under the table. Then, their guns, whirring rapidly like high-pitched vacuums, lit up and lashed out with an arching flash.

SHOOF, SHOOF, SHOOF...

Only no one was there. From inside the quantum tunnel, as they disappeared, Gilby, Lavina, and Sheckley watched the lethal rays strike and obliterate the table.

They were teleported instantaneously into a large wood-paneled room where they found themselves sitting on creaky, old-fashioned wooden pulldown stadium seats. Gilby quickly eyed the people surrounding them. Most were somber, but others chatted away with their seat neighbors like they didn't have a care in the world.

"What is this place?" asked Lavina.

"This is a courtroom, Ms. Zimberg," said Sheckley. He pointed with his mechanical arm. "Over there is the Judge's bench near the back wall. That box on the right is for the jury. When you speak with the judge, you stand on that circular dais in the middle of the room, behind the lectern, next to the defendant's table."

"Why are we here?" said Gilby, glancing around. "I thought you'd take us back to the Dating Bureau."

"Don't be silly, Mr. Gilby. You broke the law, and this is where lawbreakers go. Now, I must be leaving. I have more dates to evaluate tonight, and I have already sent my report about you to the court for review. It was a pleasure meeting you, Ms. Zimberg. And good luck." His red lens glared at Gilby and darkened. "You, not so much. When they call your name, just walk to the dais."

Collapsing air surrounded Sheckley. Lavina's hair fluttered in the breeze.

"Wait a minute, Sheckley," said Gilby. "What did—"

Sheckley and the quantum tunnel blipped out.

"Thanks for including me in your scheme," complained Lavina. She folded her arms across her chest.

"I didn't have a scheme. I was just trying to save you."

Her eyes welled up, and she lowered her gaze.

One look at her made him wish things could be different. Gilby reached out to gently touch her arm. He hated himself for subjecting her to all this danger.

"I'll get us out of here," he said, digging deep for courage so he could instill hope in her. "I promise, I'll think of something."

She dabbed her eyes with her arm. "You're lucky I like you," she said. "Now, hold my hand. I'm scared."

They sat quietly, fingers loosely interlaced, and comforted each other with occasional knowing smiles until a Beaman 622 Bailiff Robot rolled into the room. The angry-looking android, who appeared larger than other robots, wore a khaki New Hollywood Sheriff's Department uniform. Attached to his belt were a spiked nightstick and a Markey 3200 laser gun. The identification tag above his badge indicated his name was Mr. Buttz.

"Attention," growled Buttz in a loud, deep voice. "Court is now in session."

The room quieted. Gilby and Lavina looked at each other, tight-lipped.

"Please stand for the Honorable Jezper J. Throckwhistle."

Wooden seats creaked while everyone stood up.

Slowly, the upper body of a mechanical man, wearing a black judge's robe and a pair of round glasses with thick lenses, rose from inside the judge's bench on a small elevator platform until it ground to a stop. He peered out over the courtroom. "You may be seated," said the judge.

Gilby and Lavina, along with the rest of the gallery, plopped down in their noisy seats.

"Remember," said Judge Throckwhistle to the courtroom. "We live in a wonderful country. You are all fortunate to have fair trials here today because of a free and democratic society." The android smiled. "You may proceed, Mr. Buttz."

"First case," said the bailiff, "Enderson Simmons."

A grey-mustached man with a weathered face, wearing a French beret, ambled his way to the dais.

Gilby thought the man looked familiar but couldn't place him. Simmons stepped on the elevated circle.

"State your full name," demanded the judge.

"Enderson P. Simmons, your honor," said Simmons theatrically. "Perhaps you remember me. I'm the actor who played General Skinner for the government in those Dating Bureau phone calls."

Gilby brightened. It was General Skinner. They had to go easy on him. He worked for the government.

"A true patriot. You did a wonderful job, Mr. Simmons," remarked the judge.

"Thank you, your honor," said Simmons, bowing pompously in a contrived showbiz manner.

Gilby relaxed. It sounded like Judge Throckwhistle might be fair.

He turned to Lavina and whispered, "We're gonna be okay," he said, nodding his head. "Watch."

"The report states you tried to buy liquor with someone else's credits. How do you plead?"

"Not guilty, your honor."

"I think guilty," said the judge, slamming his gavel on the desk. "Prepare to die."

The crowd gasped.

Gilby gaped. His heart skipped a beat.

Lavina buried her head into his shoulder.

"What about my due process?" screamed Enderson.

"You've received your due process, sir," said the judge, his voice rising. "You were *due* in court tonight, and the *process* is how we're going to kill you."

"But... wait," pleaded Simmons.

The judge pressed a button, and a wide, red-flamed laser beam shot out from the ceiling above the dais, rendering Enderson Simmons into atoms. The room smelled like burnt sulfur.

Lavina shrieked.

Shaken, Gilby lowered his head. He couldn't speak. They were doomed, doomed, doomed. He'd never get them out of the courtroom alive.

He stared at the terrazzo floor. Partially hidden under a chewing gum wrapper was a card. A business card, and it looked familiar.

As he leaned down, his eyes widened. He couldn't believe it. Somebody had dropped Frank Popper's card.

Frantically, he snatched it up and pressed the flashing phone number. He just hoped it wasn't too late.

"Second case," yelled out Buttz, "Gilby—D for David—Ford."

Gilby froze. His knuckles, gripping the wooden seat arms, turned white.

"Come on, Mr. Ford," said the judge sternly. "Come up here. We don't have all night."

Gilby slowly stood up, wondering how far he'd get if he ran.

Lavina touched his arm. "It'll be all right," she said. A faint smile crossed her face.

He nodded, taking comfort in her affection even though he knew his minutes were numbered.

"According to the record, Mr. Ford, you had an accomplice. Is a Ms. Lavina Zimberg here?"

She took a shaky breath. "Here, your honor."

"You may join your date on the dais."

Gilby and Lavina helplessly looked at each other. Then, taking her hand, he led her past the other sitting defendants in the gallery, and they made their way to the dais. Gilby glanced back at the courtroom doors. Where was Popper? Hadn't he said he'd be there within seconds if you pressed his holonumber?

"Just step up," said the judge. "I haven't had a doubleheader in a long time."

As they stepped onto the platform, Gilby squeezed Lavina's hand.

"How do you plead?" asked the judge, shaggy eyebrows rising in anticipation.

The heavy courtroom doors banged open, disrupting the proceeding. Frank Popper, dour and determined and wearing his same rumpled Stay-Fresh™ black suit, charged into the room. "Your honor," he said. "Frank Popper, attorney-at-law. I'm representing the defendants."

"Welcome, Mr. Popper," said the judge. "I see you're practicing law again. I assume your suspension is over?"

Popper stopped at the defendant's table and clicked open his worn-out, leather-scratched briefcase. "It was a short one this time, your honor."

"How many has it been. Five times?"

"Six. But who's counting?"

Gilby felt nauseated. He cupped his forehead. Why had he called this guy?

"Please join your clients on the dais so I can hear you better," the judge said to Popper.

The attorney brushed his suit. "Need I remind you, Judge Throckwhistle, that lawyers have immunity from harm in the courtroom. Established in *Snider v. Ackerman, 1347 New Hollywood Reporter 822 (2037)*. And I quote, 'A sitting judge may not intentionally or unintentionally cause harm or death to a licensed attorney while in the course of representing his clients.'"

"Right you are, Mr. Popper," said the magistrate, smiling. "You can't blame an old judge for trying."

"Not at all, your honor," grinned Popper. "Just doing my part for transparency in this free and democratic society."

"You may proceed. How do your clients plead?"

"Let me discuss it with them."

"All right," said the judge. "You have five minutes."

Popper motioned them over, and they stepped off the rostrum and headed toward the defendant's table.

"Hey, kid," greeted Popper. "I knew you'd give me a call. I can read fieldmelders like a book." He looked at Lavina. "Who's the dame?"

Lavina held out her hand. "Lavina Zimberg," she said. "I'm his date."

Popper shook her hand, eyeing her from head to toe. He turned to Gilby. "She looks like a keeper, kid—reminds me of my second wife. I'll see what I can do."

"You think we've got a chance?" asked Gilby.

"I've got a plan. How do you plead?"

Without hesitation, both Gilby and Lavina said, "Not guilty."

"Okay, I'll tell the judge."

"Don't you need to know what happened?" asked Gilby. "About the facts?"

"Who needs facts?"

"Wait a minute," protested Gilby.

Popper stood behind the lectern. "We're ready to plead, your honor."

"Fine. Tell your clients to stand onto the dais."

"But—" said Gilby.

Bailiff Buttz towered over him; a menacing scowl etched on his robot face. "No talking unless directed by the judge," he snarled mechanically. "Now, get on the dais."

Gilby and Lavina stepped on the platform, she leaning into him, and he put his arm around her shoulders.

The judge looked at Popper. "How do your clients plead?"

"Guilty, your honor."

"What?" screamed Gilby.

Lavina clutched Gilby, which stopped him from collapsing.

"Guilty it is," said the judge. He slammed his hammer on the desk.

"Now, when are you releasing my clients and dismissing this case?" Popper asked.

The judge snarled. "Are you insane? They just pleaded guilty."

"Right, your honor. And that makes them not guilty."

"How do you figure?"

Popper stepped away from the lectern and faced Judge Throckwhistle. "Your honor, how many cases have you heard in your career? 20,000? 30—"

"Thirty-two thousand eight hundred fifty-four, to be exact," snapped the judge.

"In all those cases, to your best recollection, has anyone ever pleaded guilty?"

A menacing sneer appeared on the Judge's face. "No."

"But my clients did. That makes them the most honest defendants you've ever had in this courtroom. My clients are honest."

"That makes no sense," said the judge. He raised his eyebrows, apparently confused and trying to comprehend the logic.

"Of course, it does," said Popper. "What is your prime courtroom directive?"

"Watch it, Popper. I am not the one on trial here," said the judge, clearly irritated.

"Need I remind you that under *Symbotics v. Clevemore, 1472 New Hollywood Reporter 15 (2039)*, robot judges are required to reveal all details about their embryonic programming instructions if they are pertinent to a judicial proceeding or are contradictory to a prime courtroom directive?"

Amazed, Gilby watched the judge chafe under Popper's questioning. The robot quivered for a moment before regaining control of his body.

Eyeing Lavina, Gilby grabbed her left hand and squeezed it gently. Maybe hope existed after all.

The judge addressed their lawyer. "Belton Wagner programmed me at Judgetronics."

"And what was your basic, germinal instruction?" asked Popper.

"To protect and release honest people."

"And what is the definition of the word honesty that they programmed into you, your honor?"

Judge Throckwhistle said in a slow, mumbling voice, "Honesty is a facet of moral character that connotes positive and virtuous attributes such as integrity, truthfulness, and straightforwardness." Beads of robot oil appeared on his forehead.

"And will you admit," said Popper, "that by my clients pleading guilty, they showed integrity, truthfulness, and straightforwardness, making them honest under the definition and terms of your initial directive?"

The robot quivered again. "Yes."

"And what does the Code of Judicial Ethics, Canon 5, indicate about your prime courtroom directive?"

More beads of oil appeared on Judge Throckwhistle's brow. "To dispose of all defendants guilty of a crime."

Popper took a step toward the judge's bench. "I see," he said, holding his chin, pondering the issue. "So, if my clients are guilty of a crime, which they freely admit, you must kill them according to your prime courtroom directive?"

Gilby tensed, his shoulders tightening.

"Yes," stammered the judge.

"But how can that be? You admit they're honest. How can you kill an honest person?"

The judge fanned himself with his mechanical hand like he was overheated. "I don't know. I must think."

"And logically," Popper added, "perhaps, you've killed people who pled not guilty, but were honest, too?"

"No," crackled the judge. "They were guilty. I said so."

"Are you sure?" asked Popper, a smile on his lips.

The judge gyrated on his bench and then wobbled uncontrollably.

Gilby stared, his eyes bulging, at the sight of the rocking robot. "Your honor, do you agree honest people should not be punished?"

"I don't...think...."

"You must release my clients now," demanded Popper.

"I don't feel so good," hissed the judge.

Spinning wildly, the top of Judge Throckwhistle's head blew off like a whirling propeller, embedding in the wood-paneled wall across the room. Smoke wafted up from his neck. Lurching forward, the lifeless judge banged his open-skulled head on the bench. His thick glasses dropped to the floor and cracked.

Gilby stood stunned as if he'd had lost the ability to move. Lavina grabbed his arm; she was shaking.

The crowd screamed.

Bailiff Buttz barked at the defendants in the gallery to "Stay calm" and "Wait for the judge to recover." But no one listened. They bolted from their seats and ran out through the courtroom doors, escaping into the mall.

Popper tugged at Gilby and Lavina. "C'mon. Let's get outta here before they replace the judge, kid."

Stumbling off the dais, they dashed after Popper to the doorway.

They entered the building concourse, running by the Dating Bureau offices near the old defunct Mock-Donalds sign, past the homeless camp in the food court and along the empty gift shops and stores, until they were outside the drab vertical mall structure on Garbo Boulevard.

Hunched over and panting, Gilby breathed in the fresh night air. It smelled of Callery pear tree and garbage, another fragrance the government felt people would like. Lavina stood near him. Popper, for an older, out-of-shape man, didn't appear winded at all.

"We've got to make this quick," said Popper, pulling two oval-shaped cards and paperwork out of his coat pocket. He handed one each to Gilby and Lavina.

"What're these?" she asked.

Gilby looked at his forms and frowned. "They look like travel credits and transit papers."

"They're to Dagron-5. The rocket leaves in two hours."

"But I don't wanna go to Dagron-5," said Gilby. He crossed his arms. "Who wants to live there?"

"Maybe I do," Lavina said. "You know I've always wanted to travel."

Gilby rubbed the back of his neck. He'd always loved Earth, never wanted to leave, but in all honesty, was there any future left for him here? If he survived, what would life be like without Lavina? She was the one thing the planet couldn't provide.

"Well, kid, what's it gonna be?" said Popper. "You can't stay here. Pretty soon, the government's going to bring in another judge and track you down."

He glanced at Lavina, and a silly grin crossed her face. His heart beat faster. "You think there'd be a chance for us there?" he asked.

"We don't know each other very well," she said, "but I'd like to know you better."

He smiled. "I feel the same way about you."

Popper, appearing bored, checked his watch.

Lavina affectionately rubbed Gilby's arm. "It's not going to be easy. It could be risky, living on a lawless planet. We might never be successful. We'd have to work hard at it every day. Harder than being fieldmelders. Can you make that commitment, Gilby? For us? For a chance at happiness and love?"

"Well, it might not be as romantic as a pre-birth arranged marriage," he said, "but I'm willing to give it a shot." He looked into her eyes. "That is, if it's with you."

They fell into an embrace, her arms around his neck. He could smell the floral fragrance in her hair. Then, when her eyes beckoned, their lips touched, delicately at first, until they were both overcome by passion and kissed wildly.

Yawning, Popper leaned near them and tapped his watch. "You'd better get going."

Gilby stopped, dazed with a smile. "How'd you know to get two tickets?"

"Lucky guess. Fieldmelders usually marry fieldmelders."

"That makes sense," said Gilby, agreeing for no apparent reason. "How can we ever repay you for your services?"

"Don't worry, kid. My office already hacked your bank account. Have a nice life."

Thirty-three million miles from Earth, and passing Mars, Gilby stared out the window of the Rocketliner from the Wayfarer's Lounge. The sitting room, made to resemble an old-fashioned Victorian men's club, provided serenity to the ship's passengers on their way to Dagron-5.

Lavina, resting in a leather chair, reading a book, had fallen asleep.

Gilby turned and cast a glance at her. His heart melted again. They'd both known right away they were meant for each other. So it was no surprise that the captain had performed a marriage ceremony one month into the trip. It was the happiest day of their lives.

Picking up an open-weave thermal blanket, Gilby gently placed it over Lavina's upper body and legs. She shifted in her seat, a contented smile on her face.

Yes, sir, he thought. He and Lavina had come a long way since Earth. And in another eight months, after entering the Klemhoffer wormhole, they'd land on Dagron-5 and start life anew.

Gilby smiled. It may not be like the free and democratic society they'd just left behind, but he knew one thing for sure. There were always plenty of jobs for fieldmelders.

CHAPTER ELEVEN

CASE NUMBER EIGHT: FIVE-CENT ROMANCE

ALLEGED VIOLATION: Intentional or negligent wrongdoing
ALLEGED VIOLATION: Emotional Distress

SEPTEMBER 1983
HOLLYWOOD, CALIFORNIA

Behind a Cuban mahogany desk, C.J. Augers leaned back in his leather chair and eyed the dismayed young actor sitting in his office.

He adjusted the thick, black-framed glasses sitting on his long jowly face. At sixty-three, Augers had seen enough in the film industry to be able to counsel an artist in need, especially young performers with whom he felt he had a special rapport. And, as Executive Producer of the *Fantastic Feagley Five Fun-Time Family*

Hour, starring the less-than-fantastic Feagley Brothers, who weren't even related, Augers figured he was the right man for the job.

Frank Feagley slumped in a chair opposite him, wearing gray pants, a plaid lumberjack shirt, black suspenders, and white Reeboks. The young man, now in his late teens, tossed his mullet hair and brooded. Frank had been considered the moody one in the Fantastic Feagley Five.

Leaning forward, Augers pressed his hands on the smooth desk surface. "Now, why do you want to quit the show?" he asked.

Feagley lowered his gaze. He could barely look at C.J. "I can't talk."

"I don't know what you mean."

"I mean, Mr. Augers, there's this totally bitchin' babe in Craft Services, see, that I kinda like, and..." He squirmed in his seat. "Well, I can't talk with her. Can you believe it? A cool dude like me." He shook his head. "Every time I see her, I just don't know what to say. My mouth becomes dry, and I get all nervous inside. Then I can't remember my lines, and I stumble around like I'm some old dude like you." He raised his hand. "No offense, Mr. Augers. So, dude, I've just gotta bug out."

That was the most he'd ever heard the kid say. C.J. pursed his lips. The boy was impertinent and immature, but he couldn't afford to let Frank quit. His presence on the show brought in the teenyboppers, the twelve-to-fifteen-year-old demographic so important to sponsors and the ratings.

The familiarity of Frank's story brought back an old memory. He sighed, surrendering to the past. He knew what he'd have to say to keep Frank from leaving.

"What's the girl's name?" C.J. asked.

"Misty." He paused, clearly concerned. "You're not gonna fire her, are you?"

"No, I'm not going to fire her," he said. He motioned to the walls covered with movie posters and three Emmy Awards standing on a shelf. "Did you know that before all this, I worked on a TV show called *Doggy Dan*?"

"What does this have to do with me?" inquired Frank.

He gestured toward the boy. "Well, let me tell you."

"Way back in 1951," said C.J., "*Doggy Dan* was a TV show on the old DuMont Television Network."

"The what?" asked Frank.

"DuMont. They're defunct now. It was a TV network just like CBS and NBC, only they were based in New York City and broadcast live."

Frank rolled his eyes. "Okay, if you say so."

C.J. ignored him. "Before DuMont went under, the *Doggy Dan Show* appeared weekly on the network. They entertained kids with puppets like the Mayor of Roverville, also known as 'the Great Catsby,' and his assistant Squeaker the Mouse, a clown named Crackles, and a few costumed characters like Doggy Dan and his southern belle friend, Peachy Poodle."

Frank sighed, looked at his watch.

"No, no, you'll like this," said Augers. "When he worked, Dan wore floppy dog ears, a painted face and snout, a red bandana, blue overalls, and a hillbilly hat. His co-worker, Peachy Poodle, dressed in a polka dot gown, and had a big curly yarn wig and snout. Pretty cute. But Dan had a problem."

"What was that? Bad taste in clothes?"

Smartass.

"Dan couldn't talk to women without wearing the costume."

"You're making this up, right?" said Frank.

"No," said C.J., shaking his head. "Once he was out of character, Dan would sneak away from the studio and go straight home to avoid women. Finally, some friends told him to go see a psychiatrist."

"Did he?"

"Not at first. But loneliness, being the most crippling of emotions, finally wore Dan down. At his producer's request, he saw Dr. Pat Greenwood, a lady shrink."

Frank shrugged. "Not me, man. You gotta be a psycho to see one of those people."

Augers couldn't understand it. He usually had such a good rapport with young kids, but this Frank was really testing his patience. "So, taking a cab to Midtown, near Central Park West, Dan visited Dr. Greenwood at her office. Needless to say, Dr. Greenwood, a prim, older woman, was quite surprised that her new patient would only talk to her while dressed as a dog, wearing a furry face and floppy ears, gloved paws, and his Doggy Dan wardrobe."

"What a dweeb," said Frank.

The phone buzzed, and C.J. grabbed the receiver. He exhaled before speaking. "Yes, Jan, I can talk to her." He raised his finger to Frank, indicating it would take a minute. "Hello, dear. No, I'm not busy for lunch." He looked at his watch. "I need about thirty minutes. That's right. Just come onto the lot. There'll be a pass for you at the gate. I've gotta go. I'm in a meeting right now. Bye."

He looked at Frank, not expecting much. The kid was dense as a rock. "Where were we?"

"Dan was getting his head shrunk."

"Right," said C.J., "Dan was on the couch, talking to the wood-paneled walls filled with Dr. Greenwood's educational degrees when she interrupted him. She lowered her glasses and said firmly, 'The problem with you is, you have a classic case of gynophobia.'"

"You mean he had a vagina?" Frank exclaimed.

"No, no, no," said C.J., annoyed. "It means scared of women. It's a phobia."

"Is that what I have?" Frank said, his body tensing. "I mean not the female part."

"We don't know what you have, Frank, but Dr. Greenberg told Dan:

"'I can treat you with psychotherapy or medication for years. But what I'd rather do is have you go out into this big, beautiful world, without your Doggy Dan costume, and approach a young woman your age, a stranger—someone you don't know—and say hello. That's it, just say hello. Let's just see what happens.'"

Frank leaned back.

C.J. smiled. "He objected at first and said, 'I can't do that— I'll... I'll...'

"And Dr. Greenwood replied, 'You'll do what? Say nothing? Faint? You're an actor, so act.'"

"That's harsh," said Frank.

"'Take a little black book,' the doc said. '"Track your activity. We'll talk about it next week.'"

"What a quack."

"She wasn't a quack. It's more like tough love."

"The only kinda tough love I want is in the sack," said Frank, smirking.

"Do you want to hear this story or not?"

"Yeah, sure," the kid said, lowering his head as if to see if his navel was still there.

C.J. forced a smile. "Alright then." He paused. "Dan bought the notebook and told himself he needed to follow her advice, or at least, because he didn't want to live his life alone.

"One day after rehearsal at the Wanamaker Department Store Annex where DuMont broadcast their shows, Dan took off the Doggy Dan costume and put on his casual clothes: a sweater vest, tan trousers, penny loafers, and a white dress shirt.

"Then he stepped outside Wardrobe, headed to the elevator, and took it to the ground floor. Reaching the lobby, he walked outside, through the revolving door, to 8th and Broadway in lower Manhattan."

Frank fiddled with the lower buttons on his shirt. "Why do you think buttons are round?" he asked. "Why not square or triangular ones?"

Augers glowered at Feagley.

"What? I'm listening."

"Really?"

"Yeah, except for the boring parts."

C.J. rubbed his forehead. The kid was driving him crazy.

"So," he said, pressing on. "Dan stood on the sidewalk in front of the department store and watched people rush by in the busy daytime crowd. He saw some women he thought pretty: a brunette wearing a red tunic with black high heels and a long-haired girl in capri pants and a tight sweater.

Frank nodded. "Lookin' for some babes. Sweet."

C.J. disregarded Frank's comment. "All Dan had to do was say hello, but he couldn't do it. The idea of talking to either one without his costume made him panic, and he started to sweat."

The kid leaned forward. "Yeah, women will do that to you. What'd he do?"

"He had to escape. Dan bolted into the crowd and weaved in and out between people crossing Broadway. He ran two blocks past the Chock Full O'Nuts until he reached Astor Place. When he stopped to catch his breath, he recognized the Horn & Hardart Automat."

Frank snorted. "What kind of a stupid store only sells auto mats?"

Augers sighed.

"It's a cafeteria. A restaurant that sells food out of glass compartments."

"You mean like vending machines?"

"Yes, only nicer," said C.J., remembering. "It was a wonderful place. The entire room was full of tables you shared with other diners. The floors and countertops were marble, and there was stained glass and chrome everywhere, including machines that poured fresh-brewed coffee from Italian brass dolphin spigots. And on the walls, underneath the art deco lettering, were steel and glass vending machines that dispensed fresh food from the window boxes, except for the items at the steam table, which cost more."

Frank stared at him blankly.

"You'd deposit a nickel into the coin slot on the wall. Then you'd turn the knob and lift the little window to remove your food. And did the food ever taste good...." Augers breathed in imaginary smells. "Frankfurters, beef stew, baked beans in a pot, cherry pie. Everything."

"Did they sell burritos?"

"What?"

"If they don't have burritos, forget it," said Frank with the apparent expertise of a magazine food critic. "But only the beef and potato ones, see, cause cheese and bean burritos make you fart too much."

Augers stared at Frank in disbelief. "Fascinating."

"It's true, dude."

"Don't you wanna know why the Automat is important to the story?" said Augers, annoyed.

"You mean there's a point?"

"Yes, there's a point," he snapped. "The reason it's important is that, while standing at the corner, that's where Dan saw the girl. She appeared out of nowhere, strolling down the street, wearing a cream-colored work dress with a hunter green apron and a ribbon on her lapel. As she walked, her thick auburn hair bounced around like she'd just washed it with Prell. Dan was mesmerized."

"Been there," said Frank, casually raising his hand.

C.J. rolled his eyes. "When he saw the girl enter the Automat, Dan knew what he had to do."

"Puke?"

"No, he didn't puke. He followed her to the restaurant."

Looking back at Frank, C.J. wondered if he should just get rid of the kid and rename the show the *Fantastic Feagley Four Fun-Time Hour*, but he decided against it. Stupidity was not a valid reason to fire someone, and, besides, he wasn't that kind of person.

"Ignoring the pit in his stomach," C.J. continued, "Dan rushed toward the Automat. When he reached the entrance, he stopped. Looking through the glass doors, he scanned the room until he saw the girl walk past a cashier booth. Although he feared talking with her, he gritted his teeth, and entered the restaurant."

"I think he should have puked. It would have been more dramatic."

"What is it with you and regurgitating?"

"Hey, dude, you ever seen *The Exorcist?* That chick could seriously barf," Frank said, clearly in awe of her talent. "Now, that's drama. And I should know. I've been acting for three months."

Augers pressed a button on his phone and picked up the receiver. "Hello, Jan," he said, rubbing his forehead. "Can you bring me a glass of water and an aspirin? Thanks."

"You should visit my uncle. He's a pharmacist. He has the perfect remedy."

"What's that?" said C.J., almost afraid to ask.

"Johnny Walker Black."

The office door opened. Jan, a middle-aged woman with long brown hair and a short, tight skirt, entered holding a cup and a white pill. She handed the tablet to Augers, who put it in his mouth. He drank some water.

"I'll let you know when your wife arrives," she said.

"Thanks, Jan."

"So, if he didn't hurl, what did he do?" inquired Frank.

C.J. wished he'd never started the story. But now, he'd have to finish it.

Gathering his wits, he said, "Dan made his way through the noisy dining room, past chattering customers, and those deciding what to eat until he stood in front of the great food wall. The steel and marble compartments were organized under different types of food: pies, cakes, sandwiches, hot dishes. You name it, and they had it.

"Dan took a deep breath. His hands trembled. Just thinking about talking with the green-aproned girl almost made him give up. But he focused. He didn't want to feel small and ashamed again. Dr. Greenwood said he only had to say hello. That's it. Nothing more."

"Why doesn't he just say: Hey, babe, what's shakin'?"

"Is that what you'd say?" snapped C.J.

"Hell, no. I'd be too scared. That's why I came to see you."

"Why do you think I'm wasting my time telling you this story?"

"I thought you were having a senior thing."

Augers frowned. He'd had enough. "Okay, that's it. I tried. I can't do any more to help you. You'll have to figure it out yourself."

Feagley appeared hurt. "You mean, I'm not gonna find out what happened to Dan?"

"Afraid not," said C.J.

"But what compartment did he pick? Pie or Cake? Personally, I'd pick cake 'cause pie is too messy. You ever get pie on your face, dude, especially if you're in a pie-eating contest? Sometimes it gets in your nose, and you don't want to be using your finger to—"

"I get it," said C.J., cutting him off. The kid was an idiot. He was never going to get rid of him.

"Well, what did he choose?"

"He didn't choose either one," he said, wondering why he'd decided to answer. "Dan started with sandwiches."

"This guy is so not cool."

"He picked them because they were on the far right of the wall, and he could move toward the middle to find her. Any other questions?"

Frank shook his head.

"Good. Dan reached into his pocket and pulled out some change. After plopping a nickel into the coin slot, he turned the knob and opened the first compartment. Peering past the cinnamon-fresh apple pie, he eyed the busy kitchen area. Other women wearing similar cream-colored short-sleeve dresses and green aprons scurried about, loading the machines that filled the empty compartments with food. When he didn't see her, Dan shut the cubbyhole, moved over a column, and tried again."

"When does he meet the girl?" said Frank impatiently.

Augers ignored him. "He tried five more times until he had only two nickels left. When he slid the first coin into the slot, his gut knotted. Turning the knob, he lifted the hinged window, revealing a slice of German chocolate cake—and the girl.

"She took away his breath.

"She was prettier than he'd imagined. He gawked, unable to speak. She looked at him with movie-star brown eyes and a smile that could light up Broadway. Her perfume smelled like spring in Central Park. He stood spellbound until she said:

"'Hi, did you want your cake?'

"Dan was so panicked, his heart beating faster than a hummingbird, he slammed the hinged glass door shut."

"That's pathetic, dude."

"You could do better?"

"I'm cooler than he is," said Frank, fidgeting in his chair.

"That remains to be seen."

"Okay, man, don't have a cow. Just continue."

"Alright," said C.J., clearing his voice. "Dan immediately regretted his decision. He stood in front of the food grid feeling dejected, ashamed of himself for having failed once again. All he'd wanted to do was say hello to the girl and couldn't even do that.

"And then, out of the blue, he did something surprising, even to him. He forced his hand inside his pant pocket, pulled out his last nickel, and placed it into the coin slot. When he turned the knob and opened the door, she was still there.

"'Yes?' she asked.

"At first, he didn't respond. He just stared at the striking young girl with auburn hair standing at the other end of the cubbyhole. He tensed, wanting to talk, his mouth dryer than the Sahara, before blurting out, 'The cake,' and he slammed the hinged door shut again."

Frank looked surprised. "No way."

"Dan stood stunned. A wide smile spread across his face. He'd talked to the girl. Actually talked to her and wasn't frightened at all. He was more shocked than anyone."

"How come he could talk with her?" asked Frank.

"Now, that's a good question. The only reason he could think of was that when he spoke through the glass compartment, it protected him from talking with the girl directly. You know, it hid him, like wearing his Doggy Dan costume."

"Is this legit?"

"There's no other explanation for it."

"This dude is fucked up."

Augers adjusted his glasses. "That may be true, but it worked. So, for the next two weeks, Dan made his way from the DuMont Studios at the Wanamaker Department Store Annex to 743 Broadway for the sole purpose of saying hello to the attractive girl who worked at the Automat.

"One day, after opening up a sandwich compartment, he spied the girl and said:

"'Hello.'

"She saw him, smiled back, and said, 'No cake today? Felt like a sandwich, huh?'

"Her comment surprised Dan. He hadn't expected an actual conversation. He tried not to panic, not that it mattered. His feet were planted to the marble floor like a petrified tree."

Frank listened intently.

"When he didn't answer, the girl said:

"'That's turkey and Swiss. Did you want something else?'

"Dan gazed into her alluring brown eyes and thought he'd drown. Then shook his head and said:

"'No.'

"'You come here a lot,' she added. 'I like how you say hello to me every day. It's sweet. Nobody else does that.'

"Dan tensed, fighting off hyperventilation. His brain searched for words he couldn't locate."

"Did he puke?"

"No, he didn't puke," said C.J., exasperated. "He said, hello."

"Hello, again? What a dope."

"Surprisingly, she liked it:

"'What's your name?' she asked.

"Dan hemmed-and-hawed, shuffling his feet before spouting out:

"'Curtis.'

"She gave him a coquettish smile. 'That's a nice name, Curtis. I'm April.'

"Her amiability helped Dan relax. 'What's your last name?' he asked.

"April tilted her head. 'Guess you'll have to say hello again another day to find out.'

"Her response confused him, and he wondered if he'd said something wrong.

"April smiled. 'You have a hard time talking with girls, don't you?'

"The blood drained from Dan's face. He was mortified. But April must have sympathized with him because of what she said next."

"That she wanted to jump his bones?" said Frank.

C.J. gritted his teeth and balled his fists as if to smack the kid.

The phone buzzed, and he snatched the receiver. "Hello!" he barked. "Oh, Sorry, Jan," C.J. said apologetically. "It's been a tough morning." He glared at Frank. "She's at the gate? Okay, I'll wrap it up."

He hung up the handset and addressed Feagley. "My wife's here. We'll have to continue this later."

"But what did April say?"

Augers debated whether to finish. After reminding himself he'd started the story for reasons he could barely remember now, C.J. sighed, checked his watch, and decided he could wrap it up if this idiot didn't interrupt him anymore.

"Okay," he said. "We have ten minutes. What April said was: 'I have a hard time talking to guys, too.'

"Her comment surprised Dan, who thought she was too beautiful to have that problem. Then he wondered whether she'd only said it to make him feel better. So, he asked:

"'Well, how come you're talking with me?'

"'Because,' she said, 'I only talk with guys I like.'"

"Then she jumped his bones?" said Frank hopefully.

"No!" bellowed C.J. "Nobody jumped anybody's bones. Okay?"

"Geeze, dude. You don't have to yell."

"Do you know what their conversation means? It means they were friends. They could talk to each other. Understand?"

"Hey, I'm not stupid."

Augers didn't press the point.

"So," he continued, "over the next few weeks, Dan would visit April at the Automat and talk with her through the glass compartment. Their conversations were short, about the amount of time she could converse without getting into trouble at work. And they chatted about everything.

"He told her about growing up in Michigan after his mom died, being Doggy Dan on TV, which allowed him to act, and how he played with puppets as a child to escape his overbearing aunt.

"She told him about growing up in Greenwich Village with her parents and three brothers, her dream of attending fashion school, and how she liked to walk through the Museum of Modern Art and look at the paintings.

Frank scrunched his face. "P.U."

Augers ignored him. "She especially liked Magritte's *The False Mirror*, which she found surreal and appealing."

"Chicks, huh?" said Frank, shaking his head.

C.J. prayed he could get to the end of the story. "One day, while the two were talking, April told Dan, 'I have something to tell you, and I don't want you to get upset. After today they're moving me to the steam table in the dining room to work.'

"Dan felt his heart sink. What would happen to him? He really liked April, but they'd probably never talk again.

"April tried to reassure him things would be okay. 'It won't be so bad,' she said.

"'Easy for you to say,' he replied. 'You don't have my problem.'

"She gave him an encouraging wink. 'Why don't you come by tomorrow and see. We'll figure out a way to talk.'"

"I bet he didn't even show up," said Frank.

"Oh, he showed up all right, but not as you'd think."

"What'd he do? Get hammered? Like Steely Dan says, use the Cuervo Gold and fine Columbian." Frank pointed his index finger at C.J. "Now, that's how you seduce a hot babe, dude."

C.J. dropped his head. The kid was hopeless.

"Are you okay, Mr. Augers?" asked Frank, appearing concerned. "You seem upset."

"We're going to finish now," cut in C.J. "That is if I'm not interrupted anymore and go crazy."

Frank stared at him like he was already insane.

C.J. didn't care. He was determined to finish the story. "That night," he said, "Dan tossed and turned, agonizing about talking with April near the steam table without panicking. It wasn't until the following day, after getting dressed as Doggy Dan during rehearsal, that he had an idea.

"Dan figured if he showed up at the Automat dressed in character and explained to April that they needed him back in wardrobe after lunch, he could easily justify wearing the outfit.

"But the idea saddened him. How could he lie to April? He'd never lied to her before. His self-inflicted dilemma made him call Doctor Greenwood. But unfortunately, she was out of town at a conference, and Dan couldn't bear to make an appointment with the doctor covering her practice who didn't know him."

Frank leaned forward to interject, but Augers zinged him a death glare. Feagley sank slowly into his seat.

"When Dan arrived at the TV studio, he was still undecided about what to do. But as the morning ticked away, he became more distracted—missed marks, botched lines, and general irritability. He could barely pay attention and struggled to listen while the Great Catsby told him about losing six hundred 'smackers' on some nag at Saratoga or when Peachy Poodle revealed she wanted to join a nudist colony to save money on new clothes.

"All Dan could think about was meeting face-to-face with April in the crowded Automat dining room, not wearing his costume, no cubbyhole to protect him, unable to speak while everyone watched, staring as if he were naked."

Parched, Augers took a sip of water from the cup on his desk.

The kid yawned and slumped further into his seat.

"So," said C.J. loud enough to wake him.

Frank sprang to attention. "I hear yuh," he said, blinking his eyes rapidly.

"Dan was a mess by the time rehearsal broke for lunch. His tortured mind swirled. There was no way he could meet April without his costume. He'd freeze up. She wouldn't like him and would laugh. He dreaded the worst. When he stumbled out of the studio, wearing his Doggy Dan costume, he took the lift to the ground floor, where he exited on 8th and Broadway.

"As he made his way to the Automat, he failed to notice a group of people in front of the Wanamaker Department Store Annex who were waiting to watch a live broadcast of *Captain Video and his Space Rangers* in Studio C. The crowd immediately spotted him:

"'Where you going, Doggy Dan?' yelled out a greasy-haired teen. "Looking for a hydrant?'

"The group laughed. But Dan paid no attention. His mind still reeled about what he'd say to April."

"Why would he need a fire hydrant if he's a dude?" asked Frank.

"I'm not even going to answer that," said C.J., disgusted.

Frank looked hurt.

"Because he was dressed like a dog. Get it?"

"Got it, bro," said Frank, giving him the thumbs up.

Augers exhaled. "I'm going to finish now. Is that alright with you?"

"Whatever, dude. It's your story."

"Rushing into the intersection, Dan bolted into traffic, causing cars and taxis to screech to a halt. He wasn't alone. A whole group of people who'd waited in line for Captain Video to broadcast was now following him.

"The greasy-haired teen led. Accompanying him was some guy dressed like Captain Video, who wore an Army Surplus uniform and black leather combat boots and lugged a space gun made out of a Mopar muffler. The crowd laughed and taunted Dan. When they reached Astor Plaza on the other side of the street, the growing mob walked behind Dan straight into the Automat."

"Whoa!" said Frank.

"Dan's heart raced as he rushed across the marble floor toward the steam table.

"'It's Doggy Dan,' screamed a kid, jumping up and down. 'He's here. Doggy Dan is here.'

"Customers pivoted toward him. Youngsters danced around like he was the Pied Piper."

Frank's eyes grew wider.

"But Dan paid no attention. He was only worried about April and what he'd say to her. He tried not to panic, but fear seized him anyway.

"When he reached the edge of the busy steam table teeming with customers, April was preoccupied, ladling soup.

"'Hey, get in line, clown,' yelled a man.

"'Yeah, no cuts, Doggy Dan,' laughed the greasy-haired teen.

"April looked up and spied Dan. Their eyes met, and his heart melted. He stood transfixed, basking in the warm radiance of her smile.

"'Doggy Dan's in love,' whooped the teen.

"Laughter filled the cafeteria. The guy dressed as Captain Video pushed him forward with his space gun and barked like a drill sergeant.

"'Go on. Talk with her.'

"Snapped out of his trance, Dan scanned the room. Then, for the first time, he became aware of the large crowd around him. There were people—maybe even a hundred—laughing, teasing, and screaming at him to do something. It was his worst fear come true.

"He tried to talk, but his throat tightened. He couldn't breathe. Sweat beaded under the rim of his hat. When he felt faint, a delicate hand touched his arm.

"'Curtis,' said April, looking into his eyes. 'Curtis, it's me, April.'

"He gulped air.

"'It's all right,' she said. 'Take a breath.'

"Dan gulped down more air.

"'Let me loosen your collar,' she said. Gently reaching up, April untied the red bandana from his neck. She stroked his upper arm, which calmed him down. 'Feeling better?' she asked.

"Dan shook his head."

"Wow," Frank enthused. "It's working. What happened next?"

"April took the bandana," and said, 'Let's clean you up a bit.' Using the colorful kerchief, she wiped some sweat from his brow, and greasepaint came with it. 'You know, Curtis,' she added. 'I'm very flattered you came to talk with me today. I've never seen you in your costume before.'

"She gently rubbed away more of the theatrical makeup around his eyes. 'I really like your outfit, but it must be hot underneath that hat and ears. Let me take them off for you. Is that okay?'

"'Okay,' he murmured, stiff-necked.

"She reached up and pulled off his hat and ears, dropping them to the floor. 'That looks better,' she said.

"'It does?' he asked nervously.

"'Of course it does. You know, I realize you're working this afternoon and have to be in costume, but I like the face I see in the cubbyhole every day. You're a handsome guy!'

"Dan shook his head. 'No, I'm not.'

"Taking the bandana, she rubbed more makeup away from his nose and cheeks. 'You underestimate yourself. Here, I'll show you.' Reaching into her apron pocket, April pulled out a small, round compact. Opening the mirror, she showed Dan his face. 'See, you don't need a mask to speak with me.'

"He shook his head. 'Yes, I do. I won't be able to talk without it.'

"April smiled. 'You're doing just fine. You don't need to be nervous.' She dropped the compact back into her apron pocket. 'Here, let me clean around your chin.'

"His eyes watered up. 'You'll still like me?' Dan choked out.

"'I've always liked you,'

"A tear streaked down his cheek:

"'I think I....'

"The greasy-haired teen yelled, "Oh, c'mon, just kiss her already.'"

"Yeah, dude!" said Frank.

The fact that the kid was listening pleased C.J. A hint of a smile appeared on his face. "When April wiped away his tears, Dan struggled to talk, emotion bubbling around words he wanted to use until he choked out, 'I—.'

"April put her finger on his mouth and whispered, 'I love you, too,'

"He leaned in, meeting her welcoming lips for a kiss that was soft and sweet and lingered a little too long. Taking her in his arms, he pulled her closer, kissing her over and over, as she put her arms around his neck and held him tight."

Frank gaped, unable to speak.

The phone buzzed. Augers picked up the receiver, listened. "Thanks, Jan. Send her in."

The door swung open, and an attractive older woman with shoulder-length, graying auburn hair walked in wearing a navy-blue designer pantsuit. Her irrepressible smile lit up the room.

C.J. stood up to greet his wife.

"Hello, Curtis," said the older woman.

"Who's Curtis?" said Frank.

"Hello, dear," said C.J., pecking her on the cheek. "I'd like you to meet somebody." He pointed to Feagley. "This is Frank. One of the stars of my show."

"Nice to meet you, Frank. I'm April."

Feagley laughed. "Wow! What a coincidence. Your husband just told me a story about some chick named April."

Augers tisked. "This is her."

Frank appeared dumbfounded until the reality dawned on him. Then, a grin broke across his face. "Get outta town. You two?"

"Yes, dear," said April. "It was true love."

C.J. added, "And thirty years of therapy on my part."

"Oh, Curtis," she said, smirking. She glanced at Frank. "He understood me, and I understood him. We helped each other to be confident."

The door creaked open, and a pretty girl in her early twenties, tall and slender, wearing tight pants, black and white converse tennis shoes, and a Craft Services shirt, knocked on the door. She held a manila envelope in her hand. "Hello," she said.

"Can I help you?" inquired C.J.

"I'm Misty in Craft Services. They asked me to bring you these receipts."

"Ah, Misty." He glanced at Feagley. The kid's face was white. "Just put them on my desk."

Misty strolled into the room, placed the envelope on the desk. She noticed Frank, who appeared to be staring. "Hi, Frank. I didn't see you on set this morning."

Frank lowered his gaze. He didn't answer.

"Do you have anything to say, Frank?" asked C.J.

Raising his head, Frank helplessly looked at him.

"You really don't need to leave the show, Frank. You can do this."

Frank sighed, rubbed the back of his neck, and eyed Misty. He paused before he said in a bashful voice, "Hello."

CHAPTER TWELVE

CUPID-1637, PART FOUR

JUNE 2063
PARADISE CITY, HEAVEN

After reading the last violation, Pixel closed the red folder. His concerns over the upcoming hearing were making his head throb.

Dean, clearly bored, wandered around the room, studying the walls. "Hey, man, where's the thermostat in here? I can't find it."

"There is none," said Pixel. "All these buildings are naturally cooled at seventy-two degrees. You can't change it."

His client drew some Tic-tac-toe lines on the whiteboard attached to the wall and marked an X in the center box. He silently chuckled.

"Would you sit down, please," Pixel said sharply. "We have to finish up here and don't have much time left."

The bored Cupid's assistant took a few steps, plopped down in his chair, and spun the seat around until it stopped in front of Pixel. "So, what about these last cases? I thought they were better for me."

Pixel wasn't sure how to respond. Cupid-1637 was correct. The last few cases did seem stronger for him, especially the one involving Gilby Ford and The Dating Bureau, and the last incident concerning Frank Feagley; he had certainly lived happily-ever-after.

In both cases, the infractions seemed minor, and could easily be defended. Once again, Pixel questioned why the panel had included them.

For instance, the alleged violation claiming failure to respect authority in the Dating Bureau case appeared overly broad and ambiguous. The Cupid's Oath stated that a Cupid or Cupid's assistant "respect myself and authority." But whose authority did they mean? Was Dean supposed to have respected Earthly societal laws, which had no jurisdiction over him, or his own departmental supervisor, meaning Cupid?

And to complicate matters, the Oath failed to define any words in the document or convey any intention behind the clause in dispute.

Since courts didn't exist in heaven, there wasn't any case law he could rely on—the presumption being that if you'd already made it up to Paradise City, there wasn't any need for one. That's why the powers in charge created the hearing panels. To provide three unbiased opinions based on the evidence before rendering a decision. They would be open and interested in the type of arguments he was making.

But would they be unbiased?

Pixel rubbed his eyes, tired of his own endless questioning.

Prejudice wasn't even an issue. A pool of unbiased, fully vetted, designated angels already existed to handle the administrative hearing matters. Unless, of course, a panel of departmental supervisors superseded them. But he'd never seen that happen before.

Concerned, he wondered who was on the panel today.

"Hey, Pops," said Dean, "I'm gonna get some water." He leaned forward and stood up, rattling the quiver hanging over the chair.

"Do you even know where the water cooler is?" Pixel asked.

"I've been around a long time. I think I can figure it out."

"It's in the kitchenette. Ask my assistant Peg."

"Back in a few, Pops!"

When Dean left the room, Pixel continued to ruminate about the two cases. He figured the best defense was to argue the ambiguity surrounding the word authority and then claim his client did "help people at all times."

For example, in the Five-Cent Romance case, Frank Feagley finally talked with the girl he loved even if he drove C.J. Augers crazy in reaching that milestone. And as for Gilby Ford and Lavina Zimberg, Dean successfully matched them. They just had to leave Earth to be together in departing "a free and democratic society."

Pixel smirked. A free and democratic society. That last comment was sure to get a laugh from the panel. It never hurt to add a little levity to lighten the mood in the hearings.

But then he thought about the theater case, and his smug smile disappeared. The death of Leonard Brown had created a serious problem for the defense. One big enough to get Cupid-1637 flushed before all the other cases in the file were heard.

Had Cupid-1637 caused Leonard Brown to die in order for him to rejoin his deceased wife and daughter?

Pixel knew he'd have difficulty in claiming Dean's acts weren't intentional unless the old man's death was a suicide or of natural causes. Unfortunately, there wasn't a death certificate or an autopsy report in the file to indicate how Leonard Brown died. How could he prove Dean's innocence if no available evidence existed? It would be his client's word against a presumption he'd had a hand in the death. And to add insult to injury, Pixel had to face the hard fact that with Dean's morally questionable life on Earth, along with his poor Cupid's assistant's record, he wouldn't impress anyone as being a credible witness on his own behalf.

And then a dark thought occurred to Pixel.

Was this why there were so many violations in the file? To conceal a devastating issue like this, with little or no time to investigate, hoping that he and his client would be surprised or unprepared at the hearing to defend the case.

He prayed that wasn't true.

The door burst open, and Cupid-1637 swaggered back into the room. "Miss me?" he said, chewing gum. "Hey, I just saw that Carrie dame again in the office. Man, she's a real looker. I'm telling you, you ought to—"

Pixel glared at Dean, and he shut up. He wished his client would stop trying to match him up with Carrie as if they were one of his Cupid assignments on Earth. A more critical issue existed.

"Why the long face?" Dean asked.

"Sit down. I want to ask you something."

Cupid-1637 gingerly took his seat.

"This is important, Dean, so I want you to tell me the truth."

His eyes widened, and he clasped his hands together tightly.

"Okay," he said.

"Did you—" Pixel cleared his throat. "—Did you have anything to do with Leonard Brown's death?"

"What?" protested the romance agent. "Of course not. How can you ask such a thing? I may have been a two-bit thief on Earth, but I would never have killed anybody."

"Then how did he die?

"I don't know. Maybe it's 'cuz he hit his head or had a heart attack or something. It just happened. One second he was standing there, and then the next, he dropped to the floor." Dean suddenly sprang from his seat. He paced, waving his arms as he talked, "Me a murderer? God! I don't believe this!" Not once did he look upward and apologize to the Big Guy for saying his name in vain.

Pixel's chest tightened, and he rubbed it. Asking the question made him feel guilty. He didn't think Dean had anything to do with Leonard Brown's passing, but explain that to the panel.

Cupid-1637 leaned on the table and glared at Pixel. "What happens if they think I killed the old guy?"

"You know what happens."

"But I didn't do anything," he maintained. "I actually helped him reunite with his wife and kept him from marrying that greedy—"

Pixel interrupted. "I told you before. My file is limited. There is nothing to indicate how he died."

"Don't they keep records of these things somewhere? What kind of place is this?"

"Look, there have been one-hundred-billion people who've ever lived on Earth. So how are we going to find the death record of one guy named Leonard Brown from Los Angeles in—" Pixel looked at his watch "—the next forty-five minutes?"

There was a knock on the door. Pixel and Dean both pivoted toward the sound.

"Come in," shouted Pixel.

The door swung open, and in walked angel-in-training Judson Femur. The wide-eyed eighteen-year-old beamed. "Hi, Mr. Millet. Peg asked me to remind you about the hearing at four."

"We know," Pixel said.

Femur nodded. "Okey-dokey then. Guess I'll be going."

Maybe Judson could help.

Pixel called out to the kid before he reached the door. "Hey, do you know where the Hall of Souls is?"

Judson whirled toward Pixel. "Sure," he said. "Everybody up here knows that."

"Are you any good at doing research?"

"Well, before I died, I used to collect comic books, and then I collected *Yu-Gi-Oh* cards. But I didn't like those, so I started collecting *Beast Wars*, my favorite action figures from the *Transformers* series. But then my younger brother put them in a toilet and blew them up with a cherry bomb, so I started to collect coins. Then typewriters." Judson stroked his chin. "Or maybe it was *Hot Wheels* first, then stamps, and then typewriters. No, no. *Saved by the Bell* cards, old software manuals, and then rocks."

Pixel narrowed his eyes. "Can you?"

"Can I what?" asked Judson.

"Do some research," Pixel barked.

"Sure."

"Okay, this is important. Real important." He pointed to Dean. "This man's existence depends on it. I need you to visit the Hall of Souls right now and obtain the death summary for Leonard Brown, who died in Los Angeles during September 2006. He

285

owned a silent movie theater. That's all the information we have. We need to know how he died. Can you do that?"

"Yes."

"Do you own a cell?

"I've got a brand-new Papal iPhone."

"Good. Bring it. We need the information before the hearing starts! Call me if you find something."

"You got it, Mr. Millet," the kid said excitedly. "If I can find a mint copy of Dr. Strange in *Strange Tales*, number one twenty-six in an old trunk, and a Silver Age *Superman* comic, number two fifty-three at the Dinkytown International Comicpalooza, I can find anything."

As Femur left, Pixel frowned. He hoped the kid was trustworthy. Could he bring home the bacon?

And the clock was ticking.

CHAPTER THIRTEEN

THE HEARING

JUNE 2063
PARADISE CITY, HEAVEN

As Pixel walked down the concrete steps in front of the office building carrying the red file under his left arm, and with Cupid-1637 beside him, he noticed that the sky seemed darker than usual: a gray, dreary cloud cover that mirrored his current emotions. It seemed peculiar, especially since the Paradise City Maintenance Department hadn't programmed an overcast day to remind people what lousy weather was like on Earth. Although he wasn't a superstitious person, the bleak sky seemed like a bad omen, one which Pixel hoped wasn't related to the outcome of the upcoming hearing.

"Where to, Pops?"

Pixel pointed to a gigantic skyscraper in a business district on a hill behind a low-rise office block across the plaza. "You see that tall building with Roman pillars on the side and the winged angels blowing the elongated trumpets on top?"

"Yeah."

"The hearing is there."

"It looks like the Octavius Tower at Caesar's Palace in Las Vegas," Cupid-1637 said.

Stepping onto the flagstone walkway by the Paradise City Plaza, Pixel didn't argue the point. His client was right. The building looked garish.

"So, do they have a casino in there?" Dean asked.

Pixel tried to refocus Dean's attention instead. "Let's talk about our plan today."

"To beat the rap, right?"

"Well, it's more complicated than that." He looked at the agent of love and his messy pompadour hairdo. "Yes, our main goal is to keep you from being flushed, but our secondary goal—and this is important—is to get you transferred to another department as a lesser punishment in case you aren't allowed to remain a Cupid's assistant. So, we need to do everything possible to keep you up here."

Pixel smiled at Dean to reassure him, but it was more for himself. He just hoped his growing doubts about the hearing today weren't true.

Dean nodded. "How're you gonna keep me from getting flushed?"

They walked past the cascading, elaborate replica of the Trevi Fountain in the middle of the plaza, which Walt Disney had built once he'd arrived in heaven. Animatronic Mickey and Goofy statues, wearing floaties and inflatable wings, waved and hung ten while standing on a teetering, red-striped surfboard at the center of the ornate structure. Minnie appeared as a mermaid.

It was a Paradise City landmark. The city managers didn't like it, but kids and thirsty dogs did, so it stayed.

"Unless we have evidence," said Pixel over the sound of children laughing in the park, "we'll save the Brown case for last. Otherwise, we'll claim that they failed to train you properly as a Cupid upon your arrival, and that there were no orientation classes, no departmental employment manuals, and no continuing education courses to teach you properly."

Pixel gestured with his right hand. "Negligent supervision, if you will."

"Got-cha."

"We can also state that management failed to acknowledge and treat your unresolved emotional issues as a result of your death. Like wishing you could have properly said goodbye to your girlfriend before you died, and projecting your parental needs on others because you couldn't raise kids." Pixel pursed his lips. "It'll be tough, but that should cover the first five cases in the file. We'll deal with any out-of-pocket damages later. Maybe you can perform community services for a few hundred years."

"I don't want you mentioning stuff about Sue Woods and my longing to have kids. It's personal."

"You wanna get saved?"

"Yes."

"Then we have to mention it. We have no choice."

"Well, I don't like it, okay." He paused. "What about the other three cases?"

Pixel eyed Dean as they moved forward. "We'll claim that the Cupid Oath section is too broad and ambiguous. And that even without proper training, you did help the people you were assigned. We can say this about all the cases in the file. That leaves the Brown incident, and we all know what the problem is there."

When Pixel and Cupid-1637 reached the massive concrete staircase, they trudged up what seemed like never ending steps to the central business district.

After reaching the top, Pixel stared ahead at the garish "hearing" building. The structure towered over everything else. Besides being the oldest high-rise on the block, the builders had constructed it with the finest travertine, tuff, concrete, rebar, bricks, mortar, stone, and marble that could be obtained. And to attract attention, not that the building needed it, red neon signage at the upper part of the skyscraper spelled out:

GENESIS DEVELOPMENT CORPORATION
A 7-DAY ASSET MANAGEMENT COMPANY

Cupid-1637 pointed upward. "What's with the sign?"

"That's where the Big Guy runs his business," said Pixel.

"You mean he has an office?"

"Technically, the penthouse. But he hasn't been seen for a few thousand years."

His client shook his head. "I told you nobody up here listens."

As they approached their destination, Pixel and Dean weaved through the crowded sidewalk teeming with angels or angels-in-training on their way to meetings, the plaza, or parts unknown. All around them were businesses like the Last Supper Buffeteria, Mercury's Sandal Shoppe, Wingspan (the place to repair your molted wings), and Starbucks—which, to the surprise of no one, were everywhere. People in heaven loved their coffee.

Pixel's cell phone buzzed when they arrived at the gleaming glass revolving-door entrance to their destination.

He reached into his pocket and lifted the device near his ear. He struggled to hear the caller over the screeching traffic, honking horns, hammering jackhammers, and wailing sirens that the Paradise City managers had broadcast through nearby streetlight speakers to duplicate city sounds. Just another nostalgic touch to remind people of having lived on Earth.

"Hi Judson," said Pixel, listening carefully into his phone. "Is that you? What'd you find?"

"They don't have the records, Mr. Millet," said Judson's muffled voice. "I searched and searched, and the librarian said they're listed, but the documents are missing, and no one's signed them out."

"Crap!" He furrowed his brow. "Maybe they misplaced them. Keep looking."

"Okey-dokey," said Judson. "But if they don't have them, I have an idea."

"Do what you have to do. I'll be in the eighth-floor hearing room if you need me." He ended the call.

Dean leaned in. "Bad news?"

"They can't locate the records for Leonard Brown."

Cupid-1637 touched the back of his neck. The arrows in his quiver clattered. "I'm worried."

Pixel could see the color from Cupid-1637's face fading.

He put his hand on Dean's shoulder, which felt tense. "Don't give up hope. There's still time for Judson to find them."

Comforting his client was part of the job, but his words seemed hollow. Pixel knew it would be almost impossible to find the evidence they needed just minutes before a scheduled hearing.

But then he contemplated the issue. How could those documents have disappeared? Sure, it seemed possible due to the volume of records the Hall of Souls handled, but something wasn't right. How convenient that the information he needed today had reportedly disappeared.

Pixel rubbed his tightening chest. Could it be that someone had intentionally taken the information from Leonard Brown's file to prevent him from finding it? The thought was absurd. It was heaven, for god's sake. Who would do anything illegal up here? Yet his deep-seated faith failed to reassure him this time, and he continued to brood.

"Everything okay?" Dean asked.

"Yeah," Pixel said, gesturing to the building. "We should head up to the hearing room."

☙

After walking through the slow-spinning revolving door, Pixel and Cupid-1637 entered the building lobby and crossed the beige marble floor. Ahead of them, an original Michelangelo fresco depicting the creation of the Genesis Development Corporation covered the entire back wall near ten elevator bays. The painting showed angels hovering over a giant hand that held enormous scissors, cutting a ribbon surrounding an unnamed universe. In the left upper corner, the lettering spelled out GREAT HOMES. In the right upper corner, more lettering said GREAT PLANETS. And across the bottom in gold letters, spanning the length of the picture, it proclaimed A GREAT PLACE TO RAISE YOUR FAMILY.

His client eyed the painting. "Nice picture. What's it called?"

"*Another One Built Every Seven Days.*"

Dean shook his head. "Hey, man, seven days is too quick. I bet the craftsmanship is shoddy."

"You got that right." Pixel pressed the elevator button. His existential dread continued to weigh him down.

While he waited, his worries about the hearing mounted, and he lowered his gaze. The case was already hard enough to win, so why did it seem like someone had purposely planned for him to lose? He didn't like this feeling at all.

When the lift opened, the two stepped into the wood-paneled and carpeted elevator car. He touched the control button while Dean leaned against the handrail, appearing pensive. After the door closed, the elevator accelerated upward. Neither one spoke. They both knew the precarious stage the day had entered. Instead, each stared at the numbers lighting up above the door as they approached the eighth floor.

After the elevator door opened, Pixel stepped onto the green and black marbled lobby. His client followed.

The long and wide hallway was empty except for a lone maintenance man—an angel-in-training indicated by his tiny wings— who propelled a commercial dust mop across the shiny floor.

Pixel nodded toward the maple-colored double doors across from them. "We go in there."

They crossed the polished surface to the entrance and went in.

Although no courtrooms theoretically existed in heaven, the space still gave one the feeling of a legal proceeding. As you entered by the double doors, a one-row gallery with gravity return seats ranged against the wall for anyone who wished to watch. In front of the rear wall, directly across the room, stood an elevated judge's bench where the three panel members would sit and listen to the case. And in the middle of the floor, facing the bench, was a table where Pixel and Cupid-1637 would sit. There was no jury box.

Pixel had seen the hearing room many times before and wasn't impressed. But Cupid-1637, on the other hand, appeared awed and intimidated.

"This doesn't look anything like the room I was in the first time I had a hearing," said Dean.

"Where was that?" Pixel reached the table in the middle of the room.

"In some office with a big, fat, dopey-looking guy named Biggle and two other angels."

Pixel jerked his head back. Biggle? That was his supervisor.

"What?"

"Yeah, and they took me to this small room, see, in some office building, I don't know. And told me that even though they knew the Krieger tow truck case was an accident and couldn't discipline me about it, they said guys like me didn't belong up here; and that someday, if they ever got the power, they were gonna do something about it."

"Did you report their threat?"

"Who am I going to tell? They were just a bunch of middle-aged winged punks who thought they were tough. I've had school principals more intimidating than them. So, I just blew it off and moved on."

Pixel plopped into the leather chair. A sudden coldness rippled down his spine. Why hadn't Dean had a proper hearing on the Krieger matter, and what had Biggle been doing there? Was his boss part of a plot?

"When does this thing get started?" asked Cupid-1637.

"Any minute."

Behind the elevated desk, an ornate, carved door creaked open.

A comely female exited dressed in a conservative skirt and blouse. She marched over to Pixel in her low-heeled pumps.

The woman didn't smile. "Are you Pixel Millet?" she asked gravely.

"Yes," said Pixel.

"The panel wants you to know they're running fifteen minutes late."

"Thank you."

"You're welcome."

Before she turned, Pixel asked, "Who's on the panel today?"

Once again, without smiling: "Mr. Biggle, Mr. Dankworth, and Mr. Gastrell. Is that all?" she asked brusquely.

"No, that's it."

As the woman strolled back to the door, Pixel lowered his gaze and frowned. Beads of sweat appeared on his brow.

Holy crap! He'd been right. Something *was* up. All the panel members were head supervisors in the Department of Discipline, Mythological Gods Division. This was not good.

Cupid-1637 interrupted him. "I don't think she's your type. That Carrie chick was more your style."

"What are you talking about?" said Pixel, trying to concentrate.

Someone knocked twice from outside. "Mr. Millet," said a voice behind the entrance door.

Pixel whirled around and watched Judson Femur stick his head into the room. "Judson?"

"Hi, Mr. Millet. I just came by—"

"Did you find the records?" he said, raising his eyebrows.

"Well, no, but can you come outside into the hallway? I have to show you something. It's important."

"I don't have time." Pixel waved him away. "We're going to start the hearing in a few minutes.

"Okey-dokey. I'll tell them you'll be right out. His head popped back behind the door; the entry slammed shut.

"Judson? Judson—"

"Hey, Pops, I'll tell 'em you just stepped out for a few minutes."

Lurching out of the chair, Pixel shook his head and muttered as he marched to the door and exited the room.

☙

Once he stepped outside, Pixel spied Judson with a young family standing near some large floor-to-ceiling tinted windows. The innocent-looking teen motioned him over.

Pixel, head down, his shoes clomping on the shiny floor, reached them within seconds.

He eyed the family—a man in his early twenties, a woman around the same age with light bobbed hair and a radiant smile, and their small blond-haired girl with curls.

"What'd you want, Judson?" he asked.

"As you know," said Judson grinning, "I went to the Hall of Souls just like you asked—"

"I know, I know," said Pixel impatiently. "Then what happened?"

"Well, after I couldn't find the records, the librarian suggested I try Google Hereafter. And sure enough, after sifting through parts of the dark web, it provided me with an address."

"Whose address?"

Judson gestured with his hands toward the family. "Leonard Brown. I told you I could find anyone."

Pixel raised his eyebrows, skeptical that such a young man could be the person he needed. Then he remembered Brown had joined his wife in the silent movie with all those movie stars. He guessed they'd gotten the youth treatment up here when they died. Some people have all the luck.

"You're Leonard Brown?" asked Pixel. "The one who died in the silent movie theater?"

"Yes. And this is my wife, Claire."

"How do you do," she said.

"And I'm Katie," piped up their daughter.

Pixel extended his hand to Brown. "I'm Pixel Millet, a social worker in the Paradise City Department of Discipline."

Leonard Brown warmly grabbed Pixel's hand and shook it. "Glad to meet you."

"I'm advocating for a Cupid's assistant today involved in a romance case that secondarily centers around your death."

After exchanging some additional pleasantries, Pixel finally asked the question he'd wanted to know all afternoon.

"This may sound strange," he said. "But we need to know how you died. We were unable to find your autopsy or death records in the Hall of Souls."

"Oh, sure," said Brown. "I died from an undiagnosed congenital heart defect coupled with pulmonary hypertension."

"I knew you shouldn't have avoided seeing doctors all those years," said Claire, shaking her head.

Brown nodded. "She's right. I wasn't a good patient."

"So, you died of natural causes? My client had nothing to do with your death?"

"I'm just telling you the diagnosis they gave me."

"Who told you?"

"Some famous heart doctor with full wings. Three other angels watched him examine me after I arrived up here."

"Three angels?"

"A heavyset one who chewed Tums all the time and two others. The one with the antacids smelled like peppermint."

Pixel drew his eyebrows together. He opened his mouth to speak but then paused. Were Mr. Biggle and the two other supervisors on the panel present at Leonard Brown's examination? If so, they already knew his cause of death and wanted to flush Dean for another reason. "Do you remember what the angels looked like?"

"Sorry. It's been a long time. I'm not good with faces."

"That's true," said Claire. "He isn't. He can't remember anybody's face except for movie stars."

Leonard Brown shrugged sheepishly.

"Thanks," said Pixel. "You've both been a big help."

"I hope so," said Brown.

The hearing room door slammed open. The sound reverberated throughout the lobby, grabbing everyone's attention.

Cupid-1637 stood in the doorway, cupping his hands around his mouth to be heard. "Hey, Pops, they're getting ready to start."

Turning toward his client, Pixel shouted, "I'll be right there." Then he looked back at Leonard Brown and his family. "We may need to call you as witnesses. Can you stay here with Judson for a while in case you're needed?"

Brown cocked his head toward his wife Claire, who nodded. "I guess so."

Judson beamed. He pounded his fist into his palm. "Wow! I get to work on an actual case."

ॐ

When Pixel reentered the hearing room, the woman wearing the conservative black skirt and white blouse plugged in a red device the size and shape of an old rotary telephone and placed it on top of the elevated bench. There was a large white button in the middle of the dial.

298

After Pixel sat down at his table, Dean leaned over and asked, "Why do they need a phone?"

"In case B.G. calls. You know, the Big Guy," said Pixel, pointing upward.

"Give me a break, man. He hasn't shown up for thousands of years. Who are they kidding?"

"You ever heard of the Jewish holiday, Passover?" asked Pixel.

"Yeah."

"Well, during dinner service, they usually open a door, leave an empty chair and a cup of wine at the table for whenever the prophet Elijah shows up. It's symbolic, just like the phone. Understand?"

"So, we don't get any wine?"

"No."

"Not even Mogen David?"

"No!" snapped Pixel. "This is a hearing, not a wine bar."

"Hey, man, how am I supposed to know? It's not my fault the first disciplinary hearing I had wasn't proper."

Once again, the ornate, carved wooden door creaked open, and three male angels wearing white linen gowns marched in. Their footsteps were the only sounds heard in the quiet room.

Pixel assumed a rigid posture.

Dean slumped in his chair.

As the panel stepped onto the elevated bench, Pixel recognized the first angel as his boss, Mr. Biggle. The plump, nervous-looking man had a thinning hairline and sagging jowls; he held a bottle of chewable fruit-flavored Tums in his left hand.

Pixel then shifted his gaze to the next guy, Mr. Gastrell, who stood six inches taller than Mr. Biggle and moved his lanky frame deliberately. His slicked-back, peppery-colored hair gave off a greasy sheen, while the sneer on his sharp face made him look unpleasant. The image of Lurch from *The Addams Family* popped into Pixel's head.

Taking up the rear, Mr. Dankworth blew his nose into a handkerchief, causing a loud irritating honk. His watery and puffy, red-rimmed eyes, coupled with the weary look on his square face, made it appear as if he'd suffered from allergies a long time. Perhaps even centuries.

The three members of the panel sat down on their leather chairs: Mr. Gastrell in the middle, Mr. Biggle to his left, and Mr. Dankworth on the right. As they settled in, their chairs creaked.

Dean leaned over to Pixel and whispered, "Those were the same guys who were in my first hearing."

Pixel's stomach twinged. He *shushed* his client.

Mr. Gastrell leaned forward, hands laced together, and stared down at Pixel and Cupid-1637 with his piercing dark brown eyes. The silence in the room escalated the tension.

"Do you have something to share?" inquired Gastrell pointedly. "You seem a bit talky."

"My client just wanted to know when we were starting," chimed in Pixel. He'd just lied.

Gastrell glowered. "Indeed."

Biggle nervously popped a green Tums into his mouth.

Rising to his full Lurch-like height, Gastrell addressed the room, his piercing gaze boring into Pixel. "I am Mr. Gastrell," he said. "One of the three panelists in your hearing today. We are a diverse group who have lived in heaven for a long time. As for our backgrounds, I died during the Salem Witch Hunt from natural causes in April 1692 and was the former headmaster at the Second Colonial Church of Salem." He gestured to the left. "Over here is Mr. Biggle. During the 1929 stock market crash, he died when he accidentally fell out of a window while handling a margin call." He nodded to his right. "And this is Mr. Dankworth, who died in 1846 following Henry David Thoreau to Walden Pond, where he immediately perished from allergies." He paused. "To everyone sitting in this room, I hereby declare that the hearing of Cupid-1637 will now begin." He glared at Dean. "Is that all right with you?"

Pixel's client lowered his gaze. "Sure."

Gastrell sat down. "Before we start," he said, "let me point out this is not a legal hearing, nor is it a courtroom. We do not follow the principle of *Stare Decisis* in this jurisdiction," continued Gastrell. "We do not follow the normal court hierarchy because there are no court systems in heaven. The judgment rendered by this panel is binding. No appeals are allowed." Gastrell paused, then pinned Pixel. "I could go on and on. If you believe your client has due process here, he doesn't. The only law that applies in this hearing is how the three panelists interpret Cupid's Oath. No one else's opinion matters. If you think this is the same as on Earth, you are mistaken."

Pixel wondered if this guy thought he was a god.

"Are you ready, Mr. Millet?" asked Gastrell.

"I am."

Dankworth blew his nose and made a rude, loud sound like a wild goose. "Sorry," he said. "Pardon me."

Gastrell's face reddened, and he hesitated. Then, when all was silent, he motioned for Pixel to proceed.

Pixel stood up and faced the panel.

The angels stared back, except for Mr. Biggle, who failed to make direct eye contact and quickly looked away.

Pixel suspected he knew what that meant. His boss, of all people, part of the plan.

"My name is Pixel Millet," he said. "I am the social worker advocate for Cupid-1637. As you know, we are at today's hearing to discuss the various Cupid's Oath violations brought against my client. I should point out that Cupid-1637 was once known as Dean Webster on Earth. With the permission of the panel, I would like to occasionally refer to his Earthly name because it is pertinent to the proceeding."

"So be it," replied Gastrell.

The two other angels nodded in agreement.

Pixel glanced at Dean, who appeared unfazed by the proceeding. Then, after clearing his throat, Pixel said, "Based on the various cases in Dean Webster's disciplinary file, the following is alleged: that he exceeded his Cupid authority and failed to use resources wisely to their greatest ability; failed to use wise judgment; failed to be honest and fair; failed to make the world a better place; failed to bring love, desire, and happiness to everyone; failed to do his best to the gods and people he was helping; failed to respect authority. Further, his actions involved either intentional or negligent wrongdoing; and, at times, caused severe emotional distress to the parties involved."

Gastrell sneered. "Why not just read the entire Cupid's Oath instead? He practically broke every vow in the document. I knew witches who had fewer crimes alleged against them." He smiled as if he'd said something clever.

Mr. Dankworth and Mr. Biggle chuckled.

Pixel stretched his neck. It seemed like someone had turned on the heat.

Regrouping, he forced a smile and addressed the three angels. "I know there are many allegations here. But based on my discussions with the client and the evidence involved, we believe all of the infractions should be mitigated or absolved so that Cupid-1637—" he put his hand on Dean's shoulder "—can be acquitted without blame."

Gastrell rolled his eyes. "What could you possibly say that would convince us?"

"I intend to show the panel that Dean Webster properly handled his Cupid assignments to the best of his ability, and he soundly succeeded in uniting couples on many cases without proper training."

"What do you mean?" asked Gastrell.

"Negligent supervision," said Pixel.

Biggle opened his mouth to speak, apparently decided against it, and chewed another Tums instead.

"Continue," said Gastrell.

"In addition," Pixel said, "I will show that Dean Webster's supervisors failed to acknowledge and treat his unresolved emotional issues as a result of his untimely death in 1938, which has affected his work product."

Gastrell looked bored.

Dankworth dabbed his watery eyes with a tissue.

A feeling of discouragement overwhelmed him. The angels weren't even listening. Why were they so anxious to flush Dean?

"Finally," he said forcefully. "I intend to show that Cupid-1637 had attempted to follow the Cupid's Oath faithfully, but that the wording involved in some sections is too overly broad and ambiguous, making them unenforceable."

"Is that all?" scoffed Gastrell.

"Yes."

Gastrell leaned back in his chair, a thin smile curling his lips.

"Well, gentlemen. I think we've heard enough."

"Definitely," said Biggle, while Dankworth nodded and suppressed a sneeze.

The suddenness of their comments shocked Pixel; his heartbeat doubled. He'd been right all along about this hearing. "You can't do this."

Cupid-1637 jerked toward him, fear in his eyes. "What's happening?"

"We're going to pass sentence now," said Gastrell.

"You haven't let me present my case," Pixel hollered, surprising even himself.

Gastrell bared his teeth; he pointed at Pixel with his finger. "You come over here right now! Approach the bench."

Turning to Cupid-1637, Pixel said, "Don't say anything," then marched over to the panel.

All three angels glared at him, but Gastrell seemed overly incensed. His nostrils flared before he spoke. "What the hell do you think you're doing?" he barked.

Pixel felt his knees weaken but resolved to stay strong. In all his time as a social worker in the Paradise City Department of Discipline, Mythological Gods Division, he'd never been yelled at by one of the panel members on the bench.

"I'm advocating for my client," said Pixel.

"Are you dense?" growled Gastrell.

"No."

"Do you know why we picked you for this proceeding?"

"I haven't a clue."

"Because Biggle said you'd fall in line and give us the result we wanted."

The comment stung Pixel. He frowned, remembering that Dean had called him a shuffler earlier in the day, someone who would do anything to please his bosses. Heat flushed through him. An old feeling returned. Once again, someone had underestimated him, and that made him mad. He narrowed his eyes at Mr. Biggle. "Oh, he did, did he?"

Mr. Biggle talked with his mouth full of antacids. "Tums?" he offered sheepishly, holding up the plastic container."

"Since you don't seem to be too bright," Gastrell said. "Let me explain what's happening here."

"All right," said Pixel, his lips pressed tightly together.

"We're trying to purify heaven."

"What do you mean purify?"

"You know, weed out the undesirables." The peppery-haired leader eyed Cupid-1637. "Some people just don't belong."

"Why? Because his life wasn't so moral on Earth?"

"Need I remind you, Cupid-1637 killed Leonard Brown in his duty as a Cupid's assistant."

"No, he didn't," argued Pixel. He pointed to the entrance door across the room. "I've got Leonard Brown waiting outside in the hallway ready to testify that he died of natural causes, which were no way inflicted by my client."

Gastrell glared at his cohort and growled, "Biggle, I told you to destroy that file."

Biggle's face turned ashen, matching the color of his white gown. "I did."

Gastrell, seething, squinted at Pixel. He took a deep breath, leaned back, and steepled his fingers. "No matter," he said, trying to control his ire. "We can find another reason. That's how we handled some of the witches in my time."

"Is Dean your first victim?" said Pixel. "Is this how you flush people from heaven you don't like?"

"In case you haven't noticed," said Gastrell. "There's a power vacuum up here. And I'm going to fill it. We haven't seen leadership for thousands of years."

"What are you now? A god?"

"Not yet! But it has to start with someone."

Gastrell's statement frightened Pixel to his core. He took a step back, unable to speak.

"Now, turn around, go back to your table, and let's finish this thing," ordered Gastrell. "Or I'll flush you, too."

Turning, Pixel took a step back toward the table before noticing Carrie Lansdale, the new, good-looking transfer he'd met earlier in the day, entering the gallery. She sat down in a gravity return seat, immediately spotted him, and flashed one of her ever-friendly smiles.

Oh, great, he thought. Just in time for her to witness one of the most inglorious and treacherous acts in the annals of heaven, in which, through no fault of his own, he was complicit.

Pixel knew the panel wanted him to agree to flush Dean in order to save himself. That was their intention. They needed him to comply with their immoral deeds to give the impression he'd consented to their plan.

But that wasn't like him at all.

Throughout his life, whether it be in heaven or on Earth, he'd always performed his job to the best of his ability so he could help other people. He may not have been the most dynamic, friendly, or handsome person, but deep down, he'd needed to aid others ever since other kids had bullied him as a child. He'd had no defender. But he'd learned he could defend other victims of bullies. That's the whole reason he'd become a social worker. Why didn't anyone understand that?

If he did what the panel wanted, how could he live with himself? His decision would change the way heaven ran forever. It would hurt not just him but everyone else up here, too. The afterlife wasn't perfect, and he didn't always understand it, but it was designed that way on purpose. He knew people were up here for a reason. And he didn't want to see that destroyed.

When he reached the table, his head was spinning.

Dean leaned over and whispered, "What'd they say?"

Pixel looked into his client's frightened eyes and hesitated before saying, "They want me to flush you."

Cupid-1637 stood up, shoving his chair with such force it tipped over and crashed on the floor. "You can't do this to me," he bellowed. He appeared ready for a fight. "What about my side of the story?"

The door in back of the elevated bench slammed open; two beefy, oversized angels, whose muscles could make Hercules look like a ninety-eight-pound weakling, stepped out into the hearing room, behind Mr. Dankworth, who sneezed. The two angels' stern, unmoving expressions seemed as if they'd been fixed into place by Medusa.

"One more outburst, Mr. Webster," warned Gastrell. "And, I promise you, you won't be around long enough for a second one."

"Who cares. You're going to flush me anyway."

Gastrell glared at Pixel. "Your turn, Mr. Millet. Do you agree with the sentence?"

His heart pounding, he had to do something. Pixel bared his teeth. Then, he grabbed the red violations file and threw it at the cherry-stained bench, surprising the panel.

Gastrell ducked before the folder burst open on impact, littering the floor with paperwork.

"No, I don't!" screamed Pixel. "He doesn't deserve to be flushed."

Gastrell raised his head. "I'm warning you, Millet."

"About what? That you're going to make me disappear, too? Go ahead, flush me. I don't care. Who made you god?"

"I did," smiled Gastrell.

"Well, that pisses me off," complained Pixel. "Who are you to judge? Before we were all angels, we were people. And people aren't perfect, you know. There isn't anyone up here who can say they haven't made mistakes in life or regretted something they'd done that was morally wrong or hurt people intentionally or by accident. I know I can't." He pointed to Gastrell. "And what about you? Are you perfect? What about the innocent women who died because you called them witches to raise church membership?"

Gastrell scowled.

Pixel pointed toward his supervisor. "And you, Biggle. How many poor people did you talk out of their life savings—money they couldn't afford to lose—to invest in the stock market, only to see them go broke when it crashed?"

Biggle, mouth ajar, dropped the Tums container onto the laminated counter. Antacid tablets bounced around like jelly beans.

"And Dankworth," said Pixel, "I don't know what the hell you did, but it was probably bad."

Dankworth lowered his head, clearly ashamed. "I was Henry David Thoreau's groupie."

"I've had enough of this foolishness," snapped Gastrell.

He nodded his sharp chin at the two burly angels, who immediately pounced on both Pixel and his client.

Dean tried to stop them by throwing the first haymaker, but it was like hitting a stone wall, and he doubled over in pain, clutching his hand.

Pixel back-pedaled, trying to finish what he had to say. "Heaven's a mess," he hollered. "But we were placed up here for a reason, and that shouldn't be changed for anyone."

The two angels rushed Pixel. Dean slowed them down by holding onto their legs and was dragged across the floor.

"You know why my client made it up here?" he shouted. "Because he gave his own life saving a kid who tried to hop a freight train. And look at him now. He's even trying to help me. That's his true nature. If you don't deserve to be in heaven for those acts alone, then none of us deserve to be."

One of the muscle-bound angels grabbed Pixel with a vice-like grip. He squeezed Pixel's arms like two oranges until he couldn't handle the pain anymore and screamed. Pixel lashed out with his feet but felt himself being lifted upward, over the angel's head, to be thrown or slammed to the ground at any moment.

His pulse raced. He wondered if he could die a second time. Is this how you got flushed?

And then a booming, short telephone ring reverberated throughout the room, followed by another resonating chime. The overhead lights flashed on and off.

Everyone stopped in place, confused.

Pixel looked down from his precarious position above the angel who had lifted him. He didn't know if he was hallucinating. Had Elijah finally shown up?

Biggle pointed to the flashing red button on the Big Guy's phone, placed on the bench. "The phone. It's—it's blinking."

Gastrell's face turned pale as if a ghost had walked across his chest. "What'll we do?" said Dankworth, wiping his eyes.

"Pick it up," said Biggle, pointing. "You talk to him, Gastrell."

Gastrell wearily reached out to pick up the receiver. The blinking light flashed incessantly on his white gown, making it look as red as the Devil's skin. "Hello," he answered. "Is that you, B.G.?" Gastrell paused. "You want me to turn on the speaker? Okay." He motioned for Dankworth to flick the black switch on the side of the telephone.

"Why are you calling?" asked Gastrell. "You never use this phone."

"What in My Name is going on down there?" snapped the Big Guy with his low, resonating, authoritative voice. "And put that man down. Carefully."

The strong angel gently lowered Pixel to the floor.

Dean, dazed, stared at the ceiling and said, "Oh, my god. They really do listen up here."

"What do you mean, B.G?" said Gastrell. It's a hearing." He pointed to Cupid-1637. "He broke the—"

"What's this Cupid's Code? There was no code when I left thousands of years ago. I'm supposed to know everything up here and I didn't know about this. Who approved it?"

Gastrell pointed to Biggle. "He drafted it. I had nothing to do with it."

Biggle swallowed his Tums without chewing; he made a long and loud mucusy *harrumph* before clearing his throat. "You told me to draft it," he yelled back at Gastrell.

"This Oath makes absolutely no sense," said the Big Guy. "Who in their right mind would submit a document this poorly written?"

"But I cribbed it from the Hippocratic Oath, the Boy Scout Oath, and the Girl Scout Oath," said Biggle. "Three well-known affirmations. And the scouts make good cookies, too."

Gastrell shook his head. "You fool. Are you trying to bury us?"

Dankworth blew his nose and uttered, "As Henry David Thoreau once said, 'It's not what you look at that matters, it's what you see.'"

"Oh, shut up!" complained Gastrell. "What the hell does that even mean?"

"Well, you don't have to be belligerent about it," he said, wiping his nose.

"The only one who knows what's going on around here is that angel-in-training, the social worker," said the Big Guy. "What's your name?"

Pixel's eyes widened. His body felt numb. "Meh—me?"

"Is there any other social worker in this room?"

Carrie Lansdale cautiously raised her hand.

"Not you, lady," said the Supreme Being, sounding annoyed. "What's your name? Is it Pixel?"

"Yes, sir. Pixel Millet."

"Here is the only man who understands heaven. Of course, it's messy. It's messy because people are messy. Love is messy. It wasn't meant to be dictated by this stupid Cupid's Oath. Gastrell, do you know why people are up here?"

"Obviously not," said the peppery-haired man.

"What about you, Biggle?"

Biggle shook his head, clearly afraid to say anything.

"Dankworth?"

"Because all good things are wild and free?"

"Nice Thoreau quote but wrong."

Dankworth stared down at his hands and pouted.

"People are here," said the Booming Voice, "to continue learning. And to become the best angels they can become. That's why I gave you all free will."

"Free will," remarked the three panelists in unison, who then argued amongst themselves.

"It's still a heavily debated topic up here," said Pixel to the ceiling.

"Oh, My Name," shouted the Big Guy with evident frustration. "Silence!"

The chatter stopped immediately. Pixel's heart slammed into his gut.

"Okay," said the Divine One. "This is what we're going to do. We're not going to use the Cupid's Oath anymore. It's officially banned. And Pixel—"

"Yes," he answered.

"You're now the new supervisor in the Paradise City Department of Discipline, Mythological Gods Division. You report to me and attend every one of these future hearings. And if you have any ideas on how to make this place run a little better let me know. I'll think about it."

Adrenaline flushed through Pixel's body. His shy smile built to a broad grin; he'd finally been appreciated. "Thank you."

"And don't forget to put that Judson kid into your old position."

Judson Femur cracked open the entrance door and stuck his head inside. "Somebody call me?" he asked.

"You're now a social worker, agent-in-training," called out Pixel.

Judson raised his fist with enthusiasm. His eyes flashed like whirling pinwheels. "Thank you, sir. I'll do my best."

"I know you will. And Judson, can you send Leonard Brown and his family home now? They're not needed anymore."

"Okey-dokey," said Judson before he slammed the door shut and yelled out a loud yahoo from the hallway.

"I like that kid. A real go-getter," said the Big Guy.

"Now, as for you, Mr. Webster, you're acquitted. Keep working on being a Cupid. I think you have a unique style."

"Thanks, Pops," said Dean, bowing. "I mean, your Lordship."

"Hey, what is this? I'm not Darth Vader. Just call me B.G. if you ever meet me again."

Dean, beaming, gave him a two-finger salute.

Gastrell stood up at the judge's bench. "What about us?"

"You're not going to smite us, are you?" asked Biggle, his voice quavering.

The Divine One laughed. "Don't be ridiculous. I don't smite anyone anymore. I treat the situation like any corporate head would do. My policy is to promote you into a position of insignificance."

Gastrell stood with his arms crossed. "What?" he said.

"And as luck would have it, I have a new development in the Grand Spiral Galaxy near the planet Dagron-5. There are three supervisor positions open in the Department of Discipline, Sanitation Division. Since you have a propensity to flush, this should be a good position for you."

"But that's not fair," complained Gastrell. "We only moved forward and showed some initiative because you weren't around."

"Perhaps you've forgotten what the ABCs are of my job," said the Big Guy indignantly. "ABC—Always Be Creating. Let that be a lesson to you."

The three angels stood, apparently stunned.

"Well, get moving," ordered the Creator. "Your new jobs start tomorrow morning."

As Gastrell, Biggle, and Dankworth lumbered to the door in the back of the judge's bench, the Big Guy added, "Oh, and Dankworth, you'd better bring some extra tissues. They have some real strange allergies over there."

Dankworth stopped, wiped his eyes, then looked at the ceiling. "Disobedience is the true foundation of liberty."

"Yes. Think about that when you're cleaning a toilet," said the Supreme Being.

With their heads held low, the three disgraced angels stepped behind the door and disappeared forever from Pixel and Cupid-1637's foreseeable future.

"Well, I must be going," said the Big Guy. "I trust you can handle things, Mr. Millet?"

Pixel nodded. "Absolutely." He paused. "If I report to you, how do I get in touch, B.G.?"

"Contact the Genesis Corporation and leave a message with my office. I'll get back to you."

Dean wandered up and stood by Pixel and waved to the ceiling. "See yuh, Man."

The phone clicked, the line went dead, and the room became silent.

Only then did Pixel realize that Carrie Lansdale was still standing in the gallery.

She stood, her mouth slightly ajar, staring at him with a fixed gaze, and her hand pressed against her breastbone. "Does this always happen in your cases?" she asked. "Oh, my stars, you were so amazing. No wonder they said you were the best."

Dean nudged Pixel toward Carrie. She met him halfway, her face suffused with apparent eagerness. "Oh, and look." She pointed to his back. "You've got your full wings."

With all that had happened, Pixel hadn't even noticed. He attempted to look over his shoulder but could only see the under-tail coverts. "Yeah, I guess so," he said shyly. "I didn't expect—"

"They look good on you."

Pixel cocked his head. "You think so?"

"You deserve them. You were masterful," Carrie said, touching his wrist. "I'd love to hear more about how you came up with that speech. Weren't you afraid?"

He took a good look at Carrie. She was just as beautiful as he'd remembered. Could it be that Cupid-1637 was right? Maybe she did like him.

Carrie smiled and peeked up at him flirtatiously.

Pixel nodded. "Yeah, I was afraid, but not as much as standing here right now and asking you if you'd like to get a drink."

She laughed. "Of course, we can get a drink."

Dean tapped Pixel on the shoulder. "Hey, Pops, I'm gonna take off. Thanks for all the help, man. You're pretty good."

Pixel held out his hand, but the two hugged each other instead.

"Keep in touch," said Pixel, wondering if they'd see each other again. Cupid-1637 was positively the worst and absolutely the best client he'd ever had.

Pixel and Carrie strolled toward the hearing room entrance.

"Where do you want to go?" asked Carrie. "I'm new around here, you know."

Pixel asked with a bounce in his step, "Have you ever seen the Beatles?"

Her eyes widened. "Never."

"They're the house band over at Olidammaras in the Dungeons and Dragons sector."

"Let's go," she said as Pixel opened the door for her.

"*Yeah, yeah, yeah!*" he sang.

Just as he was about to follow Carrie out, Pixel saw Cupid-1637 raise his bow; the string was nocked with two arrows, pulled back and ready to fly.

Damn it, Dean! Pixel slammed the door shut as fast as he could, but it was too late.

One arrow hit him, and his gut fluttered.

The happy chemicals in his brain flooded his body and filled him with instant joy. He longed to know Carrie, touch Carrie, be with Carrie, and see Carrie. She was all he could think about.

And just looking at her, he could tell the second arrow had hit its mark, and she felt the same way about him.

Turning to face her, he reached out, and she gently placed her hand in his. Sparks of passion flowed between them.

When they each leaned in to kiss, Pixel knew they were in for one hell of a heavenly romance.

END

ACKNOWLEDGMENTS

A book is a team effort—my deep gratitude to everyone who helped bring these stories to light. But would like to give special thanks to the following individuals for their assistance, guidance and judgement:

Louella Nelson, author, teacher, writing mentor, and editor of this book.

Tobey Crockett PhD, editor, teacher, friend, and Founder at Yes to Positive Social Change Now, who has advised me for years about writing and editing.

Mark Onspaugh, author, and friend, for providing me with his support, encouragement and suggestions.

Veronica Van Gogh, for her graphic design expertise.

Dennis Phinney, author, who over many dinners after Lou Nelson's Wednesday Night Workshop, provided his insightful input on many of the stories in this book.

And the members of Lou Nelson's Wednesday Night Workshop: **Will Hager, Jody Pike, Michele Khoury, Kim Baccilla, and Judith Whitmore**, for their wisdom and positive feedback.

Grace Willcox, who expertly formatted the eBook and paperback editions of this book.

To my wife, **Judi Uttal**, who has been forever supportive and allowed me to pursue my writing dreams.

To my son, **Josh Copelan**, who has encouraged me to write these stories.

ABOUT THE AUTHOR

Dennis Copelan grew up in Beverly Hills, CA. His father, Jodie Copelan, was an award-winning film editor who inspired him with a love for the film industry and storytelling. Although much of his writing involves Hollywood locales and characters, Dennis had other interests growing up and attended law school. As a result, he adds that legal knowledge into his writing whenever possible. He is the author of *The Greatest Stories Never Sold,* a memoir, and *Welcome to Hollyweird,* a collection of humorous, supernatural, and horror short stories in the Twilight Zone vein. He lives in Irvine, CA with his wife Judi, son Josh, and a mini goldendoodle named Ellie.

Made in the USA
Columbia, SC
16 November 2021

49111740R00198